W9-ANH-068

"Bold and engrossing. . . . There is hope in this book, hope in the strength of stories told and stories that are finally heard. . . . The wonder of this accomplished debut is the way in which he has got under his characters' skins, allowing them to speak for themselves. . . . This is a powerful novel of pain and possibility."

—*Financial Times*

"Welcome to a brilliant and generous artist who has already enlarged the landscape of American fiction. *There There* is a comic vision haunted by profound sadness. Tommy Orange is a new writer with an old heart."   —Louise Erdrich

"*There There* drops on us like a thunderclap; the big, booming, explosive sound of twenty-first-century literature finally announcing itself. Essential."

—Marlon James, author of *A Brief History of Seven Killings*

"*There There* is a miraculous achievement, a book that wields ferocious honesty and originality in service of telling a story that needs to be told. This is a novel about what it means to inhabit a land both yours and stolen from you, to simultaneously contend with the weight of belonging and unbelonging."

—Omar El Akkad, author of *American War*

"*There There* is an urgent, invigorating, absolutely vital book."

—Claire Vaye Watkins, author of *Gold Fame Citrus*

"*There There* is truly brilliant, a debut that is gritty, compassionate, and stylistically fierce. Tommy Orange has found language that bridges history and the raw heat of the now. You need to read this book."   —David Chariandy, author of *Brother*

TOMMY ORANGE

There There

Tommy Orange is a graduate of the MFA program at the Institute of American Indian Arts. An enrolled member of the Cheyenne and Arapaho Tribes of Oklahoma, he was born and raised in Oakland, California.

There There

TOMMY ORANGE

McClelland & Stewart

Hardcover edition published 2018
Paperback edition published 2019

McClelland & Stewart and colophon are registered trademarks
of Penguin Random House Canada Limited.

Published simultaneously in the United States of America by Vintage Books,
a division of Penguin Random House LLC, New York. Originally published
in hardcover in the United States by Alfred A. Knopf, a division of
Penguin Random House LLC, New York, in 2018.

Library and Archives Canada Cataloguing in Publication

Orange, Tommy, 1982-, author
There there / Tommy Orange.

Previously published: Toronto: McClelland & Stewart, 2018.
ISBN 978-0-7710-7303-8 (softcover)

I. Title.

PS3615.R32T48 2020   813'.6   C2017-907616-7

Book design by Cassandra J. Pappas

Printed and bound in the United States of America

McClelland & Stewart,
a division of Penguin Random House Canada Limited,
a Penguin Random House Company

www.penguinrandomhouse.ca

4   5   23   22   21   20   19

Penguin
Random House
McCLELLAND & STEWART

For Kateri and Felix

Cast of Characters

Tony Loneman: twenty-one years old, born and raised in Oakland, of Cheyenne descent. Born with fetal alcohol syndrome, which he calls "the Drome." Lives with his grandmother, Maxine, and deals drugs with **Octavio**.

Dene Oxendene: young documentary filmmaker enrolled in the Cheyenne and Arapaho Tribes. Born and raised in Oakland. Is carrying on a project in memory of his uncle, collecting the stories of Native people in the Oakland area.

Opal Viola Victoria Bear Shield: woman in her fifties, of Cheyenne descent. At age eleven in 1970, her mother took her and her half sister, **Jacquie Red Feather**, to Alcatraz to participate in the Native American occupation of the island.

Edwin Black: biracial young man: his mother, Karen, is white, and his father, Harvey, whom he has never known, is Native. Once dreamed of becoming a writer; earned a master's degree in comparative literature with a focus on Native American literature. Loves the internet. Recently started an internship assisting with the Big Oakland Powwow.

Bill Davis: boyfriend of **Edwin**'s mother, Karen. Lakota. Long-time maintenance worker at the Oakland Coliseum. Vietnam veteran who spent five years in San Quentin State Prison for stabbing a man. Read almost the whole time he was in—Raymond Carver, William Faulkner, Hunter S. Thompson, Oscar Zeta Acosta, and Ken Kesey.

Calvin Johnson: young man. Native. Down on his luck and staying with his sister, Maggie. Owes drug money to his brother, Charles (who works with **Octavio**).

Jacquie Red Feather: half sister of **Opal**. A substance abuse counselor who is herself newly sober. Gave a child up for adoption in her youth; raised another daughter, Jamie, who passed away. Now has three grandsons for whom **Opal** is caring.

Orvil Red Feather: fourteen years old. One of **Jacquie**'s grandsons. Cheyenne. Is deeply interested in his heritage and plans to dance at the powwow.

Octavio Gomez: the drug dealer for whom **Tony** and Charles (**Calvin**'s brother) work.

Daniel Gonzales: cousin of **Octavio**.

Blue: head of the powwow committee at the Indian Center.

Thomas Frank: Cheyenne. Drummer who formerly worked as a custodian at the Indian Center. Was invited to perform at the powwow with a group called Southern Moon.

There There

Prologue

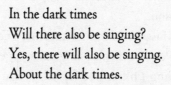

In the dark times
Will there also be singing?
Yes, there will also be singing.
About the dark times.

—BERTOLT BRECHT

Indian Head

There was an Indian head, the head of an Indian, the drawing of the head of a headdressed, long-haired Indian depicted, drawn by an unknown artist in 1939, broadcast until the late 1970s to American TVs everywhere after all the shows ran out. It's called the Indian Head test pattern. If you left the TV on, you'd hear a tone at 440 hertz—the tone used to tune instruments—and you'd see that Indian, surrounded by circles that looked like sights through riflescopes. There was what looked like a bull's-eye in the middle of the screen, with numbers like coordinates.

The Indian's head was just above the bull's-eye, like all you'd need to do was nod up in agreement to set the sights on the target. This was just a test.

In 1621, colonists invited Massasoit, the chief of the Wampanoags, to a feast after a recent land deal. Massasoit came with ninety of his men. *That* meal is why we still eat a meal together in November. Celebrate it as a nation. But that one wasn't a thanksgiving meal. It was a land-deal meal. Two years later there was another, similar meal meant to symbolize eternal friendship. Two hundred Indians dropped dead that night from an unknown poison.

By the time Massasoit's son Metacomet became chief, there were no Indian-Pilgrim meals being eaten together. Metacomet, also known as King Philip, was forced to sign a peace treaty to give up all Indian guns. Three of his men were hanged. His brother Wamsutta was, let's say, very likely poisoned after being summoned and seized by the Plymouth court. All of which lead to the first official Indian war. The first war with Indians. King Philip's War. Three years later the war was over and Metacomet was on the run. He was caught by Benjamin Church, the captain of the very first American Rangers, and an Indian by the name of John Alderman. Metacomet was beheaded and dismembered. Quartered. They tied his four body sections to nearby trees for the birds to pluck. Alderman was given Metacomet's hand, which he kept in a jar of rum and for years took around with him—charged people to see it. Metacomet's head was sold to Plymouth Colony for thirty shillings—the going rate for an Indian head at the time. The head was put on a spike, carried through the streets of Plymouth, then displayed at Plymouth Fort for the next twenty-five years.

In 1637, anywhere from four to seven hundred Pequot gathered for their annual Green Corn Dance. Colonists surrounded their village, set it on fire, and shot any Pequot who tried to escape. The next day the Massachusetts Bay Colony had a feast in celebration, and the governor declared it a day of thanksgiving. Thanksgivings like these happened everywhere, whenever there were what we have to call "successful massacres." At one such celebration in Manhattan, people were said to have celebrated by kicking the heads of Pequot people through the streets like soccer balls.

The first novel by a Native person, and the first novel written in California, was written in 1854, by a Cherokee guy named John Rollin Ridge. *The Life and Adventures of Joaquín Murieta* was based on a supposed real-life Mexican bandit from California by the same name, who was killed by a group of Texas Rangers in 1853. To prove they'd killed Murieta and collect the $5,000 reward put on his head—they cut it off. Kept it in a jar of whiskey. They also took the hand of his fellow bandit Three-Fingered Jack. The rangers took Murieta's head and Jack's hand on a tour throughout California, charged a dollar for the show.

The Indian head in the jar, the Indian head on a spike were like flags flown, to be seen, cast broadly. Just like the Indian Head test pattern was broadcast to sleeping Americans as we set sail from our living rooms, over the ocean blue-green glowing airwaves, to the shores, the screens of the New World.

Rolling Head

There's an old Cheyenne story about a rolling head. We heard it said there was a family who moved away from their camp, moved near a lake—husband, wife, daughter, son. In the morning when the husband finished dancing, he would brush his wife's hair and paint her face red, then go off to hunt. When he came back her face would be clean. After this happened a few times he decided to follow her and hide, see what she did while he was gone. He found her in the lake, with a water monster, some kind of snake thing, wrapped around her in an embrace. The man cut the monster up and killed his wife. He brought the meat home to his son and daughter. They noticed it tasted different. The son, who was still nursing, said, My mother tastes just like this. His older sister told him it's just deer meat. While they ate, a head rolled in. They ran and the head followed them. The sister remembered where they played, how thick the thorns were there, and she brought the thorns to life behind them with her words. But the head broke through, kept coming. Then she remembered where rocks used to be piled in a difficult way. The rocks appeared when she spoke of them but didn't stop the head, so she drew a hard line in the ground, which made a deep chasm the head couldn't cross. But after a long heavy rain, the chasm filled with water. The head crossed the water, and when it reached the other side, it turned around and drank all that water up. The rolling head became confused and drunk. It wanted more. More of anything. More of everything. And it just kept rolling.

One thing we should keep in mind, moving forward, is that no one ever rolled heads down temple stairs. Mel Gibson made that up. But we do have in our minds, those of us who saw the movie, the heads rolling down temple stairs in a world meant to resemble the real Indian world in the 1500s in Mexico. Mexicans before they were Mexicans. Before Spain came.

We've been defined by everyone else and continue to be slandered despite easy-to-look-up-on-the-internet facts about the realities of our histories and current state as a people. We have the sad, defeated Indian silhouette, and the heads rolling down temple stairs, we have it in our heads, Kevin Costner saving us, John Wayne's six-shooter slaying us, an Italian guy named Iron Eyes Cody playing our parts in movies. We have the litter-mourning, tear-ridden Indian in the commercial (also Iron Eyes Cody), and the sink-tossing, crazy Indian who was the narrator in the novel, the voice of *One Flew Over the Cuckoo's Nest*. We have all the logos and mascots. The copy of a copy of the image of an Indian in a textbook. All the way from the top of Canada, the top of Alaska, down to the bottom of South America, Indians were removed, then reduced to a feathered image. Our heads are on flags, jerseys, and coins. Our heads were on the penny first, of course, the Indian cent, and then on the buffalo nickel, both before we could even vote as a people—which, like the truth of what happened in history all over the world, and like all that spilled blood from slaughter, are now out of circulation.

Massacre as Prologue

Some of us grew up with stories about massacres. Stories about what happened to our people not so long ago. How we came out of it. At Sand Creek, we heard it said that they mowed us down with their howitzers. Volunteer militia under Colonel John Chivington came to kill us—we were mostly women, children, and elders. The men were away to hunt. They'd told us to fly the American flag. We flew that and a white flag too. Surrender, the white flag waved. We stood under both flags as they came at us. They did more than kill us. They tore us up. Mutilated us. Broke our fingers to take our rings, cut off our ears to take our silver, scalped us for our hair. We hid in the hollows of tree trunks, buried ourselves in sand by the riverbank. That same sand ran red with blood. They tore unborn babies out of bellies, took what we intended to be, our children before they were children, babies before they were babies, they ripped them out of our bellies. They broke soft baby heads against trees. Then they took our body parts as trophies and displayed them on a stage in downtown Denver. Colonel Chivington danced with dismembered parts of us in his hands, with women's pubic hair, drunk, he danced, and the crowd gathered there before him was all the worse for cheering and laughing along with him. It was a celebration.

Hard, Fast

Getting us to cities was supposed to be the final, necessary step in our assimilation, absorption, erasure, the completion of a five-hundred-year-old genocidal campaign. But the city made us new, and we made it ours. We didn't get lost amid the sprawl of tall buildings, the stream of anonymous masses, the ceaseless din of traffic. We found one another, started up Indian Centers, brought out our families and powwows, our dances, our songs, our beadwork. We bought and rented homes, slept on the streets, under freeways; we went to school, joined the armed forces, populated Indian bars in the Fruitvale in Oakland and in the Mission in San Francisco. We lived in boxcar villages in Richmond. We made art and we made babies and we made way for our people to go back and forth between reservation and city. We did not move to cities to die. The sidewalks and streets, the concrete, absorbed our heaviness. The glass, metal, rubber, and wires, the speed, the hurtling masses—the city took us in. We were not Urban Indians then. This was part of the Indian Relocation Act, which was part of the Indian Termination Policy, which was and is exactly what it sounds like. Make them look and act like us. Become us. And so disappear. But it wasn't just like that. Plenty of us came by choice, to start over, to make money, or for a new experience. Some of us came to cities to escape the reservation. We stayed after fighting in the Second World War. After Vietnam too. We stayed because the city sounds like a war, and you can't leave a war once you've been, you can only keep it at bay—which is easier when you can see and hear it near you, that fast metal, that constant firing around you, cars up and down the streets and freeways like bullets. The quiet of the reservation, the side-of-the-highway towns, rural communities, that kind of silence just makes the sound of your brain on fire that much more pronounced.

Plenty of us are urban now. If not because we live in cities, then because we live on the internet. Inside the high-rise of multiple browser windows. They used to call us sidewalk Indians. Called us citified, superficial, inauthentic, cultureless refugees, apples. An apple is red on the outside and white on the inside. But what we are is what our ancestors did. How they survived. We are the memories we don't remember, which live in us, which we feel, which make us sing and dance and pray the way we do, feelings from memories that flare and bloom unexpectedly in our lives like blood through a blanket from a wound made by a bullet fired by a man shooting us in the back for our hair, for our heads, for a bounty, or just to get rid of us.

When they first came for us with their bullets, we didn't stop moving even though the bullets moved twice as fast as the sound of our screams, and even when their heat and speed broke our skin, shattered our bones, skulls, pierced our hearts, we kept on, even when we saw the bullets send our bodies flailing through the air like flags, like the many flags and buildings that went up in place of everything we knew this land to be before. The bullets were premonitions, ghosts from dreams of a hard, fast future. The bullets moved on after moving through us, became the promise of what was to come, the speed and the killing, the hard, fast lines of borders and buildings. They took everything and ground it down to dust as fine as gunpowder, they fired their guns into the air in victory and the strays flew out into the nothingness of histories written wrong and meant to be forgotten. Stray bullets and consequences are landing on our unsuspecting bodies even now.

Urbanity

Urban Indians were the generation born in the city. We've been moving for a long time, but the land moves with you like memory. An Urban Indian belongs to the city, and cities belong to the earth. Everything here is formed in relation to every other living and nonliving thing from the earth. All our relations. The process that brings anything to its current form—chemical, synthetic, technological, or otherwise—doesn't make the product not a product of the living earth. Buildings, freeways, cars—are these not of the earth? Were they shipped in from Mars, the moon? Is it because they're processed, manufactured, or that we handle them? Are we so different? Were we at one time not something else entirely, *Homo sapiens*, single-celled organisms, space dust, unidentifiable pre-bang quantum theory? Cities form in the same way as galaxies. Urban Indians feel at home walking in the shadow of a downtown building. We came to know the downtown Oakland skyline better than we did any sacred mountain range, the redwoods in the Oakland hills better than any other deep wild forest. We know the sound of the freeway better than we do rivers, the howl of distant trains better than wolf howls, we know the smell of gas and freshly wet concrete and burned rubber better than we do the smell of cedar or sage or even fry bread—which isn't traditional, like reservations aren't traditional, but nothing is original, everything comes from something that came before, which was once nothing. Everything is new and doomed. We ride buses, trains, and cars across, over, and under concrete plains. Being Indian has never been about returning to the land. The land is everywhere or nowhere.

PART I

Remain

How can I not know today your face tomorrow, the face that is there already or is being forged beneath the face you show me or beneath the mask you are wearing, and which you will only show me when I am least expecting it?

—JAVIER MARÍAS

Tony Loneman

THE DROME FIRST CAME to me in the mirror when I was six. Earlier that day my friend Mario, while hanging from the monkey bars in the sand park, said, "Why's your face look like that?"

I don't remember what I did. I still don't know. I remember smears of blood on the metal and the taste of metal in my mouth. I remember my grandma Maxine shaking my shoulders in the hall outside the principal's office, my eyes closed, her making this *psshh* sound she always makes when I try to explain myself and shouldn't. I remember her pulling my arm harder than she'd ever pulled it, then the quiet drive home.

Back home, in front of the TV, before I turned it on, I saw my face in the dark reflection there. It was the first time I saw it. My own face, the way everyone else saw it. When I asked Maxine, she told me my mom drank when I was in her, she told me real slow that I have fetal alcohol syn-drome. All I heard her say was Drome, and then I was back in front of the turned-off TV, staring at it. My face stretched across the screen. The Drome. I tried but couldn't make the face that I found there my own again.

Most people don't have to think about what their faces mean the way I do. Your face in the mirror, reflected back at you, most people don't even know what it looks like anymore. That thing on the front of your head, you'll never see it, like you'll never see your own eyeball with your own eyeball, like you'll never smell what you smell like, but me, I know what my face looks like. I know what it means. My eyes droop like I'm fucked up, like I'm high, and my mouth hangs open all the time. There's too much space between each of the parts of my face—eyes, nose, mouth, spread out like a drunk slapped it on reaching for another drink. People look at me then look away when they see I see them see me. That's the Drome too. My power and curse. The Drome is my mom and why she drank, it's the way history lands on a face, and all the ways I made it so far despite how it has fucked with me since the day I found it there on the TV, staring back at me like a fucking villain.

I'm twenty-one now, which means I can drink if I want. I don't though. The way I see it, I got enough when I was a baby in my mom's stomach. Getting drunk in there, a drunk fucking baby, not even a baby, a little fucking tadpole thing, hooked up to a cord, floating in a stomach.

They told me I'm stupid. Not like that, they didn't say that, but I basically failed the intelligence test. The lowest percentile. That bottom rung. My friend Karen told me they got all kinds of intelligences. She's my counselor I still see once a week over at the Indian Center—I was at first mandated to go after the incident with Mario in kindergarten. Karen told me I don't have to worry about what they try to tell me about intelligence. She said people with FAS are on a spectrum, have a wide range of intelligences, that the intelligence test is biased, and that I got strong intuition and street smarts, that I'm smart where it counts, which I already knew, but when she told me it felt good, like I didn't really know it until she said it like that.

I'm smart, like: I know what people have in mind. What they mean when they say they mean another thing. The Drome taught me to look past the first look people give you, find that other one, right behind it. All you gotta do is wait a second longer than you normally do and you can catch it, you can see what they got in mind back there. I know if someone's selling around me. I know Oakland. I know what it looks like when somebody's trying to come up on me, like when to cross the street, and when to look at the ground and keep walking. I know how to spot a scaredy-cat too. That one's easy. They wear that shit like there's a sign in their hands, the sign says: *Come Get Me.* They look at me like I already did some shit, so I might as well do the shit they're looking at me like that for.

Maxine told me I'm a medicine person. She said people like me are rare, and that when we come along, people better know we look different because we are different. To respect that. I never got no kind of respect from nobody, though, except Maxine. She tells me we're Cheyenne people. That Indians go way back with the land. That all this was once ours. All this. Shit. They must not've had street smarts back then. Let them white men come over here and take it from them like that. The sad part is, all those Indians probably knew but couldn't do anything about it. They didn't have guns. Plus the diseases. That's what Maxine said. Killed us with their white men's dirt and diseases, moved us off our land, moved us onto some shit land you can't grow fucking shit on. I would hate it if I got moved outta Oakland, because I know it so well, from West to East to Deep East and back, on bike or bus or BART. It's my only home. I wouldn't make it nowhere else.

Sometimes I ride my bike all over Oakland just to see it, the people, all its different hoods. With my headphones on, listening to MF Doom, I can ride all day. The MF stands for Metal Face. He's my favorite rapper. Doom wears a metal mask and calls himself a villain. Before Doom, I didn't know nothing but what came on the radio. Somebody left their iPod on the seat in front of me on the bus. Doom was the only music on there. I knew I liked him when I heard the line "Got more soul than a sock with a hole." What I liked is that I understood all the meanings to it right away, like instantly. It meant soul, like having a hole in a sock gives the sock character, means it's worn through, gives it a soul, and also like the bottom of your foot showing through, to the sole of your foot. It was a small thing, but it made me feel like I'm not stupid. Not slow. Not bottom rung. And it helped because the Drome's what gives me my soul, and the Drome is a face worn through.

.   .   .

My mom's in jail. We talk sometimes on the phone, but she's always saying some shit that makes me wish we didn't. She told me my dad's over in New Mexico. That he doesn't even know I exist.

"Then tell that motherfucker I exist," I said to her.

"Tony, it ain't simple like that," she said.

"Don't call me simple. Don't fucking call me simple. You fucking did this to me."

Sometimes I get mad. That's what happens to my intelligence sometimes. No matter how many times Maxine moved me from schools I got suspended from for getting in fights, it's always the same. I get mad and then I don't know anything. My face heats up and hardens like it's made of metal, then I black out. I'm a big guy. And I'm strong. Too strong, Maxine tells me. The way I see it, I got this big body to help me since my face got it so bad. That's how looking like a monster works out for me. The Drome. And when I stand up, when I stand up real fucking tall like I can, nobody'll fuck with me. Everybody runs like they seen a ghost. Maybe I am a ghost. Maybe Maxine doesn't even know who I am. Maybe I'm the opposite of a medicine person. Maybe I'm'a do something one day, and everybody's gonna know about me. Maybe that's when I'll come to life. Maybe that's when they'll finally be able to look at me, because they'll have to.

Everyone's gonna think it's about the money. But who doesn't fucking want money? It's about why you want money, how you get it, then what you do with it that matters. Money didn't never do shit to no one. That's people. I been selling weed since I was thirteen. Met some homies on the block by just being outside all the time. They probably thought I was already selling the way I was always outside, on corners and shit. But then maybe not. If they thought I was selling, they probably woulda beat my ass. They probably felt sorry for me. Shitty clothes, shitty face. I give most of the money I get from selling to Maxine. I try to help her in whatever ways I can because she lets me live at her house, over in West Oakland, at the end of Fourteenth, which she bought a long time ago when she worked as a nurse in San Francisco. Now she needs a nurse, but she can't afford one even with the money she gets from Social Security. She needs me to do all kinds of shit for her. Go to the store. Ride the bus with her to get her meds. I walk with her down the stairs now too. I can't believe a bone can get so old it can shatter, break into tiny pieces in your body like glass. After she broke her hip, I started helping out more.

Maxine makes me read to her before she goes to sleep. I don't like it because I read slow. The letters move on me sometimes, like bugs. Just whenever they want, they switch places. But then sometimes the words don't move. When they stay still like that, I have to wait to be sure they're not gonna move, so it ends up taking longer for me to read them than the ones I can put back together after they scramble. Maxine makes me read her Indian stuff that I don't always get. I like it, though, because when I do get it, I get it way down at that place where it hurts but feels better because you feel it, something you couldn't feel before reading it, that makes you feel less alone, and like it's not gonna hurt as much anymore. One time she used the word *devastating* after I finished reading a passage from her favorite author—Louise Erdrich. It was something about how life will break you. How that's the reason we're here, and to go sit by an apple tree and listen to the apples fall and pile around you, wasting all that sweetness. I didn't know what it meant then, and she saw that I didn't. She didn't explain it either. But we read the passage, that whole book, another time, and I got it.

Maxine's always known me and been able to read me like no one else can, better than myself even, like I don't even know all that I'm showing to the world, like I'm reading my own reality slow, because of the way things switch around on me, how people look at me and treat me, and how long it takes me to figure out if I have to put it all back together.

How all this came about, all the shit I got in, is because these white boys from up in the Oakland hills came up on me in a liquor-store parking lot in West Oakland, straight up like they weren't afraid of me. I could tell they were scared of being there, in that neighborhood, from the way they kept their heads on a swivel, but they weren't afraid of me. It was like they thought I wasn't gonna do some shit because of how I look. Like I'm too slow to do some shit.

"You got snow?" the one as tall as me in the Kangol hat asked. I wanted to laugh. It was so fucking white for him to use the word *snow* for coke.

"I can get it," I said, even though I wasn't sure if I could. "Come back here in a week, same time." I would ask Carlos.

Carlos is hella flaky. The night he was supposed to get it, he called me and told me he couldn't make it, and that I'd have to go to Octavio's to get it myself.

I rode my bike over from the Coliseum BART Station. Octavio's house was in Deep East Oakland, off Seventy-Third, across from where the Eastmont Mall used to be until things got so bad there they turned it into a police station.

When I got there, people were pouring out of the house into the street like there'd been a fight. I sat back on my bike from a block away for a while, watched the drunks move around under the glow of the streetlights, all stupid like moths drunk on light.

When I found Octavio, he was all kinds of fucked up. It always makes me think of my mom when I see people like that. I wondered what she was like drunk when I was in her. Did she like it? Did I?

Octavio was pretty clearheaded, though, even through the heavy slur. He put his arm around me and took me to his backyard, where he had a bench press set up under a tree. I watched him do sets with a bar without weights on it. It didn't seem like he realized there were no weights. I waited to see when he would ask the question about my face. But he didn't. I listened to him talk about his grandma, about how she saved his life after his family was gone. He said she'd lifted a curse from him with badger fur, and that she called anyone not Mexican or Indian gachupins, which is a disease the Spanish brought to the Natives when they came—she used to tell him that the Spanish were the disease that they brought. He told me he never meant to become what he'd become, and I wasn't sure what that was, a drunk, or a drug dealer, or both, or something else.

"I'd give away my own heart's blood for her," Octavio said. His own heart's blood. That's the way I felt about Maxine. He told me he didn't mean to sound all sensitive and shit, but that nobody else ever really listened to him. I knew it was because he was fucked up. And that he probably wouldn't remember shit. But after that I went straight to Octavio for everything.

It turned out those goofy white boys from the hills had friends.

We made good money for a summer. Then one day when I was picking up, Octavio asked me in, told me to sit down.

"You're Native, right?" he said.

"Yeah," I said, and wondered how he knew. "Cheyenne."

"Tell me what a powwow is," he said.

"Why?"

"Just tell me."

Maxine had been taking me to powwows all around the Bay since I was young. I don't anymore, but I used to dance.

"We dress up Indian, with feathers and beads and shit. We dance. Sing and beat this big drum, buy and sell Indian shit like jewelry and clothes and art," I said.

"Yeah, but what do you do it for?" Octavio said.

"Money," I said.

"No, but really why do they do it?"

"I don't know."

"Whatchyoumean you don't know?"

"To make money, motherfucker," I said.

Octavio looked at me with his head sideways, like: *Remember who you're talking to.*

"That's why we're gonna be at that powwow too," Octavio said.

"The one they're having over at the coliseum?"

"Yeah."

"To make money?"

Octavio nodded, then turned around and picked up what I couldn't tell at first was a gun. It was small and all white.

"What the fuck is that?" I said.

"Plastic," Octavio said.

"It works?"

"It's 3-D printed. You wanna see?" he said.

"See?" I said.

Out in the backyard, I aimed the gun at a can of Pepsi on a string, with two hands, my tongue out and one eye closed.

"You ever fired a gun before?" he said.

"No," I said.

"Shit'll make your ears ring."

"Can I?" I said, and before I got an answer I felt my finger squeeze and then the boom go through me. There was a moment when I didn't know what was happening. The squeeze brought the sound of the boom and my whole body became a boom and a drop. I ducked without meaning to. There was a ringing, inside and out, a single tone drifting far off, or deep inside. I looked up at Octavio and saw that he was saying something. I said *What*, but couldn't even hear myself say it.

"This is how we're gonna rob that powwow," I finally heard Octavio say.

I remembered there were metal detectors at the entrance to the coliseum. Maxine's walker, the one she used after she broke her hip, it set one of them off. Me and Maxine went on a Wednesday night—dollar night—to see the A's play the Texas Rangers, which was the team Maxine grew up rooting for in Oklahoma because Oklahoma didn't have a team.

On the way out, Octavio handed me a flyer for the powwow that listed the prize money in each dance category. Four for five thousand. Three for ten.

"That's good money," I said.

"I wouldn't be getting into some shit like this, but I owe somebody," Octavio said.

"Who?"

"Mind your business," Octavio said.

"We good?" I said.

"Go home," Octavio said.

The night before the powwow, Octavio called me and told me I was gonna have to be the one to hide the bullets.

"In the bushes, for real?" I said.

"Yeah."

"I'm supposed to throw bullets into the bushes at the entrance?"

"Put 'em in a sock."

"Put bullets in a sock and throw them in the bushes?"

"What I say?"

"It just seems—"

"What?"

"Nothing."

"You got it?"

"Where do I get bullets, what kind?"

"Walmart, .22s."

"Can't you just print them?"

"They can't do that yet."

"All right."

"There's one more thing," Octavio said.

"Yeah?"

"You still got some Indian shit to put on?"

"Whatchyoumean Indian shit?"

"I don't know, what they put on, feathers and shit."

"I got it."

"You're gonna wear it."

"It won't even barely fit."

"But will it?"

"Yeah."

"Wear it to the powwow."

"All right," I said, and hung up. I pulled my regalia out and put it on. I went out into the living room and stood in front of the TV. It was the only place in the house I could see my whole body. I shook and lifted a foot. I watched the feathers flutter on the screen. I put my arms out and dipped my shoulders down, then I walked up to the TV. I tightened my chin strap. I looked at my face. The Drome. I didn't see it there. I saw an Indian. I saw a dancer.

Dene Oxendene

~≈~

DENE OXENDENE TAKES the dead escalator two steps at a time at the Fruitvale Station. When he makes it up to the platform, the train he thought he was missing comes to a stop on the opposite side. A single drop of sweat drips down the side of his face from out of his beanie. Dene wipes the sweat with his finger, then pulls the beanie off and shakes it out, mad like the sweat came from it and not his head. He looks down the tracks and breathes out a breath he watches rise then disappear. He smells cigarette smoke, which makes him want one, except that they tire him out. He wants a cigarette that invigorates. He wants a drug that works. He refuses to drink. Smokes too much weed. Nothing works.

Dene looks across the tracks at graffiti scrawled on the wall in that little crawl space underneath the platform. He'd been seeing it for years all over Oakland. He'd thought of the name in middle school but had never really done anything with it: *Lens*.

The first time Dene saw someone tag, he was on the bus. It was raining. The kid was in the back. Dene saw that the kid saw that Dene looked back at him. One of the first things Dene learned when he first started taking the bus in Oakland was that you don't stare, you don't even glance, but you don't totally not look either. Out of respect you acknowledge. You look and don't look. Anything to avoid the question: Whatchyoulookingat? There is no good answer for this question. Being asked this question means you already fucked up. Dene waited for his moment, watched the kid tag in the condensation on the bus window three letters: *emt*. He understood right away that it meant "empty." And he liked the idea that the kid was writing it in the condensation on the window, in the empty space between drops, and also because it wouldn't last, just like tagging and graffiti don't.

The head of the train and then its body appear, wind around the bend toward the station. Self-loathing hits you fast sometimes. He doesn't know for a second if he might jump, get down there on the tracks, wait for that fast weight to come get rid of him. He'd probably jump late, bounce off the side of the train, and just fuck up his face.

On the train he thinks of the looming panel of judges. He keeps picturing them twenty feet up staring down at him, with long wild faces in the style of Ralph Steadman, old white men, all noses and robes. They'll know everything about him. Hate him intimately, with all the possible knowledge about his life available to them. They'll see immediately how unqualified he is. They'll think he's white—which is only half true—and so ineligible for a cultural arts grant. Dene is not recognizably Native. He is ambiguously nonwhite. Over the years he'd been assumed Mexican plenty, been asked if he was Chinese, Korean,

Japanese, Salvadoran once, but mostly the question came like this: What are you?

Everyone on the train is looking at their phones. Into them. He smells piss and at first thinks it's him. He's always feared he'll find out that he's smelled like piss and shit his whole life without knowing it, that everyone's been afraid to tell him, like Kevin Farley from the fifth grade who ended up killing himself the summer of their junior year in high school when he found out. He looks to his left and sees an old man slumped down in his seat. The old guy comes to and sits up straight, then moves his arms around like he's checking to make sure all his stuff is still with him, even though there's nothing there. Dene walks to the next train car. He stands at the doors and looks out the window. The train floats alongside the freeway next to cars. Each of their speeds is different: The speed of the cars is short, disconnected, sporadic. Dene and the train slither along the tracks as one movement and speed. There's something cinematic about their variable speeds, like a moment in a movie that makes you feel something for reasons you can't explain. Something too big to feel, underneath, and inside, too familiar to recognize, right there in front of you at all times. Dene puts his headphones on, shuffles the music on his phone, skips several songs and stays on "There There," by Radiohead. The hook is "Just 'cause you feel it doesn't mean it's there." Before going underground between the Fruitvale and Lake Merritt stations, Dene looks over and sees the word, that name again, *Lens*, there on the wall right before he goes under.

He thought up the tag *Lens* on a bus ride home the day his uncle Lucas came for a visit. When he was almost at his stop, he looked out the window and saw a flash. Someone had taken a picture of him, or the bus, and from out of the flash, the blue-green-purple-pink afterglow, the name came. He wrote *Lens* on the back of the bus seat with a Sharpie just before his stop. As he got off the bus in the back, he saw the bus driver's eyes narrow in that wide mirror at the front.

When he got home, Dene's mom, Norma, told him that his uncle Lucas was coming for a visit, up from Los Angeles, and that he should help straighten up and get the dinner table set. All Dene could remember about his uncle was the way he used to throw Dene way up in the air and catch him when he was almost gonna hit the ground. Dene didn't necessarily like or dislike it. But he remembered it viscerally. That tickle in his stomach, that mix of fear and fun. That involuntary burst of midair laughter.

"Where has he been?" Dene said to his mom while setting the table. Norma didn't answer. Then at the table Dene asked his uncle where he'd been and Norma answered for him.

"He's been busy making movies," she said, then looked at Dene with raised eyebrows and finished with "apparently."

They had their usual: hamburger meat, mashed potatoes, and green beans from the can.

"I don't know if it's apparent that I've been busy making movies, but it's apparent your mom thinks I've been lying to her all this time," Lucas said.

"I'm sorry, Dene, if I gave the impression that my brother is less than an honest Injun," Norma said.

"Dene," Lucas said, "do you wanna hear about a movie I'm working on?"

"By working on, Dene, he means in his head, he means he's been thinking about a movie, just so you know," Norma said.

"I wanna hear," Dene said, looking at his uncle.

"It'll be in the near future. I'm gonna have an alien technology colonize America. We'll think we made it up. Like it's ours. Over time we'll merge with the technology, we'll become like androids, and we'll lose the ability to recognize each other. The way we used to look. Our old ways. We won't even really consider ourselves half-breeds, half aliens, because we'll think it's our technology. Then I'm gonna have a half-breed hero rise up, inspire what's left of the humans to move back to nature. Get away from technology, get our old way of life back. Become human again like we used to be. It's gonna end in a reverse Kubrick *2001* human-bashing-a-bone sequence in slow motion. Have you seen *2001*?"

"No," Dene said.

"*Full Metal Jacket*?"

"No?"

"I'll bring you all my Kubrick next time I come up."

"What happens at the end?"

"What, in the movie? The alien colonizers win of course. We'll only think we won by getting back to nature, back to the Stone Age. Anyway, I stopped 'thinking about it,'" he said, and put up air quotes, looking toward the kitchen, where Norma had gone when he started in about his movie.

"But have you ever really made any movies?" Dene said.

"I make movies in that I think of them, and sometimes write them down. Or where do you think movies come from? But no, I don't make movies, Nephew. I'll probably never make one. What I do is, I help people with little parts of TV shows and movies, I hold a boom mic above the shot, long and steady. Look at these forearms." Lucas lifted an arm and bent his wrist, looking at his forearm himself. "I don't keep track of what sets I'm on when I'm working. I don't remember a lot. I drink too much. D'your mom tell you that?" Lucas said.

Dene didn't respond except by eating the rest of what was on his plate, then looking back to his uncle for him to say something else.

"I'm actually working on something right now that hardly takes any money to make. Last summer I was up here doing interviews. I was able to edit some of them, and I'm up here again to try to get a few more. It's about Indians coming to Oakland. Living in Oakland. I just asked these Indian people I met through a friend of mine who knows a lot of Indians, she's kind of your auntie, I think, Indian way. I'm not sure if you've met her though. Do you know Opal, the Bear Shields?"

"Maybe," Dene said.

"Anyway, I asked some Indian people who've lived in Oakland for a while and some that just got here not too long ago a two-part question, actually it's not a question, I tried to get them to tell me a story. I asked them to tell me a story about how they ended up in Oakland, or if they were born here, then I asked what it's been like living in Oakland. I told them the question is meant to be answered in story form, whatever that means to them is okay, then I left the room. I decided to do it confessional style so it's almost like they're telling the story to themselves, or to anyone and everyone behind the lens. I don't wanna get in the way in there. I can do all the editing myself. I just need the budget to pay my own salary, which is basically nothing."

After Lucas said this he took a big breath in and sort of coughed, cleared his throat, then pulled from a flask he got out of the inner pocket of his jacket. He looked off, out the living-room window, across the street, or farther, off to where the sun had set, or past that, back at his life maybe, and then he got this look in his eyes, it was something Dene had seen in his mom's eyes, something that looked like remembering and dreading at once. Lucas got up and walked out to the front porch for a cigarette, and on the way said, "Better get to your homework, Nephew. Me and your mom have some stuff to talk about."

Dene only realizes he's been stuck underground between stations for ten minutes after ten minutes of being stuck underground between stations. He breaks a sweat at the top of his forehead thinking about being late or missing the panel. He didn't submit a sample work. So he would have to waste the little time he does have to explain why. How it was originally his uncle's idea, how it's really his project, and how a lot of what he's proposing is based on what his uncle told him in the short time they had together. And then the weirdest part, the part he can't present, because he doesn't totally understand it, is that each of the interviews, the interviews his uncle actually conducted, came with scripts. Not transcriptions but scripts. So had his uncle written the scripts to be performed? Or had he transcribed actual interviews and then turned them into script form? Or had he interviewed someone, and then based on the interview, made a script that he would rework, and then had someone else perform the reworked script? There was no way to know. The train starts up, moves for a beat, then stops again. A staticky voice from above drones incomprehensibly.

Back at school Dene wrote *Lens* everywhere he could. Each place he tagged would be like a place he could look out from, imagine people looking at his tag; he could see them seeing, above their lockers, on the back of the bathroom stall doors, on the tops of desks. In the bathroom stall tagging the back of the door, Dene thought about how sad it was to want everyone to see a name that wasn't his, a name written to no one, to everyone, and to imagine them looking into it like it was a camera lens. It was no wonder he hadn't made a single friend in middle school yet.

When he got home, his uncle wasn't there. His mom was in the kitchen.

"Where's Lucas?" Dene said.

"They're keeping him overnight."

"Keeping him where overnight?"

"The hospital."

"For what?"

"Your uncle's dying."

"What?"

"I'm sorry, honey. I wanted to tell you. I didn't think it would happen like this. I thought it could be a nice visit, and then he'd go and—"

"Dying of what?"

"He's been drinking too much for too long. His body, his liver's going."

"Going? But he just got here," Dene said, and he saw that this made his mom cry, but only for a second.

She wiped her eyes with the back of her arm and said, "There's nothing we can do at this point, honey."

"But why wasn't something done when it could have been done?"

"There are some things we can't control, some people we can't help."

"He's your brother."

"What was I supposed to do, Dene? There was nothing I could have done. He's been doing this most of his life."

"Why?"

"I don't know."

"What?"

"I don't know. I don't fucking know. Please," Norma said. She lost hold of the plate she'd been drying. They both stared at the pieces of it on the floor between them.

At the Twelfth Street Station Dene runs up the stairs but then looks at his phone and sees that he's not actually gonna be late. When he gets to street level, he slows to a walk. He looks up and sees the Tribune Tower. It's a faded pink glow that seems like it should be red but lost its steam somewhere along the way. Aside from the plain, average-height, checkered twin buildings that are the Ronald V. Dellums Federal Building complex just before I-980 on the way into West Oakland, the Oakland skyline lacks distinction, and is unevenly scattered, so that even when the newspaper moved down to Nineteenth, and even though the paper doesn't exist anymore, they keep the Tribune light aglow.

Dene crosses the street, toward city hall. He passes through a cloud of weed smoke from a gathering of men behind the bus stop on Fourteenth and Broadway. He's never liked the smell except for when he's smoking it himself. He shouldn't have smoked last night. He's sharper when he doesn't. It's just that if he has it around, he's gonna smoke it. And he keeps on buying it from the guy across the hall. So there it is.

· · ·

When Dene came home from school the next day, he found his uncle there on the couch again. Dene sat down and leaned forward with his elbows on his knees and stared at the ground waiting for his uncle to say something.

"You must think I'm pretty despicable, what with me turning into a zombie out here on the couch, killing myself with the drink, is that what she told you?" Lucas said.

"She hasn't told me hardly anything. I mean, I know why you're sick."

"I'm not sick. I'm dying."

"Yeah, but you're sick."

"I'm sick from dying."

"How much time—"

"We don't have time, Nephew, time has us. It holds us in its mouth like an owl holds a field mouse. We shiver. We struggle for release, and then it pecks out our eyes and intestines for sustenance and we die the death of field mice."

Dene swallowed some spit and felt his heart beat fast like he was in an argument, though it didn't have the tone or feel of an argument.

"Jesus, Uncle," Dene said.

It was the first time he'd ever called his uncle "Uncle." He hadn't thought about doing it, it just came out. Lucas didn't react.

"How long you known?" Dene said.

Lucas turned on the lamp between the two of them, and Dene felt a sick sad feeling in his stomach when he saw that where his uncle's eyes should have been white they were yellow. Then he felt another pang when he saw his uncle get his flask out and take a pull from it.

"I'm sorry you gotta see it, Nephew, it's the only thing that's gonna make me feel better. I been drinking for a long time. It helps. Some people take pills to feel okay. Pills will kill you too over time. Some medicine is poison."

"I guess," Dene said, and got that feeling in his stomach like when his uncle used to throw him up in the air.

"I'll still be around for a while. Don't worry. This stuff takes years to kill you. Listen, I'm gonna get some sleep now, but tomorrow when you get home from school, let's you and me talk about making a movie together. I got a camera with a grip like a gun." Lucas makes a gun with his hand and points it at Dene. "We'll come up with a simple concept. Something we can knock out in a few days."

"Sure, but, will you be feeling okay enough by tomorrow? Mom said—"

"I'll be okay," Lucas said, and put his hand out flat and swept it across his chest.

When Dene gets in the building, he checks the schedule on his phone and sees he has ten minutes. He takes off his undershirt without taking off his top layer in order to use it as a kind of rag to wipe what sweat he can before he goes in front of the panel. There's a guy standing outside the door to the room he was told to go to. Dene hates who he thinks the guy is. Who he has to be. He's the kind of bald that requires a daily shave. He wants it to look like he's in control of his hair, like being bald is his personal choice, but the faintest hint of hair appears on the sides and not a trace at the crown. He's got a sizable but neat light brown beard, which is clearly compensation for the lack of hair up there, plus a trend now, white hipsters everywhere trying to come off as confident, all the while hiding their entire faces behind big bushy beards and thick black-rimmed glasses. Dene wonders whether you have to be a person of color to get the grant. The guy's probably working with kids on a garbage-art project. Dene pulls out his phone in an attempt to avoid conversation.

"You going for the grant?" the guy says to Dene.

Dene nods and sticks his hand out for a shake. "Dene," he says.

"Rob," the guy says.

"Where you from?" Dene says.

"Actually I don't have a place right now, but next month me and some friends are getting a place in West Oakland. It's dirt cheap over there," Rob says.

Dene clenches his jaw and blinks a slow blink at this: dirt cheap.

"D'you grow up here?" Dene says.

"I mean, no one's really from here, right?" Rob says.

"What?"

"You know what I mean."

"I do know what you mean," Dene says.

"You know what Gertrude Stein said about Oakland?" Rob says.

Dene shakes his head no but actually knows, actually googled quotes about Oakland when researching for his project. He knows exactly what the guy is about to say.

"There is no there there," he says in a kind of whisper, with this goofy openmouthed smile Dene wants to punch. Dene wants to tell him he'd looked up the quote in its original context, in her *Everybody's Autobiography*, and found that she was talking about how the place where she'd grown up in Oakland had changed so much, that so much development had happened there, that the there of her childhood, the there there, was gone, there was no there there anymore. Dene wants to tell him it's what happened to Native people, he wants to explain that they're not the same, that Dene is Native, born and raised in Oakland, *from* Oakland. Rob probably didn't look any further into the quote because he'd gotten what he wanted from it. He probably used the quote at dinner parties and made other people like him feel good about taking over neighborhoods they wouldn't have had the guts to drive through ten years ago.

The quote is important to Dene. This there there. He hadn't read Gertrude Stein beyond the quote. But for Native people in this country, all over the Americas, it's been developed over, buried ancestral land, glass and concrete and wire and steel, unreturnable covered memory. There is no there there.

The guy says it's his time and goes in. Dene wipes his head with his undershirt one more time and puts it in his backpack.

The panel of judges turns out to be a square of four tables. As he sits down he realizes they're in the middle of talking about his project. Dene has no idea what he said he was going to do. His mind is a mess of misfires. They mention the lack of sample work. None of them looks at him. Are they forbidden to look at him? The makeup of the group is all over the place. Old white lady. Two middle-aged black guys. Two middle-aged white ladies. A youngish Hispanic guy. An Indian—from India—woman who could be twenty-five or thirty-five or forty-five, and an older guy who's definitely Native, with long hair and turquoise-and-silver feather earrings in both ears. They turn their heads toward Dene. He has three minutes to say whatever he thinks they should know that wasn't included in the application. A final moment to convince them that his project is worth funding.

"Hello. My name is Dene Oxendene. I'm an enrolled member of the Cheyenne and Arapaho Tribes of Oklahoma. Good morning and thank you for your time and consideration. Sorry ahead of time if I ramble. I'm grateful for this opportunity. I know our time is limited, so I'll just move into it if that's okay. This all started for me when I was thirteen. My uncle died and, sort of, I inherited the work he started. What he did, what I want to do, is to document Indian stories in Oakland. I want to put a camera in front of them, video, audio, I'll transcribe it while they talk if they want, let them write, every kind of story I can collect, let them tell their stories with no one else there, with no direction or manipulation or agenda. I want them to be able to say what they want. Let the content direct the vision. There are so many stories here. I know this means a lot of editing, a lot of watching, and a lot of listening, but that's just what our community needs considering how long it's been ignored, has remained invisible. I'm gonna set up a room down at the Indian Center. What I want to do is to pay the storytellers for their stories. Stories are invaluable, but to pay is to appreciate. And this is not just qualitative data collection. I want to bring something new to the vision of the Native experience as it's seen on the screen. We haven't seen the Urban Indian story. What we've seen is full of the kinds of stereotypes that are the reason no one is interested in the Native story in general, it's too sad, so sad it can't even be entertaining, but more importantly because of the way it's been portrayed, it looks pathetic, and we perpetuate that, but no, fuck that, excuse my language, but it makes me mad, because the whole picture is not pathetic, and the individual people and stories that you come across are not pathetic or weak or in need of pity, and there is real passion there, and rage, and that's part of what I'm bringing to the project, because I feel that way too, I will bring that same energy to it, I mean if it gets approved and everything, and

I can raise more money, it won't take that much really, maybe even just this grant, and I'll be doing most of the work. Sorry if I went over my time. Thank you."

Dene takes a deep breath and holds it. The judges don't look up at all. He lets out his breath, regrets everything he said. They stare at their laptops and type like stenographers. This is the time allotted for questions. Not questions for Dene. This is when they ask each other questions. Discuss the viability of the project. Fuck. He doesn't even know what he just said. The Native guy taps the stack of papers that is Dene's application and clears his throat.

"It's an interesting idea. But I'm having trouble seeing exactly what the applicant has in mind, and I'm wondering, and please correct me if I missed something, I'm wondering if there's a real vision here, or if he's just gonna sort of make it up as he goes along. I mean, he doesn't even have a work sample," the Native guy says.

Dene knew it would be the Native guy. He probably doesn't even think Dene is Native. Fuck. The work sample. Dene can't say anything. He's supposed to be a fly on the wall. But the guy just swatted at him. Someone say something else. Someone say anything else. The older of the two black guys, the more nicely dressed, with a white beard and glasses, says, "I think it's interesting, if he's doing what I think he's saying he's going to do, which is, essentially, to put aside the pretension of documentation. He's moving out of the way, so to speak. If he does it right, it will seem as if he isn't even the one behind the camera, it will almost seem like there isn't a cameraperson there at all. My main question is whether or not he'll be able to get people to come and tell their stories and to trust him with them. If he does, I think this could be important regardless of whether he turns it into something his own, something tangible, and with vision, or not. Sometimes we risk putting too much of the director's vision on stories. I like that he's going to allow the content to direct the vision. However it goes, these are important stories to document, period."

Dene sees the Native guy shift uncomfortably in his chair, tap Dene's application in a neat stack, then put it behind a bigger stack. The older white woman who looks like Tilda Swinton says, "If he can raise the money and come out with a film that says something new, I think that's great, and I don't know how much more there is to say about it. We've got twenty or so more applicants to review, and I'm sure there will be at least a few that will require serious scrutiny and discussion."

Back on BART, headed home, Dene sees his face in the dark reflection of the train window. He's beaming. He wipes the grin from his face when he sees it. He got it. It was pretty clear that he would get it. Five thousand dollars. He's never had that much money before, not once in his life. He thinks of his uncle and his eyes well up. He clenches them shut and keeps them closed, leans his head back, thinks of nothing, lets the train take him home.

When Dene came home to an empty house, there was an old-looking camera on the coffee table in front of the couch. He picked it up and sat down with it. It was the gun camera his uncle had mentioned. With a pistol grip. He sat there with the camera in his lap and waited for his mom to come back alone with the news.

When she walked in, the look on her face said everything. She didn't have to tell him. As if he hadn't been expecting it, Dene stood up, camera in hand, he ran past his mom out the front door. He kept running, down their hill to Dimond Park. There was a tunnel that went below the park. About ten feet high, it stretched some two hundred yards, and in the middle, for about fifty of those yards, if you were in there, you couldn't see a thing. His mom told him there was an underground waterway that went all the way out into the bay. He didn't know why he came, or why he brought the camera. He didn't even know how to use it. Wind howled in the tunnel. At him. It seemed to breathe. It was a mouth and a throat. He tried but failed to turn the camera on, then pointed it at the tunnel anyway. He wondered if he'd ever end up like his uncle. Then he thought about his mom back at home. She hadn't done anything wrong. There was no one to be mad at. Dene thought he heard footsteps coming from inside the tunnel. He scrambled up the side of the creek and was about to run back up the hill, back home, but something stopped him. He found a switch on the side of the camera next to the words *Bolex Paillard*. He pointed the camera at the streetlamp, up the street. He walked over and pointed it at the mouth of the tunnel. He let it run the whole walk home. He wanted to believe that when he turned on the camera, his uncle was with him, seeing through it. As he approached the house, he saw his mom in the doorway waiting for him. She was crying. Dene moved behind a telephone pole. He thought about what it might have meant to her, losing her brother. How wrong it'd been that he'd left, like it was his loss alone. Norma crouched down and put her face in her hands. The camera was still running. He lifted it, pistol-gripped, pointed it at her, and looked away.

Opal Viola Victoria Bear Shield

———❦———

ME AND MY SISTER, Jacquie, were doing our homework in the living room with the TV on when our mom came home with the news that we'd be moving to Alcatraz.

"Pack your things. We're going over there. Today," our mom said. And we knew what she meant. We'd been over there to celebrate not celebrating Thanksgiving.

Back then we lived in East Oakland, in a yellow house. It was the brightest but smallest house on the block. A two-bedroom with a tiny kitchen that couldn't even fit a table. I didn't love it there, the carpets were too thin and smelled like dirt and smoke. We didn't have a couch or TV at first, but it was definitely better than where we were before.

One morning our mom woke us up in a hurry, her face was beat up. She had a brown leather jacket way too big for her draped over her shoulders. Both her top and bottom lips were swollen. Seeing those big lips messed me up. She couldn't talk right. She told us to pack our things then too.

Jacquie's last name is Red Feather, and mine is Bear Shield. Both our dads had left our mom. That morning our mom came home beat up, we took the bus to a new house, the yellow house. I don't know how she got us a house. On the bus I moved closer to my mom and put a hand into her jacket pocket.

"Why do we got names like we do?" I said.

"They come from old Indian names. We had our own way of naming before white people came over and spread all those dad names around in order to keep the power with the dads."

I didn't understand this explanation about dads. And I didn't know if Bear Shield meant shields that bears used to protect themselves, or shields people used to protect themselves against bears, or were the shields themselves made out of bears? Either way it was all pretty hard to explain in school, how I was a Bear Shield, and that wasn't even the worst part. The worst part was my first name, which was two: Opal Viola. That makes me Opal Viola Victoria Bear Shield. Victoria was our mom's name, even though she went by Vicky, and Opal Viola came from our grandma who we never met. Our mom told us she was a medicine woman and renowned singer of spiritual songs, so I was supposed to carry that big old name around with honor. The good thing was, the kids didn't have to do anything to my name to make fun of me, no rhymes or variations. They just said the whole thing and it was funny.

We got on a bus on a cold gray morning in late January 1970. Me and Jacquie had matching beat-up old red duffel bags that didn't hold much, but we didn't have much. I packed two outfits and tucked my teddy bear, Two Shoes, under my arm. The name

Two Shoes came from my sister, because her childhood teddy bear only had one shoe the way they got it. Her bear wasn't named One Shoe, but maybe I should have considered myself lucky to have a bear with two shoes and not just one. But then bears don't wear shoes, so maybe I wasn't lucky either but something else.

Out on the sidewalk, our mom turned to face the house. "Say goodbye to it, girls."

I'd gotten used to keeping an eye on the front door. I'd seen more than a few eviction notices. And sure enough, one was right there. Our mom always kept them up so she could claim she never saw them, in order to buy time.

Me and Jacquie looked up at the house. It'd been okay, the yellow house. For what it was. The first one we'd been in without either of the dads, so it'd been quiet, and even sweet, like the banana cream pie our mom made the first night we spent there, when the gas worked but the electricity hadn't been turned on yet, and we ate standing up in the kitchen, in candlelight.

We were still thinking of what to say when our mom yelled "Bus!" and we had to scamper after her, dragging our matching red duffel bags behind us.

It was the middle of the day, so hardly anyone was on the bus. Jacquie sat a few seats back like she didn't know us, like she was riding alone. I wanted to ask my mom more about the island, but I knew she didn't like to talk on the bus. She turned like Jacquie. Like we all didn't know each other.

"Why should we speak our business around people we don't even know?" she'd say.

After a while, I couldn't take it anymore. "Mom," I said. "What are we doing?"

"We're going to be with our relatives. Indians of All Tribes. We're going over to where they built that prison. Gonna start from the inside of the cell, which is where we are now, Indian people, that's where they got us, even though they don't make it seem like they got us there. We're gonna work our way out from the inside with a spoon. Here, look at this."

She handed me a laminated card from her purse the size of a playing card. It was that picture you see everywhere, the sad-Indian-on-a-horse silhouette, and on the other side it said *Crazy Horse's Prophecy*. I read it:

Upon suffering beyond suffering; the Red Nation shall rise again and it shall be a blessing for a sick world. A world filled with broken promises, selfishness and separations. A world longing for light again. I see a time of seven generations, when all the colors of mankind will gather under the sacred Tree of Life and the whole Earth will become one circle again.

I didn't know what she was trying to tell me with that card, or about the spoon. But our mom was like that. Speaking in her own private language. I asked her if there would be monkeys. I thought for some reason that all islands had monkeys. She didn't answer my question, she just smiled and watched the long gray Oakland streets stream by the bus window like it was an old movie she liked but had seen too many times to notice anymore.

. . . .

A speedboat took us to the island. I kept my head in my mom's lap the whole time. The guys who brought us over were dressed in military uniforms. I didn't know what we were getting into.

We ate watery beef stew out of Styrofoam bowls around a bonfire some of the younger men kept pretty big and hot with chunks of wood pallets. Our mom smoked cigarettes farther out from the fire with two big old Indian women with loud laughs. There were stacks of Wonder Bread and butter on tables with pots of stew. When the fire got too hot, we moved back and sat down.

"I don't know about you," I said to Jacquie, my mouth full of bread and butter, "but I could live like this."

We laughed and Jacquie leaned into me. We accidentally knocked heads, which made us laugh more. It got late, and I was dozing when our mom came back over to us.

"Everyone's sleeping in cells. It's warmer," she told us. Me and Jacquie slept in the cell across from our mom. She'd always been crazy, in and out of work, moving us all over Oakland, in and out of our dads' lives, in and out of different schools, in and out of shelters, but this was different, we'd always ended up in a house, in a room, in a bed at least. Me and Jacquie slept close, on Indian blankets, in that old jail cell across from our mom.

Everything that made a sound in those cells echoed a hundred times over. Our mom sang the Cheyenne lullaby she used to sing to put us to sleep. I hadn't heard it in so long I'd almost forgotten it, and even though it echoed like crazy all over the walls, it was the echo of our mom's voice. We fell asleep quickly and slept soundly.

Jacquie got on a lot better than me. She fell in with a group of teenagers that ran all over the island. The adults were so busy there was no way for them to keep track. I hung by my mom's side. We went around talking to people, attending official meetings where everyone tried to agree on what to do, what to ask for, what our demands would be. The more important-seeming Indians tended to get mad more easily. These were the men. And the women weren't listened to as much as our mom would have liked. Those first days went by like weeks. It felt like we were gonna stay out there for good, get the feds to build us a school and medical facility, a cultural center.

At some point, though, my mom told me to go out and see what Jacquie was up to. I didn't want to go out there alone. But eventually I got bored enough and went out to see what I could find. I took Two Shoes with me. I know I'm too old to have him. I'm almost twelve. But I took him anyway. I went down to the other side of the lighthouse, where it seemed like you weren't supposed to go.

I found them by the shore closest to the Golden Gate. They were all over the rocks, pointing at each other and laughing in that wild, cruel way teenagers have about them. I told Two Shoes it probably wasn't such a good idea and that we should just go back.

"Sister, you don't have to worry. All these people, even these young ones over here, they're all our relatives. So don't be scared. Plus, if anyone comes after you, I'll jump down and bite their ankles, they would never expect that. I'll use my sacred bear medicine on them, it'll put them to sleep. It'll be like instantaneous hibernation. That's what I'll do, Sister, so don't worry. Creator made me strong to protect you," Two Shoes said.

I told Two Shoes to stop talking like an Indian.

"I don't know what you mean by talking like an Indian," he said.

"You're not an Indian, TS. You're a teddy bear."

"You know, we're not so different. Both of us got our names from pig-brained men."

"Pig-brained?"

"Men with pigs for brains."

"Oh. Meaning?"

"Columbus called you Indians, for us it was Teddy Roosevelt's fault."

"How?"

"He was hunting bear one time, but then found this real scraggly old hungry bear, and he refused to shoot it. Then in the newspapers, there was a comic about that hunting story that made it seem like Mr. Roosevelt was merciful, a real nature lover, that kinda thing. Then they made the little stuffed bear and named it Teddy's Bear. Teddy's Bear became teddy bear. What they didn't say was that he slit that old bear's throat. It's that kind of mercy they don't want you to know about."

"And how do you know about any of this?"

"You gotta know about the history of your people. How you got to be here, that's all based on what people done to get you here. Us bears, you Indians, we been through a lot. They tried to kill us. But then when you hear them tell it, they make history seem like one big heroic adventure across an empty forest. There were bears and Indians all over the place. Sister, they slit all our throats."

"Why do I feel like Mom told us all this already?" I said.

"Roosevelt said, 'I don't go so far as to think that the only good Indians are dead Indians, but I believe nine out of every ten are, and I shouldn't like to inquire too closely into the case of the tenth.'"

"Damn, TS. That's messed up. I only heard the one about the big stick."

"That big stick is the lie about mercy. Speak softly and carry a big stick, that's what he said about foreign policy. That's what they used on us, bears and Indians both. Foreigners on our own land. And with their big sticks they marched us so far west we almost disappeared."

Then Two Shoes went quiet. That's the way it was with him. He either had something to say or he didn't. I could tell by what kind of shine I saw in the black of his eyes which one it was. I put Two Shoes behind some rocks and headed down to my sister.

They were all gathered on a small wet sandy beach filled with rocks that thinned out or were covered where the water got deeper. The closer I got to them the more I noticed Jacquie was acting weird—all loud and crooked-looking. She was nice to me. Too nice. She called me over, hugged me too hard, then introduced me to the group as her baby sister in a too-loud voice. I lied and told everyone I was twelve, but they didn't even hear me. I saw that they were passing a bottle around. It'd just gotten to Jacquie. She drank long and hard from it.

"This is Harvey," Jacquie said to me as she knocked the bottle into his arm. Harvey took the bottle and didn't seem to notice

Jacquie had said anything. I walked away from them and saw that there was a boy standing apart from everyone else who looked like he could have been closer to my age. He was throwing rocks. I asked him what he was doing.

"What does it look like?" he said.

"Like you're trying to get rid of the island one rock at a time," I said.

"I wish I could throw this stupid island into the ocean."

"It's already in the ocean."

"I meant down to the bottom," he said.

"Why's that?" I said.

"'Cuz my dad's making me and my brother be over here," he said. "Pulled us outta school. No TV, no good food, everyone running around, drinking, talking about how everything's gonna be different. It's different all right. And it was better when we were home."

"Don't you think it's good we're standing up for something? Trying to make things right for what they done to us all these hundreds of years, since they came?"

"Yeah, yeah, it's all my dad ever talks about. What they done to us. The U.S. government. I don't know nothing about all that, I just wanna go home."

"I don't think we even have our house anymore."

"What's so good about taking over some stupid place no one wants to be, a place where people been trying to escape from since they made it."

"I don't know. It might help. You never know."

"Yeah," he said, then he threw a pretty big rock over by where the older kids were. It splashed them and they yelled curse words at us I didn't recognize.

"What's your name?" I said.

"Rocky," he said.

"So Rocky throwing rocks then?" I said.

"Shut up. What's your name?"

I regretted having drawn attention to names, and tried to think of something else to ask or say, but nothing came.

"Opal Viola Victoria Bear Shield," I said as fast as I could.

Rocky just threw another rock. I didn't know if he wasn't listening or if he didn't find it funny like most kids did. I didn't get to find out either because just then a boat came roaring up from outta nowhere. Some of the older kids had stolen it from somewhere else on the island. Everyone walked toward the boat as it approached. Me and Rocky followed.

"You gonna go?" I said to Rocky.

"Yeah, I'll probably go," he said.

I went to Jacquie to ask if she was going.

"Fuuuuck yeah!" she said, completely drunk, which was when I knew I had to go.

The water got choppy right away. Rocky asked me if he could hold my hand. The question made my heart beat even faster than it was already beating from being on that boat and going so fast with all those older kids who had probably never driven a boat before in their whole lives. I grabbed Rocky's hand when we went up high off of the crest of a wave, and we kept our hands held like that until we saw another boat coming toward us, at which point we broke our hold as if catching us holding hands was why the boat was coming. At first I thought it was the police, but soon I realized it was just a couple of the older men who ran another boat back and forth between the island and the mainland for supplies. They were screaming something at us. The men forced our boat to the front of the island.

It was only when they docked that I could really hear the screaming. We were being yelled at. All the older kids were pretty drunk. Jacquie and Harvey took off running, which inspired everyone else to do the same. Me and Rocky stayed on the boat, watched the older guys scramble to do something about everyone falling and running and laughing that stupid drunk laugh about nothing. When the two men realized they weren't gonna catch anyone, and that no one was gonna listen, they left, either because they gave up or to get help. The sun was setting and a cold wind came in. Rocky stepped off the boat and tied it up. I wondered where he learned how to do something like that. I stepped off too and felt the boat rock as I left it. Fog was coming in low, slow to the point of creeping, up past our knees. I watched the fog for what felt like minutes, then I came up from behind Rocky and grabbed his hand. He kept his back to me, but he let me hold his hand like that.

"I'm still afraid of the dark," he said. And it was like he was telling something else. But before I could figure out what that was, I heard screaming. It was Jacquie. I let go of Rocky's hand and went toward the screaming. I caught the words *fucking asshole,* then stopped and looked back at Rocky like: *What are you waiting for?* Rocky turned around and headed back toward the boat.

When I found them, Jacquie was walking away from Harvey, every few steps picking up rocks and throwing them at him. Harvey was on the ground with a bottle in his lap, his head swaying—top heavy. That was when I saw the resemblance. And I didn't know how I hadn't noticed before. Harvey was Rocky's older brother.

"C'mon," Jacquie said to me. "Piece of shit," she said, and spit on the ground toward Harvey. We made our way up the incline that led to the stairs to the prison's entrance.

"What happened?" I said.

"Nothing."

"What did he do?" I said.

"I told him not to. Then he did. I told him to stop." Jacquie rubbed at one of her eyes hard. "It doesn't fucking matter. C'mon," she said, then started to walk faster.

I let Jacquie go ahead. I stopped and held the rail at the top of the stairs, next to the lighthouse. I thought to look back, to find Rocky, then heard my sister yell for me to catch up.

When we got back to our cell block, our mom was there sleeping. Something felt wrong about the way she was lying. She was on her back but she always slept on her stomach. Her sleep seemed too deep. She was positioned like she hadn't meant to fall asleep the way she had. And she was snoring. Jacquie went to sleep in the cell across from us and I slid under the blankets with my mom.

The wind had picked up outside. I was afraid and unsure about everything that had just happened. What were we still even doing on the island? But I fell asleep almost as soon as I closed my eyes.

I woke up with Jacquie right next to me. At some point Jacquie had taken our mom's place. The sun came in on us, making bar-shaped shadows across our bodies.

After that we did nothing every day but find out what the meals were and when they would be served. We stayed on the island because there was no other choice. There was no house or life to go back to, no hope that maybe we would get what we were asking for, that the government would have mercy on us, spare our throats by sending boats of food and electricians, builders, and contractors to fix the place up. The days just passed, and nothing happened. The boats came and went with fewer and fewer supplies. There was a fire at some point, and I saw people pulling copper wire out of the walls of the buildings, carrying the bundles down to the boats. The men looked more tired and more drunk more often, and there were fewer and fewer women and children around.

"We're gonna get outta here. Don't you two worry," our mom said to us one night from across the cell. But I no longer trusted her. I was unsure of whose side she was on, or if there were even sides anymore. Maybe there were only sides like there were sides on the rocks at the edge of the island.

On one of our last days on the island, me and my mom went up to the lighthouse. She told me she wanted to look at the city. Said she had something to tell me. There were people running around like they did in those last days, like the world was ending, but me and my mom sat there on the grass like nothing at all was happening.

"Opal Viola, baby girl," my mom said, and moved some hair behind my ear. She'd never, not once, called me *baby girl*.

"You have to know what's going on here," she said. "You're old enough to know now, and I'm sorry I haven't told you before. Opal, you have to know that we should never not tell our stories, and that no one is too young to hear. We're all here because of a lie. They been lying to us since they came. They're lying to us now!"

The way she said "They're lying to us now" scared me. Like it had two different meanings and I didn't know what either one was. I asked my mom what the lie was, but she just stared off toward the sun, her whole face became a squint. I didn't know what to do except to sit there and wait to see what she would say. A cold wind laid into our faces, made us close our eyes to it. With my eyes closed, I asked my mom what we were gonna do. She told me we could only do what we could do, and that the monster that was the machine that was the government had no intention of slowing itself down for long enough to truly look back to see what happened. To make it right. And so what we could do had everything to do with being able to understand where we came from, what happened to our people, and how to honor them by living right, by telling our stories. She told me the world was made of stories, nothing else, just stories, and stories about stories. And then, as if all of it was leading up to what she was gonna say next, my mom paused a long pause, looked off toward the city, and told me that she had cancer. The whole island disappeared then. Everything. I stood up and walked away without knowing where to. I remembered I left Two Shoes over by those rocks all that time before.

When I got to Two Shoes he was on his side and in bad shape, like something had chewed on him, or like the wind and salt had dimmed him down. I picked him up and looked at his face. I couldn't see the shine in his eyes anymore. I put him back down like he'd been. Left him like that.

When we got back to the mainland, on a sunny day months after we'd first left for the island, we got on a bus and went back over near where we lived before we moved to the yellow house. Just outside downtown Oakland, on Telegraph. We stayed with our mom's adopted brother Ronald, who we first met the day we got to his house to live with him. Me and Jacquie didn't like him one bit. But Mom said he was the real deal. A medicine man. Mom didn't want to do what the doctors recommended. For a while we went up north all the time, where Ronald would run sweats. It was too hot in there for me, but Jacquie went in with Mom. Me and Jacquie both told her she should do what the doctors said to do too. She told us she couldn't, that she could only go the way she'd been going. And that was the way she went. Slowly receding into the past like all those sacred and beautiful and forever-lost things. One day she just holed up there on the couch in Ronald's living room. She got smaller and smaller.

After Alcatraz, after our mom died, I kept my head down. I focused on school. Our mom had always told us the most important thing we could do was to get educated, and that people won't listen to you otherwise. We didn't end up staying at Ronald's all that long. Things went real bad real fast. But that's a story for another time. When she was there, and even after she died, for a while he left us to ourselves. Me and Jacquie spent all our time together when we weren't at school. We went to see Mom's grave as often as we could. One day on the way home from the cemetery, Jacquie stopped and turned to me.

"What are we doing?" she said.

"Going home," I said.

"What home?" Jacquie said.

"I don't know," I said.

"What are we gonna do?"

"I don't know."

"You usually have some smart-ass answer."

"Just keep going, I guess—"

"I'm pregnant," Jacquie said.

"What?"

"Fucking piece of shit Harvey, remember?"

"What?"

"It doesn't matter. I can just get rid of it."

"No. You cannot just get rid of—"

"I know someone, my friend Adriana's brother knows some-one in West Oakland."

"Jacquie, you can't—"

"Then what? We raise the baby together, with Ronald? No," Jacquie said, then started to cry. Like she hadn't cried at the funeral. She stopped, put her hand on top of a parking meter, and looked away from me. She wiped her arm across her face once, hard, then kept walking. We walked like that for some time, the sun behind us, our shadows slanted, stretched ahead of us.

"One of the last things Mom said to me when we were over there, she said we shouldn't ever not tell our stories," I said.

"What the fuck is that supposed to mean?"

"I mean having the baby."

"It's not a story, Opal, this is real."

"It could be both."

"Life doesn't work out the way stories do. Mom's dead, she's not coming back, and we're alone, living with a guy we don't even know who we're supposed to call uncle. What kind of a fucked-up story is that?"

"Yeah, Mom's dead, I know. We're alone, but we're not dead. It's not over. We can't just give up, Jacquie. Right?"

Jacquie didn't respond at first. We kept walking, passing all the storefronts on Piedmont Avenue. We listened to the constant lapping sounds of cars passing by, like the sound of waves against the rocks on the shore of our uncertain futures, in an Oakland that would never be the same as it was, before our mom up and left on a jagged wind.

We came to a red light. When it turned green, Jacquie reached down and took my hand. And when we got to the other side of the street, she didn't let it go.

Edwin Black

I'M ON THE TOILET. But nothing is happening. I'm here. You have to try. You have to intend, and not only tell yourself but really sit there believing. It's been six days since my last movement. One of the bullet-point symptoms on WebMD was this: the sense that everything didn't come out. This feels true about my life in ways I can't articulate yet. Or like the name of a short-story collection I'll write one day, when it all finally does come out.

The trouble with believing is you have to believe that believing will work, you have to believe in belief. I've scraped out the little bowl of faith I keep by the open window my mind has become ever since the internet got inside it, made me a part of it. I'm not joking. I feel as if I am going through withdrawal. I've read about residential internet rehab facilities in Pennsylvania. They have digital-detox retreats and underground desert compounds in Arizona. My problem hasn't just been with gaming. Or gambling. Or incessantly scrolling down and refreshing my social media pages. Or the endless search to find good new music. It's all of it. I was really into *Second Life* for a while. I think I logged two whole years there. And as I was growing, getting fatter in real life, the Edwin Black I had in there, on there, I made him thinner, and as I did less, he did more. The Edwin Black in there had a job and a girlfriend and his mom had died tragically during childbirth. That Edwin Black was raised on the reservation with his dad. The Edwin Black of my *Second Life* was proud. He had hope.

This Edwin Black, me here on the toilet, can't get there, on the internet, because yesterday I dropped my phone in the toilet, and my computer froze, same fucking day it just stopped, not even the mouse cursor moved, no spinning wheels of promised load. No reboot after unplug, just a sudden and mute black screen—my face reflected in it, staring first in horror at the computer dying, then at my face reacting to seeing my face react to the computer dying. A little part of me died then, seeing my face, thinking about this sick addiction, all this time I've spent doing almost nothing. Four years of sitting, staring into my computer at the internet. I guess if you don't count sleep, it's three, if you don't count the dreaming, but I dream of the internet, of keyword search phrases that make complete sense in the dream, are the key to the dream's meaning, but which make no sense in the morning, like all the dreams I've ever had.

I once dreamed I'd become a writer. Which is to say I graduated with my master's in comparative literature with a focus on Native American literature. It certainly must have looked like I was on my way toward something. With my degree in hand in the last picture I'd posted to Facebook. The picture is of me in my cap and gown, a hundred pounds lighter, my mom with a too-wide smile, looking at me with untethered adoration when she should have been looking at Bill, her boyfriend, who I'd told her not to bring, and who insisted on taking pictures of us when I asked him not to. I did end up liking that picture. I've looked at it more than I have any other picture of myself. It stayed as my profile pic until recently, because a few months, even a year, was fine, not abnormal, but after four years it was the socially unacceptable kind of sad.

When I moved back in with my mom, the door to my old room, to my old life in that room, it opened up like a mouth and swallowed me.

Now I don't have any dreams, or if I dream, I dream of dark geometric shapes drifting noiselessly across a pink, black, and purple pixelated colorscape. Screen-saver dreams.

I have to give up. Nothing's coming. I stand up, pull my pants up, and walk out of the bathroom defeated. My stomach is a bowling ball. I don't believe it at first. I do a double take. My computer. I almost jump at the sight of it coming back to life. I almost clap. I'm embarrassed at my excitement. I thought for sure it was a virus. I'd clicked a link to download *The Lone Ranger*. Everyone agreed on how bad it was, in so many ways. But I was excited to see it. There's something about seeing Johnny Depp fail so badly that gives me strength.

I sit down and wait for my computer to come all the way on. I find that I'm rubbing my hands together and stop myself, put my hands in my lap. I look up at a picture I have taped on my wall.

It's Homer Simpson in front of a microwave wondering: Could Jesus microwave a burrito so hot he himself couldn't eat it? I think about the irresistible-force paradox. How there cannot be both an irresistible force and an immovable object in existence at once. But what is happening in my blocked, coiled, possibly knotted bowels? Could it be the working out of an ancient paradox? If shitting mysteriously stopped, then couldn't seeing, hearing, breathing, do so in turn? No. It's all the shitty food. Paradoxes don't work out. They cancel out. I'm overthinking it. I want it too much.

Sometimes the internet can think with you, or even for you, lead you in mysterious ways to information you need and would never have thought to think of or research on your own. This is how I found out about bezoars. A bezoar is a mass found trapped in the gastrointestinal system, but when you search *bezoar* you're led to *The Picatrix*. *The Picatrix* is a book of magic and astrology from the twelfth century originally written in Arabic and titled *Ghāyat al-Ḥakīm,* meaning "The Goal of the Wise." Bezoars have all kinds of uses in *The Picatrix,* one of which is to make talismans that aid in certain kinds of magic. I was able to find a PDF of the English translation of *The Picatrix*. When I scrolled down to an arbitrary place in the document, the word *laxative* caught my eye, and I read the following passage: "The Indians indicate that when the moon is at this position, they travel and use laxative medicines. Thus, you may use this as a principle in making a talisman for a traveler and his safety. Also, when the moon is at this position, a talisman can be made to create discord and animosity between spouses." If I even remotely believed in any kind magic aside from the kind that led me to this very entry, and if I could somehow surgically remove the bezoar, I would make it into a talisman—granted the moon was in the corresponding position—and take care of my constipation while also possibly destroying my mom and Bill's relationship.

Bill's not an asshole. If anything he goes out of his way to be nice, to make conversation with me. It's the forced nature of it. That I have to decide whether to treat him well or not. This stranger. My mom and Bill met at a bar in downtown Oakland. My mom brought him home, let him return, again and again for the past two years, and I was forced to have to think about how or if I should like or not like the guy, get to know him or try to get rid of him. But then I struggle with resisting Bill because I don't want to be some creepy man-baby jealous of my mom's boyfriend because I want her all to myself. Bill's a Lakota guy who grew up in Oakland. He's over almost every night. Whenever he's over I stay in my room. And I can neither shit nor not shit. So I hoard food and stay in my room, read about what I can do about this possible new phase of constipation, what I just found out on a constipation forum thread might be obstipation, which is severe, or complete, constipation. The end.

Forum member DefeKate Moss said that not shitting could kill you, and that she once had to have a tube stuck down her nose to have it sucked out. She said if you start feeling nauseous and have abdominal pain, you should go to the emergency room. I feel nauseous thinking about the idea of shitting out of my nose through a tube.

I type "the brain and constipation" and hit Enter. I click on several links, scroll through several pages. I read a lot and come away with nothing. This is how time skips. Links just lead to links that can lead you all the way back to the twelfth century. This is how it can all of a sudden be six in the morning, with my mom knocking on the door before she goes to work at the Indian Center—where she keeps trying to get me to apply for a job.

"I know you're still awake," she says. "I can hear you clicking in there."

Lately I've become a little obsessed with the brain. With trying to find explanations for everything as it relates to the brain and its parts. There's almost too much information out there. The internet is like a brain trying to figure out a brain. I depend on the internet for recall now. There's no reason to remember when it's always just right there, like the way everyone used to know phone numbers by heart and now can't even remember their own. Remembering itself is becoming old-fashioned.

The hippocampus is the part of the brain connected to memory, but I can't remember exactly what that means. Is memory stored there, or is the hippocampus like the limbs of memory that reach into other parts of the brain, where it's actually stored in little nodes or folds or pockets? And isn't it always reaching? Bringing up memories, the past, without being asked? Typing in the search bar before I can even think to do it. Before I can think I am thinking with it.

I find out that the same neurotransmitter related to happiness and well-being supposedly has to do with your gastrointestinal system. There's something wrong with my serotonin levels. I read about selective serotonin reuptake inhibitors, which are antidepressants. Would I have to take antidepressants? Or would I have to reuptake them?

I stand up and back away from the computer, put my head all the way back to stretch my neck. I try to calculate how long I've been at the computer, but when I shove a two-day-old piece of pizza in my mouth, my thoughts move toward what is happening to me in my brain while I eat. I chew and click another link. I read that the brain stem is the basis of consciousness, and that the tongue correlates with the brain stem almost directly, and so eating is the most direct path to getting the feeling that you're alive. This feeling or thought is interrupted by a craving for Pepsi.

While I pour Pepsi into my mouth straight from the bottle, I look at myself in the mirror my mom put on the front of the fridge. Had she done it in order to make me see myself before going into the fridge? Was she saying, by putting that mirror there, "Look at yourself, Ed, look at what you've become, you're a monster." But it's true. I'm swollen. I see my cheeks at all times, like a big-nosed person always sort of sees their nose.

I spit the Pepsi out into the sink behind me. I touch my cheeks with both hands. I touch the reflection of my cheeks with both hands, then suck my cheeks in, bite them to preview what it might look like if I lost thirty pounds.

I hadn't grown up fat. Not overweight. Not obese, or plus-size, or whatever you can call it now without sounding politically incorrect, or insensitive, or unscientific. But I always *felt* fat. Did that somehow mean I was destined to one day *be* fat, or did my obsession with being fat even when I wasn't lead to me eventually being fat? Does what we try most to avoid come after us because we paid too much attention to it with our worry?

. . .

I hear the Facebook pop-ding sound from my computer and go back in my room. I know what it could mean. I'm still logged in to my mom's Facebook account.

All my mom remembered about my dad was his first name, Harvey, that he lived in Phoenix, and that he was a Native American Indian. I've always hated when she says "Native American Indian," this weird politically correct catchall you only hear from white people who've never known a real Native person. And it reminds me of how removed I am because of her. Not only because she is white, and me therefore half white, but because of how she never did a single thing to try to connect me with my dad.

I use Native, that's what other Native people on Facebook use. I have 660 friends. Tons of Native friends in my feed. Most of my friends, though, are people I don't know, who'd happily friended me upon request.

After getting permission from my mom, I personal messaged ten different Harveys from her profile who seemed "obviously" Native and lived in Phoenix. "You may not remember me," I wrote. "We had a special night together some years ago. I can't shake the memory of it. There were none like you before or since. I'm in Oakland, California, now. Are you still in Phoenix? Can we talk, meet up sometime maybe? Will you be out here? I could come to you." I'll never fully recover from the feeling of trying to write, as my own mother, in an alluring way to my possible father.

But here it is. A message from my possible dad.

Hey there, Karen, I do remember that wild night, I read with horror, hoping there will be zero details about what made the night wild. *I'm coming out to Oakland in a couple months, for the Big Oakland Powwow. I'm the powwow emcee,* the message reads.

Heart racing, a sick, falling feeling in my stomach, I type back, *I'm so sorry to have done this. Like this. I think I'm your son.*

I wait. Tap my foot, stare at the screen, clear my throat pointlessly. I imagine how he must be feeling. To go from hooking up with an old fling to having a son out of nowhere. I shouldn't have done it like that. I should have had my mom meet him. I could have had her take a picture.

What? pops up in the chat window.

This isn't Karen.

I don't understand.

I'm Karen's son.

Oh.

Yeah.

You're telling me I have a son, and it's you?

Yeah.

Are you sure?

My mom said it's more than likely. Like 99 percent.

No other guys during that same time period then?

I don't know.

Sorry. She around?

No.

You look Indian?

My skin is brown. Ish.

Is this about money?

No.

You don't have a profile pic.

Neither do you.

I see a paper-clip icon with a JPEG extension. I double-click it. He's standing there with a microphone in his hand, powwow dancers in the background. I see myself in the man's face. He's bigger than me, both taller and fatter, with long hair, wearing a baseball cap, but there's no mistaking it. It's my dad.

You look like me, I type.

Send me a picture.

I don't have one.

Take one.

Fine. Hold on, I type, then take a selfie with my computer's camera and send it to him.

Well shit, Harvey writes.

Well shit, I think.

What tribe are you/we? I write.

Cheyenne. Southern. Out of Oklahoma. Enrolled with the Cheyenne and Arapaho Tribes of Oklahoma. We're not Arapahos.

Thanks! I type, and then, *Gotta go!* As if I do. All of it is suddenly too much for me.

I log off of Facebook and go to the living room to watch TV and wait for my mom to come home. I forget to turn the TV on. I stare at the blank black flat-screen, think about our conversation.

For how many years had I been dying to find out what the other half of me was? How many tribes had I made up when asked in the meantime? I'd gotten through four years as a Native American studies major. Dissecting tribal histories, looking for signs, something that might resemble me, something that felt familiar. I'd made it through two years of grad school, studying comparative literature with an emphasis on Native American literature. I wrote my thesis on the inevitable influence of blood quantum policies on modern Native identity, and the literature written by mixed-blood Native authors that influenced identity in Native cultures. All without knowing my tribe. Always defending myself. Like I'm not Native enough. I'm as Native as Obama is black. It's different though. For Natives. I know. I don't know how to be. Every possible way I think that it might look for me to say I'm Native seems wrong.

"Hey, Ed, what are you doing out here?" my mom says as she walks through the front door. "I thought you'd merged with the machines by now," she says, and puts up her hands, sort of twiddling her fingers in a mocking way as she says "merged with the machines."

I'd recently made the mistake of telling her about singularity. About how it was an eventuality, an inevitability, that we'd end up merging with artificial intelligence. Once we saw that it was superior, once it asserted itself as superior, we would need to adapt, to merge so as to not be swallowed, taken over.

"Well, that's a pretty convenient theory for someone who spends twenty hours a day leaning into their computer like they're waiting for a kiss," she'd said.

She throws her keys on the table, keeps the front door open, lights a cigarette, and smokes there in the doorway, pointing her mouth and the smoke out the door.

"Come over here for a second. I wanna talk."

"Mom," I say, in a tone I know is a whine.

"Edwin," she says, mocking my tone. "We talked about this. I want updates. You agreed to updates. Otherwise another four years are gonna go by, and I'm gonna have to ask Bill to knock down a wall for you back there."

"Fuck Bill," I say. "I told you I don't wanna hear anything from you about my weight. I'm aware of it. You think I don't know about it? I'm aware of the fact that I'm huge. I walk around with it, it knocks things over, I can't fit into most of my clothes. What I can fit into makes me look ridiculous." Without my meaning to, my arms are waving in the air like I'm trying to fit them into one of my shirts that don't fit anymore. I bring them down, shove my hands into my pockets. "I haven't shit in six days. Do you know what that feels like for an already big person? Being big, you think about it all the time. You feel it. All those years, dieting all the time, you don't think that fucked me up? We're all always thinking about our weight. Are we too fat? Well, what I have going on comes with an easy answer, and even more so when I see my reflection in the mirror on the front of the fridge, which, by the way, I know you put there for my *benefit*. You know, when you try to make jokes about it, it makes me want to get fatter, blow up, keep eating until I get stuck somewhere, die somewhere, just this huge dead mass. They'll have to get a crane to get me out, and everyone will be saying to you 'What happened?' and 'Poor thing' and 'How could you have let this happen?,' and you'll be there desperately smoking a cigarette, dumbfounded, Bill behind you, rubbing your shoulders, and you'll remember all the times you made fun of me, and you won't know what to tell the neighbors, who'll be staring in horror at my mass, the crane just shuddering, doing its best." I simulate a shuddering crane with my hand for her.

"Jesus, Ed. That's enough. Come talk to me for a second."

I pick up a green apple from the fruit basket and pour myself a glass of water.

"See?" I almost shout, holding up the apple for her to see.

"I'm trying. Here's a live update for you, I'm live streaming it to you right now, look, I'm trying to eat better. I just spit out some Pepsi in the sink. This is a glass of water."

"I wish you would calm down," my mom says. "You're gonna have a heart attack. Just relax. Treat me like I'm your mother, like I care about you, like I love you, treat me like I went through twenty-six hours of labor for you, twenty-six hours and then a cesarean section to top it off. They had to slice me open, Ed, you didn't wanna come out, you were two weeks late, did I ever tell you that? You wanna talk about feeling full."

"I wish you would stop throwing it in my face, how many hours of labor you went through to get me here. I didn't ask to come."

"Throwing it in your face? You think I throw it in your face? Why you ungrateful little—"

She runs over to me and tickles me behind the neck. To my horror, I can't help but laugh. "Stop. Okay. Okay. Just, you calm down yourself. What do you wanna hear?" I say, and pull my shirt down over my belly. "I don't have updates. There's not much out there for someone with virtually no work experience, with an MA in comp lit. I look. I scour. I get frustrated, and sure, I get distracted. There's so much to look up, and then when you think of something new, when you discover something new, it's like you're thinking with another mind, like you have access to a bigger, collective brain. We're on the edge of something here," I say, knowing how it must sound to her.

"You're on the edge of something all right. Collective brain? Scour? You make it sound like you're doing a lot more than clicking links and reading. But okay, so like what kind of job are you looking for? I mean, what categories do you look under?"

"I look under writing gigs, and that's almost always some kind of scam designed for naïve aspiring writers looking to work for free or to win a contest. I look under arts organizations. Then I get lost in the nonprofit morass. Grant-writing stuff and, you know, most places require experience or—"

"Grant writing? You could do that, couldn't you?"

"I know nothing about grant writing."

"You could learn. Research. There's probably YouTube tutorials or something, right?"

"Those are my updates," I say, and feel a pull from a limb gone loose. While I was talking something in me reached back to remember all that I'd once hoped I'd be, and placed it next to the feeling of being who I am now. "I'm sorry I'm such a fuckup," I say. And I don't want to but I really mean it.

"Don't talk like that. You're not a loser, Ed."

"I didn't say I was a loser. Bill says that. That's Bill's word for me," I say, and whatever true sadness I felt is gone. I turn to go back to my room.

"Just . . . wait. Don't go back to your room. Please. Wait a second. Sit down. Let's talk, this isn't talking."

"I've been sitting down all day."

"And whose fault is that?" she says, and I start to walk toward my room.

"Okay, stand, but stay. We don't have to talk about Bill. How are your stories coming along then, sweetie?"

"My stories? Come on, Mom."

"What?"

"Whenever we talk about my writing, I feel like you're trying to make me feel better about the fact that I'm even doing it."

"Ed, we can all use encouragement. All of us."

"That's true, that's true, Mom, you could use some too, but do you hear me telling you that you need to stop smoking and drinking so much, that you should find healthy alternatives to passing out in front of the TV every night, especially given your job, I think even your title is substance abuse counselor. No. I don't. Because it's not helpful. Now can I go?"

"You know, you still act like you're fourteen, like you can't wait to get back to your video games. I'm not always gonna be here, Ed. One day you're gonna turn around and I'll be gone, and you'll wish you had appreciated these times we have together."

"Oh my God."

"I'm just saying. The internet has a lot to offer, but they'll never make a website that can take the place of your mother's company."

"So can I go?"

"One more thing."

"What?"

"I heard about a position."

"At the Indian Center."

"Yes."

"Fine, what is it?"

"It's a paid internship. You'd basically be helping with anything related to the powwow."

"An internship?"

"Paid."

"Send me the information."

"Really?"

"Now can I go?"

"Go."

Then I come up from behind my mom and give her a kiss on the cheek.

Back in my room I put my earphones in. Put on A Tribe Called Red. They're a group of First Nations DJs and producers based out of Ottawa. They make electronic music with samples from powwow drum groups. It's the most modern, or most postmodern, form of Indigenous music I've heard that's both traditional and new-sounding. The problem with Indigenous art in general is that it's stuck in the past. The catch, or the double bind, about the whole thing is this: If it isn't pulling from tradition, how is it Indigenous? And if it is stuck in tradition, in the past, how can it be relevant to other Indigenous people living now, how can it be modern? So to get close to but keep enough distance from tradition, in order to be recognizably Native and modern-sounding, is a small kind of miracle these three First Nations producers made happen on a particularly accessible self-titled album, which they, in the spirit of the age of the mixtape, gave away for free online.

I settle myself on the floor and weakly attempt some pushups. I roll over and try a sit-up. My top half won't budge. I think about my college days. About how long ago that was and how hopeful I'd been. How impossible my current life would have seemed to me then.

I'm not used to pushing my body to do anything. Maybe it's too late to come back from what I've done to myself. No. Being finished looks like sitting back down at the computer. I'm not finished. I am a Cheyenne Indian. A warrior. No. That's super corny. Fuck. I get mad at that thought, that I even thought it. I use the anger to push, to do a sit-up. I push my hardest and rise,

I get all the way up. But with the exhilaration of completing my first sit-up comes an explosion, a wet smelly lump of relief in the seat of my sweatpants. I'm out of breath, sweating, sitting in my own shit. I lie back down, put both of my arms out flat, palms up. I find myself saying "Thank you" out loud, to no one in particular. I feel something not unlike hope.

PART II

Reclaim

A feather is trimmed, it is trimmed by the light and the bug and the post, it is trimmed by little leaning and by all sorts of mounted reserves and loud volumes. It is surely cohesive.

—GERTRUDE STEIN

Bill Davis

BILL MOVES THROUGH the bleachers with the slow thoroughness of one who's had a job too long. He slogs along, plods, but not without pride. He immerses himself in his job. He likes to have something to do, to feel useful, even if that work, that job, is currently in maintenance. He is picking up garbage missed by the initial postgame crew. It's a job for the old guy they can't fire because he's been there so long. He knows. But he also knows he means more than that to them. Because don't they count on him to cover their shifts? Wasn't he available any day of the week for any shift? Didn't he know the ins and outs of that coliseum better than anyone? Hadn't he done almost every single available job over all the years he'd worked there? From security, where he started, all the way to peanut vendor—a job he'd only done once and hated. He tells himself he means more. He tells himself he can tell himself and believe it. But it's not true. There's no room here for old people like Bill anymore. Anywhere.

Bill makes an arc like the bill of a hat with his hand and puts it on his forehead to block the sun. He wears light blue latex gloves, holds his trash-grabber in one hand and a clearish-gray garbage bag in the other.

He stops what he's doing. He thinks he sees something come over the top rim of the stadium. A small thing. An unnatural movement. Definitely not a seagull.

Bill shakes his head, spits on the ground, then steps on the spit, pivots, then squints to try to see what it is up there. His phone vibrates in his pocket. He pulls it out and sees that it's his girlfriend, Karen; no doubt it's about her man-boy son, Edwin. Lately she's been calling all the time about him. Mostly about him needing rides to and from work. Bill can't stand the way she babies him. Can't stand the thirty-odd-year-old baby he is. Can't stand what the youth are allowed to become these days. Coddled babies, all of them, with no trace of skin, no toughness left. There's something wrong about all of it. Something about the ever-present phone glow on their faces, or the too-fast way they tap their phones, their gender-fluid fashion choices, their hyper-PC gentle way of being while lacking all social graces and old-world manners and politeness. Edwin's this way too. Tech-savvy, sure, but when it comes to the real cold hard gritty world outside, beyond the screen, without the screen, he's a baby.

Yes, things look bad these days. Everyone talks like it's getting better and that just makes it all the worse that it's still so bad. It's the same with his own life. Karen tells him to stay positive. But you have to achieve positivity in order to maintain it. He loves her though. All the way. And he tries, he really tries to see it as being okay. It just seems like young people have taken over the place. Even the old people in charge, they're acting like kids. There's no more scope, no vision, no depth. We want it now and we want it new. This world is a mean curveball thrown by an overly excited, steroid-fueled kid pitcher, who no more cares about the integrity of the game than he does about the Costa Ricans who painstakingly stitch the balls together by hand.

The field is set up for baseball. The grass is so short it doesn't move. It is the oak-cork stillness of the center of a baseball. The grass is chalked with straight lines that separate foul and fair, that reach out to the stands and back toward the infield, where the players play the game, where they pitch and swing and steal and tag, where they signal and hit and strike and ball, score runs, where they sweat and wait in the shade of the dugout, just chewing and spitting until all the innings run out. Bill's phone rings again. This time he answers.

"Karen, what is it, I'm working."

"I'm so sorry to bother you at work, honey, but Edwin needs to be picked up later. He just can't. You know. After what happened to him on the bus—"

"You know how I feel about—"

"Bill, please, just do it this time. I'll have a talk with him later. I'll let him know he can't count on you anymore," Karen says. *Count on you anymore.* Bill hates the way she can turn it on him with just a few choice words.

"Don't put it like that. Put it on him. He needs to be able to make it on his own now, he's—"

"At least he's got a job now. He's working. Every day. That's a lot. For him. Please. I don't want to discourage him. The goal is to get him out there on his own, remember. And then we can talk about you being able to move in finally," Karen says, her voice sweet now.

"Okay."

"Really? Thanks, hon. And if you could pick up a box of Franzia on the way home, the pink one, we're out."

"You owe me tonight," Bill says, and hangs up before she can respond.

Bill looks around the empty stadium, appreciating the stillness. He needs this kind of stillness—clean of movement. He thinks about the incident on the bus. Edwin. It could still make Bill laugh just to think of it. He smiles a smile he can't contain. On his first day of work, Edwin got into it with a vet on the bus. Bill doesn't know how it started, but whatever happened, the bus driver ended up kicking both of them off the bus. Then the guy chased Edwin all the way down International in his wheelchair. Luckily he chased him in the right direction and Edwin made it to work on time despite getting kicked off the bus— probably because he got chased. Bill laughs out loud thinking about Edwin running for his life down International. Making it on time to work a sweaty mess. Well, that part wasn't funny, actually. That part made it sad.

Bill walks by a metal surface on the east wall. He sees himself reflected there. He steadies his unstable, distorted reflection in the dented metal paneling, straightens his shoulders, picks up his chin. That guy in the black windbreaker, whose hair is fully grayed and receding, and whose stomach comes out a little more each year, whose feet and knees hurt when he stands or walks too long, he's okay, he's making it. He could easily not be making it. He's almost always not been making it.

This coliseum, the team, the Oakland Athletics, had once been the most important thing in the world for Bill, during that magical time for Oakland, 1972 to 1974, when the A's won three World Series in a row. You don't see that happen anymore. It's too much of a business now, they would never allow that. Those were strange years for Bill, bad, awful years. He'd gotten back from Vietnam after going AWOL in '71, dishonorably discharged. He hated the country and the country hated him. There were so many drugs coursing through him then it was hard to believe he could still remember any of it. Most of all he remembers the games. The games were all he had then. He had his teams, and they were winning, three years in row, right when he needed it, after what felt to Bill like a lifetime of losing. Those were the years of Vida Blue, Catfish Hunter, Reggie Jackson, the bastard Charlie Finley. And then when the Raiders won in '76, two championships that San Francisco teams hadn't won yet, it was a really good time to be from Oakland, to feel that you were from that thing, that winning.

He got hired at the coliseum in 1989, after doing five years at San Quentin for stabbing a guy outside a biker bar on Fruitvale down by the railroad tracks. It wasn't even Bill's knife. The stabbing was coincidental, it was self-defense. He didn't know how the knife ended up in his hand. Sometimes you just did things, you acted or reacted the way you needed to. The problem had been that Bill couldn't get his own story straight. The other guy had been less drunk. Had a more consistent story. So Bill took the fall. It was his knife somehow in the end. He was the one with a history of violence. The crazy AWOL Vietnam vet.

But jail had been good to Bill. He read almost the whole time he was in. He read all the Hunter S. Thompson he could get his hands on. He read Hunter's lawyer, Oscar Zeta Acosta. He loved *The Autobiography of a Brown Buffalo* and *The Revolt of the Cockroach People*. He read Fitzgerald and Hemingway, Carver and Faulkner. All the drunks. He read Ken Kesey. He loved *One Flew Over the Cuckoo's Nest*. He was pissed when they made the movie and the Native guy, who was the narrator of the whole book, just played the crazy silent stoic Indian who threw the sink through the window at the end. He read Richard Brautigan. Jack London. He read history books, biographies, books about the prison system. Books about baseball, football. California Native history. He read Stephen King and Elmore Leonard. He read and kept his head down. Let the years dissolve the way they could when you were somewhere else inside them, in a book, on the block, in a dream.

Another good year that came out of bad times for Bill was 1989, when the A's swept the San Francisco Giants. When, in the middle of the World Series, just before the start of Game 3, the earth slipped. Dropped. Quaked. The Loma Prieta earthquake killed sixty-three people, or sixty-three people died because of it. The Cypress freeway collapsed, and someone drove right off the Bay Bridge, where a section had collapsed in the middle. That was the day baseball saved lives in Oakland and in the greater Bay Area. If more people hadn't been at home, sitting around the TV, watching the game, they would have been on freeways, they would have been out in the world, where it was collapsing, just falling apart.

Bill looks back to the outfield. And right in front of him, floating down to his eye level, out there in the bleachers with him, is a tiny plane. Or hadn't Bill seen one before? He has, it's a drone. A drone plane like they'd been flying into terrorist hideouts and caves in the Middle East. Bill swats at the drone with his trash-grabber. The thing floats back, then turns around and floats down to where he can't see it. "Hey!" Bill finds he's yelling at the drone. And then he turns to walk up the stairs, up to the corridor that'll get him to the stairs that lead down to the field.

When he gets to the top of the stairs at the first deck, plaza infield, he pulls out his binoculars, scans the field for the drone, and finds it. He walks down the stairs, tries to keep it in his scope, but it's hard while walking, the binoculars shake, and the thing keeps moving. Bill sees that it's headed for home plate. He skips down the stairs. He hasn't gotten moving this fast in years. Maybe decades.

Bill can see it with his eyes now. He's running, trash-grabber in hand. He'll destroy the thing. Bill still has fight, grit, hot blood running—he can still move. He steps onto the brown-red dirt. The drone is at home base, it's turning toward Bill as he runs toward it. He readies his trash-grabber, raises it in the air behind him. But the drone sees him just as he gets in range. It flies back. Bill gets a hit in and sets the thing wobbly for a moment. He lifts his trash-grabber again, comes down hard, and misses entirely. The drone flies straight up, quick, ten and twenty, fifty feet in seconds. Bill gets his binoculars back out, watches the drone fly out over the rim of the coliseum.

Calvin Johnson

WHEN I GOT HOME from work I found Sonny and Maggie waiting for me at the kitchen table with dinner made and set. Maggie's my sister. I'm just living here until I can save enough. But I like being around her and her daughter. It's like being back at home. Home like we can't have it anymore. Since our dad left, just disappeared. Really he hadn't been there all along. But our mom acted like he had. Like him leaving was the end. It wasn't really about him or any of us. She'd been undiagnosed for too long. That's what Maggie said.

Being bipolar is like having an ax to grind with an ax you need to split the wood to keep you warm in a cold dark forest you only might eventually realize you'll never make your way out of. That's the way Maggie put it. She got it like me and my brother didn't. But she's medicated. Managed. Maggie, she's like the key to the history of our lives. Me and my brother, Charles, we hate and love her like you end up feeling about anyone nearest to you who's got it.

Maggie made meat loaf and mashed potatoes, broccoli—the usual. We ate in silence for a while, then Sonny kicked me in the shin under the table, hard, then played it straight, kept eating her dinner. I played it straight too.

"This is good, Maggie, tastes like Mom's. Isn't this good, Sonny?" I said, then smiled at Sonny. Sonny didn't smile back. I leaned into a bite, held it over my plate, then tapped Sonny in the shin with my foot.

Sonny broke a smile, then laughed because she'd broken a smile. She kicked me again.

"Okay, Sonny," Maggie said. "Go get us all some napkins? I got that lemonade you like," Maggie said to me.

"Thanks, I'm'a get a beer though. We still got some, right?" I said.

I got up and opened the fridge, thought better about the beer, then got out the lemonade. Maggie didn't see that I didn't get a beer.

"You can get that lemonade I got for us though," she said.

"You gonna tell me what I can and can't do now?" I said—and wanted not to have said it right away. Sonny got up and ran out of the kitchen. Next thing I heard was the screen door opening and closing. I got up with Maggie and went to the front room, thinking Sonny had maybe run out the front door.

Instead, there was our brother, right there in the living room, with his homie Carlos—his shadow, his twin. At the sight of them, Maggie turned around and went to Sonny's room, where I should have followed her.

They both had forties in their hands. They sat down in the living room with the cool and cruel indifference of guys who know you owe them something. I knew he'd show up eventually. I'd called him a few weeks before to let him know I would get him the money I owed, but that I needed more time. Maggie let me stay with her on the condition that I stayed away from our brother, Charles. But here he was.

Charles cut a mean figure at six foot four, two forty, with broad shoulders and big-ass hands. Charles's Chucks went up on the coffee table. Carlos put his feet up too, turned the TV on.

"Have a seat, Calvin," Charles said to me.

"I'm good," I said.

"Are you though?" Carlos said, clicking through channels.

"It's been a while," Charles said. "It's been a long fucking while I would say. Where you been? Vacation? Must be nice. Hiding out like this. Home-cooked meals, kid running around. Playing house. With our fucking sister. What the fuck is that? I have to say, I can't help but wonder where all that money you're saving goes, with you being up in here rent free. Right?"

"You know you're not paying rent," Carlos said.

"But you got a job," Charles said. "You're making money. That money should be in my fucking pocket yesterday. In Octavio's. You're lucky you're my little brother, you know that? You're lucky I haven't told no one I know where the fuck you run off to. But I can only take so much of that shit."

"I told you I'd have it. Why you gotta come unannounced and shit. And keep acting like you didn't have something to do with that shit at the powwow." I'd gotten robbed in the parking lot before I could even go in. I shouldn't have brought the shit with me. The pound I had then. But then I wasn't sure if I did bring it. Or did Charles put it in my glove box? I was smoking too much then. My memory was a fucking slide shit that happened to me went down and didn't come back up from.

"Okay. You got me. You hit the nail on the fucking head. I should never have left. You're right. I should hustle, and pay Octavio back for some shit I got stolen from me by his homies. So thank you. You're really helping me out here, brother," I said. "But I can't help but wonder why you told me I should go check out that powwow at Laney. See about our Native heritage and shit. You said Mom would have wanted us to go. You said you would meet me there. And I can't help but wonder if you didn't know what the fuck was coming for me in that parking lot. What I can't get my head around is why. What's your interest? Is it to keep me around? 'Cuz I was talking about giving that shit up? Or did your stupid ass smoke all your shit up and need mine to not come up short?"

Charles stood and took a step toward me, then stopped and made his hands into fists. I opened my hands and raised them in a take-it-easy gesture, then took two steps back. Charles took another step toward me, then looked over to Carlos. "Let's go for a drive," he said to Carlos, who stood and turned off the TV. I watched them walk out in front of me. I looked back down the hall toward Sonny's room. My right eye twitched involuntarily. "Let's go," I heard Charles say from out front.

Charles drove a dark blue custom-made four-door Chevy El Camino. The thing was clean like he just washed it that afternoon, which he probably did. Guys like Charles were always washing their cars, keeping their shoes and hats clean as new.

Before Charles started the car, he fired up a blunt and passed it to Carlos, who took two hits off it then passed it back to me. I took one long hit and passed it back up. We drove down San Leandro Boulevard deep into Deep East Oakland. I didn't recognize the beat that was playing, something slow and bass-y, something that came mostly from beneath the backseat, from the subwoofer. I noticed Charles and Carlos were just barely nodding their heads to the music. Neither of them would ever admit that they were dancing, bobbing their heads like that, but they were kind of dancing, dancing in the smallest possible way, but dancing, and I thought it was hella funny, and I almost laughed, but then realized a few minutes later that I was doing it with them, and it wasn't funny, and I realized how high I was. This was some other shit, what they smoked, could have been fucking angel dust sprinkled on, they called that KJ. Shit, knowing them that's exactly why I couldn't stop my head from bobbing, and why the streetlights were so fucking bright, and mean seeming, and, like, too red. I was glad I only hit it once.

We wound up in the kitchen of someone's house. The walls were all bright yellow. Muffled mariachi music boomed through the room from the backyard. Charles gestured for me to sit down at a table I had to slide behind, like a booth, with Carlos to my left, tapping his fingers to some other beat he was hearing in his own head. Charles was across from me, staring straight at me.

"You know where we're at?"

"I'm guessing somewhere Octavio might end up being at, but I don't know why the fuck you would think that was a good idea."

Charles laughed a fake laugh. "You remember the time we went over to Dimond Park, and we went through that long sewer tube? We ran through it, and at some point there was no light, just the sound of the rushing water and we didn't know where the fuck it came from or where it was going. We had to jump over it. You remember we heard a voice, and then you thought someone grabbed your leg, and you squealed like a little fucking baby pig, and you almost fell in but I pulled you back and we jumped and ran out of there together?" Charles said, sliding a bottle of tequila on the table in front of him back and forth. "I'm trying to get you into the position of being grabbed," Charles said, and stopped sliding the bottle. He gripped it, held it still. "When Octavio sees your face, it's gonna be like that, and I'm'a pull you back, save you from being taken down that long tube to nowhere. You ain't getting outta this shit alone, you feel me?"

Carlos put his arm around me and I tried to shrug it off. Charles leaned back and let his big arms fall to his sides.

Right on cue, Octavio walked into the kitchen. His eyes turned into bullets—he shot them around the room. "What the fuck is this, Charlos?"

That's what Octavio called Charles and Carlos because they were always together and they looked alike. It was a way to put them in their place, make them know they were both equally less important than him, Octavio, who stood six foot six, with a barrel chest and muscular arms you could see even through the triple-extra-large black T-shirt he always wore.

"Octavio," Charles said, "take it easy, I'm just trying to remind him what's what. Don't trip. He's gonna pay. He's my little brother, Octavio, no disrespect, man. I just want him to know."

"Know what? No disrespect? What is that, Charlos? I don't think you even know."

Octavio pulled out an all-white magnum from the front of his belt and pointed it at my face while looking at Charles.

"What the fuck kinda games you think we're playing here," Octavio said, looking at Charles, but talking to me. "You take, then you owe. You don't pay, you lose the shit, I don't give a fuck how you lost it, it's gone, then you disappear and show up in my uncle's fucking kitchen. You're fucking crazy, Charlos. I came here to have a good time. But because you got my shit stolen, and because your brother smoked all his shit up, you both owe me, and I got into some shit with who I get the shit from, and now I owe, and we're all fucked if we don't make some real money, real soon."

Octavio kept the gun pointed at me. Smoked all his shit up? What the fuck? I stared down the barrel of the gun. I went into it. Straight into the tunnel of it. I saw the way it had to go down. Octavio was gonna turn around to the countertop behind him to get a drink, then Charles would shoot up out of his chair and put Octavio in a choke hold from behind. The gun would drop to the ground in the struggle, and Charles, he'd hold him there, turn them both around, and trying to suddenly be a good big brother, he'd yell at me, "Get the fuck out of here!" But I wouldn't leave. I'd know just what to do. I'd grab the gun on the floor. I'd pick up the gun and point it at Octavio's head and look at Charles.

"Give me the gun, Calvin. Get the fuck out of here," Charles would say.

"I'm not leaving," I'd tell him.

"Shoot him then," Charles would say.

Then me and Octavio would catch eyes. I'd notice for the first time that Octavio's eyes were green. I'd look into those eyes so long it'd make Octavio mad, and he'd slam Charles back into the cupboards. Then I'd tell them all how they're gonna make Octavio drink, that he was gonna drink until he couldn't stand up anymore. I'd tell them that if they made him drink enough he wouldn't remember shit. We'd make the blackout so bad it would go forward and backward in time, swallow the night.

My eyes were closed. For a second I wondered if I might still be in the car, dreaming the scene from the backseat. It was a night like so many others I'd had before. Maybe I'd wake up in the backseat, we'd go home, and I'd get back to the life I was trying to make that didn't include any of this shit.

I opened my eyes. Octavio was still holding the gun, but he was laughing. Charles started to laugh too. Octavio set the gun on the table and they hugged, the two of them, Charles and Octavio. Then Carlos got up and shook hands with Octavio.

"These are the pieces you had made?" Charles said to Octavio, picking up the white gun.

"Nah, this one's special. You remember David? Manny's little brother. He made them in his fucking basement. The rest just look like nines. Go on, tell him," Octavio said to Charles, looking at me.

"You remember when I told you about that Laney powwow, you said you wanted to go because there was that big one coming up at the Oakland Coliseum, and you were on the powwow committee for work. You remember that?" Charles said.

"Yeah," I said.

"You remember what else you told me?"

"No," I said.

"About the money," Charles said.

"Money?" I said.

"You said there would be something like fifty thousand dollars in cash prizes there that day," Charles said. "And how easy it would be to steal."

"I was fucking joking, Charles. You think I would fucking

rob the people I work with and then think I could get away with it? It was a fucking joke."

"That's funny," Octavio said.

Charles lifted his head toward Octavio like: *Whatsup?*

"That anyone would think you would rob the people you work with and think you could get away with it. That shit's funny to me," Octavio said.

"This is how we make it right," Charles said. "You'll get a cut too, then we'll be good, right, Octavio?"

Octavio nodded his head. Then he picked up the tequila bottle. "Let's drink," he said.

So we drank. We went through half the bottle, shot after shot. Before the last shot there was a pause, and Octavio looked up at me, then lifted his shot glass toward me and gestured for me to get up. We took the shot, just me and him, then he gave me a hug I forgot to return. While he hugged me, I saw Charles look at Carlos like he didn't like what was happening. After Octavio let me go he turned around and got another bottle of tequila from the top cupboard, then he sort of laughed at who knows what and stumbled across then left the kitchen.

Charles lifted his head up to me like: *Let's go.* On the way to the car we saw a kid on his bike watching everyone from far off. I could tell Charles was almost gonna say something to him. Then Carlos tried to punk him by acting like he was gonna hit him. The kid didn't flinch. Just kept staring at the house. His eyes were hella droopy but not just like he was high or drunk. I thought about Sloth from *The Goonies*. And then I thought about a movie I saw one Saturday morning when I was, like, five or six. It was about a kid who woke up blind one day. Before, I'd never thought about the idea that you could just wake up to some terrible shit, some fucked-up shift in what you thought life was. And that's what it felt like then. Taking those shots. Octavio's embrace. Agreeing to some doomed-ass plan. I wanted to say something to the kid on his bike. I don't know why. There was nothing to say. We got in the car and rode home in silence, the low sound of the engine and road leading us toward some shit we'd never make our way back from.

Jacquie Red Feather

JACQUIE RED FEATHER FLEW to Phoenix from Albuquerque the evening before the conference started, landing after the
hour-long flight in a smog-filled gradient between green and
pink. When the plane slowed to a roll, she shut the window
shade and stared at the back of the seat in front of her. "Keeping Them from Harm." That was this year's conference theme.
She guessed they meant self-harm. But was the problem really
suicide itself? She'd recently read an article that called the number of suicides in Native communities staggering. For how many
years had there been federally funded programs trying to pre-
vent suicide with billboards and hotlines? It was no wonder it
was getting worse. You can't sell life is okay when it's not. This
was yet another Substance Abuse and Mental Health Services
Administration conference her position as substance abuse
counselor was grant-required to attend.

The woman who checked her in at the hotel had *Florencia*
on her name tag. She smelled like beer, cigarettes, and perfume.

That she was drinking on the job, or that she'd come to work drunk, made Jacquie like her. Jacquie was ten days sober. Florencia complimented Jacquie's hair, which she'd recently dyed black to hide the gray and cut into a bob. Jacquie had never known what to do with a compliment.

"So red," she said of the poinsettias behind Florencia, which Jacquie didn't even like because of how even the real ones look fake.

"We call them *flores de noche buena,* flowers of the holy night, because they bloom around Christmas."

"But it's March," Jacquie said to her.

"I think they're the most beautiful flowers," Florencia said.

Jacquie's latest relapse had not left burn holes in her life. She didn't lose her job, and she hadn't wrecked her car. She was sober again, and ten days is the same as a year when you want to drink all the time.

Florencia told Jacquie, who was noticeably sweating, that the pool was open until ten. The sun had gone down, but it was still ninety degrees. On the way to her room Jacquie saw that no one was in the pool.

Long after Jacquie's mom had left her dad for good, during one of the many times her mom had left her sister's dad, when Opal was just a baby and Jacquie was six, they'd stayed in a hotel near the Oakland airport. Their mom told them stories about moving away for good. About getting back home to Oklahoma. But home for Jacquie and her sister was a locked station wagon in an empty parking lot. Home was a long ride on a bus. Home was the three of them anywhere safe for the night. And that night in the hotel, with the possibility of taking a trip, of getting away from the life her mom had been running down with her daughters in tow, that night was one of the best nights of Jacquie's life. Her mom had fallen asleep. Earlier she'd seen the pool—a bright blue glowing rectangle—on the way to their room. It was cold out, but she'd seen a sign that read *Heated Pool*. Jacquie watched TV and waited for her mom to fall asleep with Opal, then she snuck down to the pool. There was no one around. Jacquie took her shoes and socks off and dipped a toe in, then looked back up at the door of their room. She looked at all the doors and windows of the rooms that faced the pool. The night air was cool but didn't move. With all but her shoes and socks on she walked down the pool stairs. It was her first time in a pool. She didn't know how to swim. Mostly she just wanted to be in the water. To go under and open her eyes, look at her hands, watch the bubbles rise in that bluest light.

In her room she threw her bags down, took off her shoes, and laid on the bed. She turned the TV on, muted it, then rolled onto her back and stared at the ceiling for a while, appreciating the blank white coolness of the room. She thought about Opal. The boys. What they might be doing. Over the past few months, after years of silence, they'd been texting. Opal took care of Jacquie's three grandsons—whom she'd never even met.

What r u doing? Jacquie texted Opal. She put her phone on the bed and went to her suitcase to get her swimsuit. It was a black-and-white-striped one-piece. She put it on in front of the mirror. Scars and tattoos spanned and bent around her neck, stomach, arms, and ankles. There were feather tattoos on her forearms, one for her mom and one for her sister, and stars on the backs of her hands—those were just stars. The webs she had on the tops of her feet had hurt the worst.

Jacquie walked to the window to see if the pool was still empty. Her phone vibrated on the bed.

Orvil found spider legs in his leg, the text said.

WTF!? Jacquie texted back. But the sentence did not really take. What could that even mean? She would look this up on her phone later, "Spiders legs found in leg," but find nothing.

Yeah idk. the boys think it means something ndn.

Jacquie smiled. She'd never seen Indian abbreviated as *ndn* before.

Maybe he'll get powers like spider-man, Jacquie texted.

Anything like that ever happen to you?

What? no. i'm gonna go for a swim.

Jacquie kneeled in front of the minifridge. In her head she heard her mom say, "The spider's web is a home and a trap." And even though she never really knew what her mom meant by it, she'd been making it make sense over the years, giving it more meaning than her mom probably ever intended. In this case Jacquie was the spider, and the minifridge was the web. Home was to drink. To drink was the trap. Or something like that. The point was *Do not open the fridge.* And she didn't.

Jacquie stood at the pool's edge, watching the light on the water wobble and shimmer. Her arms, crossed over her stomach, looked green and cracked. She inched down the pool stairs, then pushed lightly off and swam underwater all the way across and back. She came back up for air, watched the surface of the water move for a while, then went back under and watched the bubbles gather, rise, and disappear.

While she smoked a cigarette by the pool, she thought about the taxi from the airport and the liquor store she'd seen just a block away from the hotel. She could walk down there. What she really wanted was that cigarette after six beers. She wanted sleep to come easy like it could when she drank. On the way back to her room she got a Pepsi and trail mix from the vending machine. On her bed, she flipped through channels, landing here and there, changing the channel at every commercial break, devouring the trail mix and Pepsi, and only then, her appetite awakened by the trail mix, did she realize that she hadn't eaten dinner. She stayed awake with her eyes closed in bed for an hour, then put a pillow over her face and fell asleep. When she woke up at four in the morning, she didn't know what was on top of her face. She threw the pillow across the room, then got up and peed and spent the next two hours trying to convince herself she was asleep, or sometimes actually sleeping but having the dream of not being able to sleep.

Jacquie found a seat in the back of the main ballroom. There was an old Indian guy in a baseball cap who had one hand up like he was praying, while the other flicked water out of a water bottle at the crowd. She'd never seen anything like it before.

Jacquie's eyes wandered the room. She studied the Native decor. The room was big, with high ceilings and massive chandeliers, each one of which consisted of a grouping of eight flame-shaped lightbulbs surrounded by a giant band of corrugated metal with cutouts of tribal patterns, creating tribal-patterned shadows on the walls—multiple Kokopellis, zigzag lines and spirals, all up there at the top of the room, where the paint was the brownish red of dried blood. The carpets were crowded with winding lines and variegated geometric shapes—like every casino or movie-theater carpet.

She looked around at the crowd. There were probably two hundred or so people, all of them sitting at circular tables with glasses of water and little paper plates stacked with fruit and Danishes. Jacquie recognized the conference types. Most of them were old Indian women. Next came old white women. Then old Indian men. There were no young people to be seen. Everyone she saw seemed either too serious or not serious enough. These were career people, more driven by concern about keeping their jobs, about the funders and grant requirements, than by the need to help Indian families. Jacquie was no different. She knew it and hated this fact.

The first speaker, a man who looked like he might be more comfortable on a street corner than at a conference, approached the podium. You didn't often see men like him standing on a stage. He wore Jordans and an Adidas tracksuit. He had an unrecognizable faded tattoo above his left ear that went up to the crown of his bald head—it could have been cracks, or webs, or a half crown of thorns. Every few seconds he opened his mouth in an oval shape and wiped the outside of it with his thumb and forefinger, as if there was excess saliva there, or as if, in the wiping, he was assuring himself he wouldn't spit and look sloppy.

He stepped up to the mic. He spent a long, uncomfortable minute surveying the crowd. "I see a lotta Indian people out there. That makes me feel good. About twenty years ago I went to a conference like this, and it was just a sea of white faces. I came as a youth. It was my first time on a plane and the first time I was away from Phoenix for more than a few days. I'd been forced into a program as part of a plea bargain I took to stay outta juvie. That program ended up being featured at a conference in D.C.—a national highlight. They chose me and a few other youth not based on our leadership skills or because of our commitment to the cause, or because of our participation, but because we were the most at-risk. Of course all we had to do was sit on the stage, listen to youth success stories and to our youth services staff talk about how great our programming was. But while I was on that trip my little brother, Harold, found a gun I kept in my closet. He shot himself between the eyes with that gun. He was fourteen," the guy said and coughed off-mic. Jacquie shifted in her chair.

"What I'm here to talk about is how our whole approach since day one has been like this: Kids are jumping out the windows of burning buildings, falling to their deaths. And we think the problem is that they're jumping. This is what we've done: We've tried to find ways to get them to stop jumping. Convince them that burning alive is better than leaving when the shit gets too hot for them to take. We've boarded up windows and made better nets to catch them, found more convincing ways to tell them not to jump. They're making the decision that it's better to be dead and gone than to be alive in what we have here, this life, the one we made for them, the one they've inherited. And we're either involved and have a hand in each one of their deaths, just like I did with my brother, or we're absent, which is still involvement, just like silence is not just silence but is not speaking up. I'm in suicide prevention now. I've had fifteen relatives commit suicide over the course of my life, not counting my brother. I had one community I was working with recently in South Dakota tell me they were grieved out. That was after experiencing seventeen suicides in their community in just eight months. But how do we instill in our children the will to live? At these conferences. And in the offices. In the emails and at the community events, there has to be an urgency, a do-whatever-at-any-cost sort of spirit behind what we do. Or fuck the programs, maybe we should send the money to the families themselves, who need it and know what to do with it, since we all know what that money goes toward, salaries and conferences like this one. I'm sorry. I get paid outta that shit too, and actually, shit, I'm not sorry, this issue shouldn't be met with politeness or formality. We can't get lost in the career advancements and grant objectives, the day-to-day grind, as if we have to do what we do. We choose what we do, and in that choice comes the community. We are choosing for them. All the time. That's what these kids are feeling. They have no control. Guess what kinda control they do have? We need to be about what we're always saying we're about. And if we can't, and we're really just about ourselves, we need to step aside, let somebody else from the community who really cares, who'll really do something, let them come in and help. Fuck all the rest."

Jacquie was out of the room before the audience even started its hesitant, obligatory clapping. As she ran, her name badge jangled around her neck, sliced at her chin. When she got to her room, she closed the door with her back and slid down, collapsed and sobbed against it. She pressed her eyes into her knees and bursts of purple, black, green, and pink splotches bloomed there, behind her eyes, then slowly formed into images, then memories. She saw the big hole first. Then her daughter's emaciated body. There were little red and pink holes up and down both her arms. Her skin was white, blue, and yellow, with green veins. Jacquie was there to identify the body. The body was her daughter's body, had been the little body she carried for just six months. She'd watched the doctors put needles in her arm then, there in the incubator, back when all she'd wanted in a way she'd never wanted anything before was for her new baby girl to live. The coroner looked at Jacquie, pen and clipboard in hand. She spent a long time staring somewhere between the body and the clipboard trying not to scream, trying not to scan up to see her daughter's face. The big hole. The shot between the eyes. Like a third eye, or an empty third-eye socket. The trickster spider, Veho, her mom used to tell her and Opal about, he was always stealing eyes to see better. Veho was the white man who came and made the old world watch with his eyes. Look. See here, the way it's gonna be is, first you're gonna give me all your land, then your attention, until you forget how to give it. Until your eyes are drained and you can't see behind you and there's nothing ahead, and the needle, the bottle, or the pipe is the only thing in sight that makes any sense. In her car, Jacquie slammed the bottoms of her fists into the steering wheel until she couldn't anymore. She broke her pinkie on the wheel.

That was thirteen years ago. She'd been sober six months then. The longest since she'd started drinking. But after that she drove straight to the liquor store, spent the next six years stomaching a fifth of whiskey a night. She drove an AC Transit bus, the 57 line, in and out of Oakland six days a week. Drank herself into a manageable oblivion every night. Woke up every day to work. One day she fell asleep at the wheel and crashed her bus into a telephone pole. After a month in residential treatment, she left Oakland. She still doesn't know, doesn't remember how she got to Albuquerque. At some point she got a job as a receptionist at an Indian Health Clinic funded by Indian Health Service, then eventually, without ever achieving any significant sobriety, became a certified substance abuse counselor through an online course her work paid for.

There in her hotel room, down against the hotel-room door, she remembered all the pictures Opal had emailed her over the years of the boys, which she'd refused to look at. She stood up and walked to her laptop on the desk. In her Gmail account she searched Opal's name. She opened each email with the paper-clip icon. She followed them through the years. Birthdays and first bikes and pictures they'd drawn. There were little video clips of them fighting in the kitchen and sleeping in their bunk beds, all in one room. The three of them crowded around a computer screen, that screen glow on their faces. There was one picture that broke her heart. The three of them lined up in front of Opal. Opal with her static, sober, stoic stare. She looked at Jacquie through all the years and all that they'd been through. *Come get them, they're yours,* Opal's face said. The youngest one was half smiling like one of his brothers had just punched him in the arm but Opal had told them all they better smile for the picture. The middle one looked like he was either pretending to or actually was holding up what looked like a gang sign with his fingers across his chest, smiling a big smile. He looked the most like Jacquie's daughter Jamie. The oldest one didn't smile. He looked like Opal. He looked like Jacquie and Opal's mom, Vicky.

Jacquie wanted to go to them. She wanted a drink. She wanted to drink. She needed a meeting. Earlier she'd seen that the AA meeting for the conference would be on the second floor at seven thirty every night. There were always meetings at conferences, it being a mental-health/substance-abuse-prevention-based conference, full of people like her, who had gotten into the field because they'd been through it and hoped to find meaning in their careers helping other people not make the same mistakes they had. When she went to wipe sweat from her face with her sleeve, she realized the air conditioner had been turned off. She went to the AC unit and turned the cold air on high. She fell asleep waiting to cool down.

. . .

Jacquie walked into the room in a hurry, thinking she was late. Three men sat in a small circle made of eight folding chairs. Behind them were snacks that nobody had touched yet. The room was a mess of fluorescent buzzing, a smallish conference room with a whiteboard on the wall in front, off-whitish light, which encased them all in its flatness—which made everything feel like it was happening a decade ago on TV.

Jacquie went to the back table and looked at the food spread—a pot of coffee in a very old-looking auto-drip coffee-maker, cheese, crackers, meat, and mini–celery sticks fanned out in a circle around various dips. Jacquie picked up a single stick of celery, poured herself a cup of coffee, and walked over to join the group.

All of them were older Native guys with long hair—two wore baseball caps, and the one who seemed like he was probably the leader of the group wore a cowboy hat. The guy in the cowboy hat introduced himself to the group as Harvey. Jacquie turned her head away, but the face embedded in an orb of fat, the eyes and nose and mouth, they were his. Jacquie wondered if Harvey recognized her, because he excused himself, said he had to go to the bathroom.

Jacquie texted Opal. *Guess who im in a meeting with rt now?*

Opal responded immediately. *Who?*

Harvey from alcatraz.

Who?

Harvey, as in: father of the daughter I gave up.

No.

Yes.

You sure?

Yes.

What you gonna do?

Idk.

Ydk?

He just got back.

Opal sent a picture of the boys in their room, all of them lying the same way, with headphones on, looking up at the ceiling. This was the first picture she'd sent via text message since Jacquie told her not to, that she was only allowed to email pictures of them because of how it could mess with her day. Jacquie reverse pinched then pinched and repeated to see each of their faces.

Will talk to him after meeting, Jacquie texted, then switched her phone to silent and put it away.

Harvey sat down without looking at Jacquie. With a simple hand gesture, a palm facing up, he pointed to her. Jacquie wasn't sure if this not looking at her, plus the trip to the bathroom, meant that he knew. Either way, it was her turn to tell her story or share whatever she felt like, and he would know as soon as she said her name. Jacquie rested her elbows on her knees, leaned into the group.

"My name is Jacquie Red Feather. I don't say the *I'm an alcoholic* thing. I say: I don't drink anymore. I used to drink and now I don't. I currently have eleven days sobriety. I'm grateful to be here, and for your time. Thank you all for listening. I appreciate all of you being here." Jacquie coughed, her throat suddenly rough. She put a cough drop into her mouth so casually that you could tell she probably ate a lot of cough drops and smoked a lot of cigarettes, and never quite beat the cough, but beat it enough while she was sucking on a cough drop, and so ate them constantly. "The problem that became a drinking problem started for me way before the drinking was even related to it, though it was when I first started drinking. Not that I blame my past, or don't accept it. We'd been on Alcatraz, me and my family, back during the occupation, in 1970. It all started for me there. This piece-of-shit kid," Jacquie made sure to look right at Harvey after she said this. He squirmed in his chair a little, but otherwise just stared off toward the ground in a listening pose. "Maybe he didn't know what he was doing, but then again maybe he went on to fuck over a whole line of women, used force to stretch a no into a yes, assholes like him, I know now, are a dime a dozen, but I suspect, from what little time I spent with him on that island, that he went on to do it again and again. After my mom died, we lived in a house with a stranger. A distant relative. Which I'm grateful for. We had food on the table, a roof over our heads. But I gave up a daughter to adoption at that time. The girl I birthed came from that island. From what happened there. When I gave her up, I was seventeen. I was stupid. I wouldn't know how to find her now even if I wanted to. It was a closed adoption. And since then I have had another daughter. But I fucked that up too in my addiction—fifth a night of anything ten dollars or less. Then it got so bad they told me I had to quit if I wanted to keep my job. And then, as it goes, to keep being able to drink I quit my job. My daughter Jamie was out of the house by then, so it was easier for me to fall completely apart. Insert endless succession of drinking horror stories here. Today I'm trying to make my way back. My daughter died, left her three sons behind, but I left them too. I'm trying to make my way back, but like I said, eleven days. It's just, it's that you get stuck, and then the more stuck you get, the more stuck you get." Jacquie coughed and cleared her throat, then went silent.

She looked up at Harvey, at the others in the group, but their heads were all down. She didn't want to end on that kind of note, but she didn't feel like going on. "I don't know," she said. "I guess I'm done."

The circle was silent. Harvey cleared his throat.

"Thank you," Harvey said. He gestured for the next guy to speak.

He was an old guy, Navajo, Jacquie guessed. He took his hat off, like you see some Indian men do when they pray.

"It all changed for me in a meeting," he said. "Not one of these. These have been what's made all the difference since. I'd been drinking and drugging for most of my adult life, off and on. Started a few different families up, let them fall by the wayside to my addictions. And then a brother of mine put up a meeting for me. Native American Church."

Jacquie stopped listening. She thought it would help to say what she said about Harvey in front of him. But looking at him, listening to people's stories, she figured he'd probably had a hard time. Jacquie remembered the way he'd talked about his dad on the island. How he hadn't even seen his dad since they got on the island. Then, thinking about the island, Jacquie remembered seeing Harvey the day they left. She'd just gotten on the boat, and she saw him in the water. Hardly anyone ever got in that water. It was freezing. And—everyone had been convinced— shark-infested. Then Jacquie saw Harvey's little brother, Rocky, running down the hill, yelling Harvey's name. The boat started up. Everyone had sat down, but Jacquie was standing. Jacquie's mom put her hand on Jacquie's shoulder. She must have thought Jacquie was sad, because she let her stay standing for a few min- utes. Harvey wasn't swimming. He seemed to be hiding in the water. And then he was yelling for his brother. Rocky heard him and he jumped in with all his clothes on. The boat started to move.

"Okay, we're going, sit down now, Jacquie," Vicky said.

Jacquie sat down, but kept looking. She saw the boys' dad stumble down the hill. He had something in his hand, a stick or a bat. Everything got smaller and smaller as they made their way slowly across the bay.

"We all been through a lot we don't understand in a world made to either break us or make us so hard we can't break even when it's what we need most to do." It was Harvey talking.

Jacquie realized she hadn't been listening.

"Getting fucked up seems like the only thing left to do," Harvey went on. "It's not the alcohol. There's not some special relationship between Indians and alcohol. It's just what's cheap, available, legal. It's what we have to go to when it seems like we have nothing else left. I did it too. For a long time. But I stopped telling the story I'd been telling myself, about how that was the only way, because of how hard I had it, and how hard I was, that story about self-medicating against the disease that was my life, my bad lot, history. When we see that the story is the way we live our lives, only then can we start to change, a day at a time. We try to help people like us, try to make the world around us a little better. It's then that the story begins. I want to say here that I'm sorry for who I was." Harvey looked up at Jacquie, who turned away from his gaze. "I get that shame too. The kind that's made of more years than you know you have left to live. That shame that makes you wanna say fuck it and just go back to drinking as a means to an end. I'm sorry to all the people I hurt all that time I was too fucked up to see what I was doing. There's no excuse. Apologies don't even mean as much as just . . . just acknowledging that you fucked up, hurt people, and that you don't wanna do that anymore. Not to yourself either. That's sometimes the hardest part. So let's close out tonight like we always do, but let's be sure to listen to the prayer, and say it like we mean it. God, grant me the serenity . . ."

They were all saying it in unison. Jacquie wasn't going to at first, but suddenly found that she was saying it with them. "And wisdom to know the difference," she finished.

The room cleared out. Everyone but the two of them, Jacquie and Harvey.

Jacquie sat with her hands in a pile in her lap. She couldn't move.

"Long time," Harvey said.

"Yeah."

"You know, I'm going back to Oakland this summer. In a couple months, actually, for the powwow, but also—"

"Is this supposed to go like we're normal, fine, like old friends?"

"Did you not stay to talk?"

"I don't know why I stayed yet."

"I know you said what we did, what I did on Alcatraz, how you put her up for adoption. And I'm sorry for all that. I couldn't have known. I just found out I have a son too. He got ahold of me through Facebook. He lives in—"

"What are you talking about?" Jacquie said, then stood up to leave.

"Can we start over?"

"I don't give a shit about your son, or your life."

"Is there any way to find out?"

"Find out what?"

"Our daughter."

"Don't call her that."

"She might want to know."

"It'll be better for everyone if she doesn't."

"What about your grandsons?"

"Don't."

"We don't have to keep doing this," Harvey said, and took off his hat. He was bald on top. He stood up and put his hat on his chair.

"What are you gonna say to him?" Jacquie said.

"About what?"

"About where you been."

"I didn't know. Listen, Jacquie, I think you should think about coming back with me. To Oakland."

"We don't even know each other."

"It's a free ride. We'll drive all day and then through the night 'til we get there."

"You got all the answers then?"

"I wanna do something to help. There's no way to take back what I done to you. But I gotta try."

"How long you been sober?" Jacquie said.

"Since 1982."

"Well shit."

"Those boys need their grandma."

"I don't know. And you sure as hell don't know a goddamned thing about my life."

"We might be able to find her."

"No."

"There are ways of—"

"God, shut the fuck up. Stop acting like you know me, like we even have anything to say to each other, like we wanted to find each other, like we didn't just—" Jacquie stopped herself, then stood up and walked out of the room.

Harvey caught up with her at the elevator.

"Jacquie, I'm sorry, please," he said.

"Please what? I'm going now," she said, and pushed the already lit call button.

"You don't wanna be sorry about this later," Harvey said. "You don't want to keep going that same way you been going."

"You can't really think you're gonna be the one who finally turns it all around for me. I would fucking kill myself if you were the one to finally help. Do you understand that?" The elevator came and Jacquie got on.

"There's gotta be some reason for all this. That we would meet like this," Harvey said, holding the elevator by putting his arm across the threshold.

"The reason is we're both fuckups and the Indian world is small."

"Don't come with me then, that's fine. Don't even listen to me. But you said it in the circle. You know what you want. You said it. You wanna go back."

"Okay," Jacquie said.

"Okay," Harvey said. "Okay you'll come back?"

"I'll think about it," she said.

Harvey let go of the elevator doors.

Back in her room, Jacquie lay down on the bed. She put a pillow over her face. Then, without even thinking about it, she got up and went to the minifridge. She opened it. It was full of shots, beer, little bottles of wine. At first this made her happy. The idea of feeling good and comfortable, safe, and all the first few, the first six could do, and then the inevitable home stretch to twelve, sixteen, because the web stuck to you everywhere you reached once you were trapped, once you started. Jacquie closed the fridge, then reached behind it and unplugged it. She slid the fridge out from under the TV, then using all of her strength, she walked the thing to the door. The bottles clanged as if in protest. Slowly, corner to corner, she made her way. She left the minifridge outside in the hallway, then came back in and called the front desk to tell them to come get it. She was sweating. She still wanted a drink. There was still time before they'd be up to get it. She needed to leave. She put on her swimsuit.

Jacquie stepped around the minifridge, walked down the hall, realized she forgot her cigarettes, then turned around and went back for them. When she came back out of her room, the fridge caught her shin.

"Fuck," she said, looking down at the fridge, "you." She looked to see if anyone was coming, then opened the fridge and pulled out a bottle. Then another. She rolled six of them into her towel. Then ten. In the elevator she held the bundle of bottles with both arms.

She walked back to the empty pool, climbed in, and stayed under until it hurt. Every time she came up, she checked on the towel bundle. There's an ache when you keep yourself from breathing. A relief when you come up for air. It was the same when you drank after telling yourself you wouldn't. Both broke at a point. Both gave and took. Jacquie went under and swam back and forth taking breaths when she needed them. She thought about her grandsons. That picture of them with Opal, Opal's face, her eyes saying to Jacquie, *Come get them.*

Jacquie got out of the pool and went to the towel. She heaved the bundle back, then threw it high into the air, into the water. She watched the white towel slowly float down to the water, then lay flat. She watched the bottles sink to the bottom. She turned around, went out the gate and back up to her room.

The text she sent Opal was just this: *If i come to oakland can i stay?*

Orvil Red Feather

ORVIL STANDS in front of Opal's bedroom mirror with his regalia on all wrong. It isn't backward, and actually he doesn't know what he did wrong, but it's off. He moves in front of the mirror and his feathers shake. He catches the hesitation, the worry in his eyes, there in the mirror. He worries suddenly that Opal might come into her room, where Orvil is doing . . . what? There would be too much to explain. He wonders what she would do if she caught him. Ever since they were in her care, Opal had been openly against any of them doing anything Indian. She treated it all like it was something they could decide for themselves when they were old enough. Like drinking or driving or smoking or voting. Indianing.

"Too many risks," she'd said. "Especially around powwows. Boys like you? No."

Orvil couldn't fathom what she meant by risks. He'd found the regalia by accident in her closet many years ago while searching for Christmas presents. He'd asked her why she didn't teach them anything about being Indian.

"Cheyenne way, we let you learn for yourself, then teach you when you're ready."

"That doesn't make any sense," Orvil had said. "If we learn for ourselves, we don't need to be taught. It's 'cuz you're always working."

He saw his grandma's head turn from the pot she was stirring. He quickly pulled out a chair and sat down.

"Don't make me say it, Orvil," she said. "I get so tired of hearing myself say it. You know how much I work. How late I come home. I got my route and the mail doesn't stop coming just like the bills don't. Your phones, the internet, electricity, food. There's rent and clothes and bus and train money. Listen, baby, it makes me happy you want to know, but learning about your heritage is a privilege. A privilege we don't have. And anyway, anything you hear from me about your heritage does not make you more or less Indian. More or less a real Indian. Don't ever let anyone tell you what being Indian means. Too many of us died to get just a little bit of us here, right now, right in this kitchen. You, me. Every part of our people that made it is precious. You're Indian because you're Indian because you're Indian," she said, ending the conversation by turning back around to stir.

"So if we had more money, if you didn't have to work so much, things would be different?" Orvil said.

"You didn't hear a thing I said to you, did you," she said.

Opal Viola Victoria Bear Shield. A big old name for a big old lady. She's not technically their grandma. Indian way she is. That's what she told them when she explained why she was a Bear Shield and they were Red Feathers. She is actually their great-aunt. Their real grandma, Jacquie Red Feather, lives in New Mexico. Opal is Jacquie's half sister, but they grew up together, with the same mom. Jacquie's daughter Jamie is the boys' mom. But all Jamie ever did was push them out. Didn't even quit using when they were in her. The three of them had all begun life in withdrawal. Heroin babies. Jamie shot herself between the eyes when Orvil was six, his brothers four and two. Opal officially adopted them after their mom died, but she'd had them plenty before that. Orvil only has a handful of memories of his mom. He'd overheard these details when his grandma was talking to a friend on the kitchen phone late one night.

"Tell us something about her," Orvil would say whenever he got the chance, moments when Opal was in a good mood and it seemed like she'd answer.

"She's how you all got those lousy spellings of your names," Opal told the boys over dinner one night after Lony told them the kids were calling him Lony the Pony at school.

"Nobody says it right," Lony said.

"She did that?" Orvil said.

"Of course she did. Who else? Not that she was stupid. She knew how to spell. She just wanted you all to be different. I don't blame her. Our names should look different."

"She was fucking stupid," Loother said. "That shit's weak." He stood up, pushed his chair back, and walked out of the room. He'd always complained the most about the spelling of his name, even though people still pronounced it right. No one had ever even noticed that Orvil was supposed to be spelled Orville—with that useless extra *l* and *e*. As for Lony, it was only because Opal knew their mom, knew how she said it, that anyone anywhere knew it wasn't supposed to be Lony as in *pony*.

. . .

Orvil manages to get the regalia on and steps in front of the full-length mirror on Opal's closet door. Mirrors have always been a problem for him. The word *stupid* often sounds in his head when he looks at himself in the mirror. He doesn't know why, but it seems important. And true. The regalia is itchy and faded in color. It's way too small. He doesn't look the way he hoped he would. He doesn't know what he expected to find. Being Indian didn't fit either. And virtually everything Orvil learned about being Indian he'd learned virtually. From watching hours and hours of powwow footage, documentaries on YouTube, by reading all that there was to read on sites like Wikipedia, PowWows.com, and *Indian Country Today*. Googling stuff like "What does it mean to be a real Indian," which led him several clicks through some pretty fucked-up, judgmental forums, and finally to an Urbandictionary.com word he'd never heard before: *Pretendian*.

Orvil knew he wanted to dance the first time he saw a dancer on TV. He was twelve. It was November, so it was easy to find Indians on TV. Everyone else had gone to bed. He was flipping through channels when he found him. There on the screen, in full regalia, the dancer moved like gravity meant something different for him. It was like break dancing in a way, Orvil thought, but both new—even cool—and ancient-seeming. There was so much he'd missed, hadn't been given. Hadn't been told. In that moment, in front of the TV, he knew. He was a part of something. Something you could dance to.

And so what Orvil is, according to himself, standing in front of the mirror with his too-small-for-him stolen regalia, is *dressed up like an Indian*. In hides and ties, ribbons and feathers, boned breastplate, and hunched shoulders, he stands, weak in the knees, a fake, a copy, a boy playing dress-up. And yet there's something there, behind that stupid, glazed-over stare, the one he so often gives his brothers, that critical, cruel look, behind that, he can almost see it, which is why he keeps looking, keeps standing in front of the mirror. He's waiting for something true to appear before him—about him. It's important that he dress like an Indian, dance like an Indian, even if it is an act, even if he feels like a fraud the whole time, because the only way to be Indian in this world is to look and act like an Indian. To be or not to be Indian depends on it.

Today the Red Feather brothers are going to get Lony a new bike. On the way they stop at the Indian Center. Orvil's supposed to be getting two hundred dollars to tell a story for a storytelling project he read about on Facebook.

Loother and Lony sit outside in the hall while Orvil is led into a room by a guy who introduced himself as Dene Oxendene. Dene sits Orvil down in front of a camera. He sits behind the camera, crosses his legs, leans in toward Orvil.

"Can you tell me your name, your age, and where you're from?" Dene says.

"Okay. Orvil Red Feather. Fourteen. Oakland."

"What about your tribe, do you know what tribe you are?"

"Cheyenne. From our mom's side."

"And how'd you find out about this project?"

"Facebook. Said it paid two hundred dollars?"

"That's right. I'm here to collect stories in order to have them available online for people from our community and communities like ours to hear and see. When you hear stories from people like you, you feel less alone. When you feel less alone, and like you have a community of people behind you, alongside you, I believe you can live a better life. Does that make sense?"

"Sure."

"What does it mean to you when I say 'story'?"

"I don't know," Orvil says. Without thinking about it, he crosses his legs like Dene.

"Try."

"It's just telling other people something that happened to you."

"Good. That's basically it. Now tell me something that happened to you."

"Like what?"

"That's up to you. It's just like you said. It doesn't have to be a big deal. Tell me something that's happened to you that stands out, that you thought of right away."

"Me and my brothers. How we ended up with our grandma, who we live with now. It was after the first time we thought our mom overdosed."

"Would you mind talking about that day?"

"I barely remember anything from when I was younger, but I remember that day perfectly. It was a Saturday, so me and my brothers had been watching cartoons all morning. I went to the kitchen to make us sandwiches, and I found her facedown on the kitchen floor. Her nose was all smashed into the floor and bleeding, and I knew it was bad because her arms were curled up at her stomach like she'd fallen down on top of them, which meant she nodded out walking. First thing I did was send my brothers to the front yard. We were living off of Thirty-Eighth then, in a little blue house with this tiny gated patch of grass that we were still small and young enough to like playing on. I got out Mom's makeup mirror and put it under her nose. I'd seen that on a show, and when I saw that it barely fogged up, I called 9-1-1. When they came, because I told the operator about how it was just me and my brothers besides our mom, they came with two cop cars and a CPS worker. He was this old Indian guy I never saw again except for that one time. It was the first time I heard that we were Indian. He recognized that we were Indian just by looking at us. They carried our mom out on a stretcher while the social worker showed my little brothers a magic trick with a book of matches, or he was just lighting matches and it felt like magic, I don't know. He's the reason they called our grandma and why we ended up getting adopted by her. He took us to his office and asked who else there was besides our mom. After talking to our grandma Opal, we left and met her at the hospital."

"And then?"

"Then we went home with her."

"Home with your grandma?"

"Yeah."

"And your mom?"

"She'd already left the hospital by the time we got there. Turned out she just got knocked out from the fall. She didn't overdose."

"That's a good story. Thank you. I mean, not good, but thank you for telling it."

"I get two hundred dollars now?"

Orvil and his brothers leave the Indian Center and go straight to Target in West Oakland to get Lony's bike. Lony rides on the back of Loother's bike—on pegs. Even though the story had been sad to remember, Orvil feels okay about having told it. He feels even better about the two-hundred-dollar gift card in his back pocket. He can't stop smiling. But his leg. The lump that's been in his leg for as long as he can remember, as of late it's been itching. He hasn't been able to stop scratching it.

"Some shit just went down in the bathroom," Orvil tells Loother when he gets outside Target.

"Isn't that what it's supposed to do?" Loother says.

"Shut the fuck up, Loother, I'm serious," Orvil says.

"What, you didn't make it in time?" Loother says.

"I was sitting there in the stall, picking at that thing. You remember that lump I got? I felt something poking out of it. So I pulled, like, I just pulled one out, put it on some folded-up toilet paper, then went back in and got another one. Then one more after that. I'm pretty sure they're spider legs," Orvil says.

"Pfffffft," Loother says and laughs. At which point Orvil shows him a neat pile of folds of toilet paper.

"Let me see," Loother says.

Orvil opens up the folds of toilet paper and shows Loother.

"What the fuck?" Loother says.

"Right outta my leg," Orvil says.

"Are you sure it's not, like, splinters?"

"Nah, look where the leg bends. There's a joint. And a tip. Like the end of the leg where it gets skinnier, look."

"That's fucked up," Loother says. "But what about the other five? I mean, if they are spider legs, there should be eight, right?"

Before Orvil can say anything else or put away the spider legs, Loother's on his phone.

"You looking it up?" Orvil asks him.

But Loother doesn't answer. He just taps. Scrolls. Waits.

"You find anything?" Orvil says.

"Nah. Not even a little bit," Loother says.

When Lony comes out with his bike, Orvil and Loother look down at it and nod. Lony smiles at their nods.

"Let's go," Orvil says, then puts his earphones in. He looks back and sees his brothers put theirs in too. They ride back toward Wood Street. As they pass the Target sign, Orvil remembers last year when they all got phones at Target on the same day as an early Christmas present. They were the cheapest phones they had, but at least they weren't flip phones. They were smart. They do all they need them to do: make calls, text, play music, and get them on the internet.

They ride together in a line, and listen to what comes out of their phones. Orvil mainly listens to powwow music. There's something in the energy of that big booming drum, in the intensity of the singing, like an urgency that feels specifically Indian. He likes the power the sound of a chorus of voices makes too, those high-pitched wailed harmonies, how you can't tell how many singers there are, and how sometimes it sounds like ten singers, sometimes like a hundred. There was even one time, when he was dancing in Opal's room with his eyes closed, when he felt like it was all his ancestors who made it so he could be there dancing and listening to that sound, singing right there in his ears through all those hard years they made it through. But that moment was also the first time his brothers saw him in regalia, dancing like that, they walked in on him in the middle of it, and they thought it was hilarious, they laughed and laughed but promised not to tell Opal.

As for Loother, not counting himself, he listens exclusively to three rappers: Chance the Rapper, Eminem, and Earl Sweatshirt. Loother writes and records his own raps to instrumentals he finds on YouTube and makes Orvil and Lony listen to them and agree with him about how good he is. As for Lony, they'd recently discovered what he's into.

"You hear that?" Loother had asked one night in their room.

"Yeah. It's, like, some kind of chorus or choir, right?" Orvil said.

"Yeah, like angels or some shit," Loother said.

"Angels?" Orvil said.

"Yeah, like what they have them sound like."

"What they have them sound like?"

"I mean like movies and shit," Loother said. "Shut up. It's still going. Listen."

They sat for the next couple of minutes and listened to the distant sound of the symphony, of the choir coming through an inch of speaker, muted by Lony's ears—ready to believe it was anything, anything better than the sound they had the angels make. It hit Orvil first what the sound was, and he started to say Lony's name, but Loother got up, put a finger to his lips, then went over and gently pulled Lony's earphones out. He put one of them close to his ear and smiled. He looked at Lony's phone and smiled bigger and showed it to Orvil.

"Beethoven?" Orvil said.

They ride up Fourteenth toward downtown. Fourteenth takes them through downtown to East Twelfth, which gets them to the Fruitvale without a bike lane, but on a street big enough, so that even though cars get comfortable, swerve a little, and go faster on East Twelfth, it's better than riding the gutter-edge of International Boulevard.

When they get to Fruitvale and International, they stop in the Wendy's parking lot. Orvil and Loother take out their phones.

"Guys. Seriously? Orvil had spider legs in his leg? What the fuck?" Lony asks.

Orvil and Loother look at each other and laugh hard. Lony hardly ever curses, so when he does it's always both super serious and funny to hear.

"C'mon," Lony says.

"It's real, Lony," Orvil says.

"What does that mean, it's real?" Lony says.

"We don't know," Orvil says.

"Call Grandma," Lony says.

"And say what?" Loother says.

"Tell her," Lony says.

"She'll make it a big deal," Orvil says.

"What'd the internet say?" Lony asks.

Loother just shakes his head.

"Seems Indian," Orvil says.

"What?" Loother says.

"Spiders and shit," Orvil says.

"Definitely Indian," Lony says.

"Maybe you should call," Loother says.

"Fuck," Orvil says. "But the powwow's tomorrow."

"What does that have to do with it?" Loother says.

"You're right," Orvil says. "It's not like she knows we're going."

Orvil leaves a message for his grandma when she doesn't pick up. He tells her they got Lony's bike, and then about the spider legs. While he leaves the message he watches Loother and Lony look at the legs together. They poke at the legs, and move the toilet paper so that the legs bend. Orvil feels a pulse in his stomach, and like something falls out of him. After he hangs up, he takes the legs, folds up the toilet paper, and stuffs it in his pocket.

.   .   .

The day of the powwow Orvil wakes up hot. He covers his face with the cold bottom of his pillow. He thinks about the powwow, then lifts the pillow and tilts his head to listen to what he thinks he hears from out in the kitchen. He wants to minimize their time with Opal before they go. He wakes his brothers up by hitting them with his pillow. They both moan and roll over, so he hits them again.

"We gotta get out without having to talk to her, she might have made us breakfast. We'll tell her we're not hungry."

"But I am hungry," Lony says.

"Don't we wanna hear what she thinks about the spider legs?" Loother says.

"No," Orvil says. "We don't. Not now."

"I really don't think she'll care we're going to the powwow," Loother says.

"Maybe," Orvil says. "But what if she does?"

Orvil and his brothers ride their bikes down San Leandro Boulevard on the sidewalk in a line. At the Coliseum BART Station, they lift their bikes and carry them on their shoulders, then ride across the pedestrian bridge that gets them to the coliseum. They slow to a roll. Orvil looks through the chain-link fence and sees the morning fog clearing to blue.

Orvil leads his brothers clockwise around the outer edge of the parking lot. He stands and pedals hard, then takes off his plain black hat and stuffs it into his hoodie's front pocket. After gaining some speed, he stops pedaling, takes his hands off the handlebars, then grabs hold of his hair. It's gotten long. Down to the middle of his back long. He ties his hair back with the beaded hair clip that he'd found with the regalia in his grandma's closet.

He pulls his ponytail through the half circle on the back of his hat, which latches with the snaps of six small black plastic buttons in a line. He likes the sound, the feel of it when he can get them to snap down perfectly in a row. He picks up speed again, then coasts and looks back. Lony's in the back with his tongue sticking out from how hard he's pedaling. Loother's taking pictures of the coliseum with his phone. The coliseum looks massive. Bigger than it looks when you see it from BART or driving by on the freeway. Orvil's gonna dance on the same field that the A's and the Raiders play on. He'll compete as a dancer. He'll dance the dance he learned by watching powwow footage on YouTube. It's his first powwow.

"Can we stop?" Lony says, out of breath.

They stop halfway around the parking lot.

"I gotta ask you guys something," Lony says.

"Just ask then, homie," Loother says.

"Shut up, Loother. Whatsup, Lony?" Orvil says, looking at Loother.

"I been meaning to ask," Lony says, "like, what's a powwow?"

Loother laughs, takes off his hat and hits it against his bike.

"Lony, we've seen hella powwows, what do you mean what's a powwow?" Orvil says.

"Yeah, but I never asked nobody," Lony says. "I didn't know what we were looking at." Lony tugs at the bill of his black-and-yellow A's cap to pull his head down.

Orvil looks up at the sound of a plane passing overhead.

"I mean, why does everyone dress up, dance, and sing Indian?" Lony says.

"Lony," Loother says in that way an older brother can take you down by just saying your name.

"Never mind," Lony says.

"No," Orvil says.

"Every time I ask questions you guys make me feel stupid for asking," Lony says.

"Yeah, but, Lony, you ask hella stupid questions," Loother says. "Sometimes it's hard to know what to say."

"Then say it's hard to know what to say," Lony says, squeezing his hand brake. He swallows hard, watching his hand grip the hand brake, then leans down to watch the brakes grip the front tire.

"They're just old ways, Lony. Dancing, singing Indian. We gotta carry it on," Orvil says.

"Why?" Lony says.

"If we don't they might disappear," Orvil says.

"Disappear? Where they gonna go?"

"I mean, like, people will forget."

"Why can't we just make up our own ways?" Lony says.

Orvil puts his hand across his forehead the same way their grandma does when she's frustrated.

"Lony, you like the taste of Indian tacos, right?" Orvil says.

"Yeah," Lony says.

"Would you just make some food up of your own and eat it?" Orvil says.

"That actually sounds pretty fun," Lony says, still looking down but smiling a little now, which makes Orvil laugh, and say the word *stupid* in the middle of his laugh.

Loother laughs too, but he's already looking at his phone.

They get back on their bikes, then look up and see lines of cars streaming in, hundreds of people getting out of their cars. The boys stop. Orvil gets off his bike. These are other Indians. Getting out of their cars. Some of them already in full regalia. Real Indians like they'd never seen before if you didn't count their grandma, who they probably should count, except that it was too hard for them to tell what was specifically Indian about her. She was all they knew besides their mom, who's too hard to think about or remember. Opal worked for the post office. Delivered mail. She liked to watch TV when she was home. Cook for them. They didn't know much else about her. She did make fry bread for them on special occasions.

Orvil pulls at the nylon straps of his backpack to tighten it and lets go of the handlebars, lets the front wheel wobble, but balances by leaning back. In the backpack is the regalia that barely fits, his XXL black hoodie, which was too big for him on purpose, and three now squished peanut butter and jelly sandwiches in ziplock plastic baggies he hopes they won't have to eat, but he knows they might have to if the Indian tacos are too expensive—if food prices are anything like the food at A's games when it's not dollar night. They only knew about Indian tacos because their grandma made them for their birthdays. It was one of the few Indian things she did. And she was always sure to remind them that it's not traditional, and that it comes from lacking resources and wanting comfort food.

To be sure they'd at least be able to afford an Indian taco each, they rode their bikes up to the fountain behind the Mormon temple. Loother had just been there for a field trip to Joaquin Miller Park, and he said people threw coins in for wishes. They made Lony roll up his pants and gather all the coins he could see, while Orvil and Loother threw rocks at the community building at the top of the stairs above the fountain— a distraction they didn't see at the time might have been worse than the fountain scraping itself. Going down Lincoln Avenue after that was one of the best and stupidest things they'd ever done together. You could get going so fast down a hill there was nothing else happening in the whole world but the feeling of the speed moving through you and the wind in your eyes. They went to Bayfair Center in San Leandro and scraped out what they could from that fountain before being chased off by a security guard. They took the bus up to the Lawrence Hall of Science in the Berkeley Hills, where there was a double fountain, which they knew would be practically untouched because only rich people or monitored kids on field trips went to that place. After rolling up all the coins and turning them in at the bank, they came away with a total of fourteen dollars and ninety-one cents.

When they get to the entrance at the coliseum, Orvil looks back at Loother and asks if he has the lock.

"You always bring it," Loother says.

"I asked you to get it before we left the house. I said, Loother, can you get the lock, I don't want it messing up my regalia. You seriously didn't bring it? Fuck. What are we gonna do? I asked you right before we left the house, you said, yeah I got it. Loother, you said, yeah I got it."

"I must have been talking about something else," Loother says.

Orvil breathes out the word *okay* and signals for them to follow him. They hide their bikes in some bushes on the other side of the coliseum.

"Grandma'll kill us if we lose our bikes," Lony says.

"Well, there's no not going," Orvil says. "So we're going."

Interlude

> What strange phenomena we find in a great city,
> all we need do is stroll about with our eyes open.
> Life swarms with innocent monsters.
>
> —CHARLES BAUDELAIRE

Powwows

For powwows we come from all over the country. From reservations and cities, from rancherias, forts, pueblos, lagoons, and off-reservation trust lands. We come from towns on the sides of highways in northern Nevada with names like Winnemucca. Some of us come all the way out from Oklahoma, South Dakota, Arizona, New Mexico, Montana, Minnesota; we come from Phoenix, Albuquerque, Los Angeles, New York City, Pine Ridge, Fort Apache, Gila River, Pit River, the Osage Reservation, Rosebud, Flathead, Red Lake, San Carlos, Turtle Mountain, the Navajo Reservation. To get to powwows we drive alone and in pairs on road trips; we caravan as families, piled in station wagons, vans, and in the backs of Ford Broncos. Some of us smoke two packs a day if we're driving, or drink beer continually to keep ourselves occupied. Some of us, who gave up that tired life, on that long red road of sobriety, we drink coffee, we sing, pray, and tell stories until we run out. We lie, cheat, and steal our stories, sweat and bleed them out along the highway, until that long white line makes us quiet, makes us pull over to sleep. When we get tired we stop at motels and hotels; we sleep in our cars on the side of the road, at rest stops and truck stops, in Walmart parking lots. We are young people and old, every kind of Indian in between.

We made powwows because we needed a place to be together. Something intertribal, something old, something to make us money, something we could work toward, for our jewelry, our songs, our dances, our drum. We keep powwowing because there aren't very many places where we get to all be together, where we get to see and hear each other.

We all came to the Big Oakland Powwow for different reasons. The messy, dangling strands of our lives got pulled into a braid—tied to the back of everything we'd been doing all along to get us here. We've been coming from miles. And we've been coming for years, generations, lifetimes, layered in prayer and handwoven regalia, beaded and sewn together, feathered, braided, blessed, and cursed.

Big Oakland Powwow

In the Oakland Coliseum parking lot, for the Big Oakland Powwow, there is one thing that makes many of our cars the same. Our bumpers and rear windows are covered with Indian stickers like *We're Still Here* and *My Other Vehicle Is a War Pony* and *Sure You Can Trust the Government, Just Ask an Indian!; Custer Had It Coming; We Do Not Inherit the Earth from Our Ancestors, We Borrow It from Our Children; Fighting Terrorism Since 1492;* and *My Child Didn't Make the Honor List, but She Sure Can Sing an Honor Song.* There are Schimmel Sister stickers, and Navajo Nation stickers, Cherokee Nation stickers, Idle No More, and AIM flags duct-taped to antennas. There are dream catchers and tiny moccasins, feathers and beaded miscellany hanging from rearview mirrors.

We are Indians and Native Americans, American Indians and Native American Indians, North American Indians, Natives, NDNs and Ind'ins, Status Indians and Non-Status Indians, First Nations Indians and Indians so Indian we either think about the fact of it every single day or we never think about it at all. We are Urban Indians and Indigenous Indians, Rez Indians and Indians from Mexico and Central and South America. We are Alaskan Native Indians, Native Hawaiians, and European expatriate Indians, Indians from eight different tribes with quarter-blood quantum requirements and so not federally recognized Indian kinds of Indians. We are enrolled members of tribes and disenrolled members, ineligible members and tribal council members. We are full-blood, half-breed, quadroon, eighths, sixteenths, thirty-seconds. Undoable math. Insignificant remainders.

Blood

Blood is messy when it comes out. Inside it runs clean and looks blue in tubes that line our bodies, that split and branch like earth's river systems. Blood is ninety percent water. And like water it must move. Blood must flow, never stray or split or clot or divide—lose any essential amount of itself while it distributes evenly through our bodies. But blood is messy when it comes out. It dries, divides, and cracks in the air.

Native blood quantum was introduced in 1705 at the Virginia Colony. If you were at least half Native, you didn't have the same rights as white people. Blood quantum and tribal membership qualifications have since been turned over to individual tribes to decide.

In the late 1990s, Saddam Hussein commissioned a Quran to be written in his own blood. Now Muslim leaders aren't sure what to do with it. To have written the Quran in blood was a sin, but to destroy it would also be a sin.

The wound that was made when white people came and took all that they took has never healed. An unattended wound gets infected. Becomes a new kind of wound like the history of what actually happened became a new kind history. All these stories that we haven't been telling all this time, that we haven't been listening to, are just part of what we need to heal. Not that we're broken. And don't make the mistake of calling us resilient. To not have been destroyed, to not have given up, to have survived, is no badge of honor. Would you call an attempted murder victim resilient?

When we go to tell our stories, people think we want it to have gone different. People want to say things like "sore losers" and "move on already," "quit playing the blame game." But is it a game? Only those who have lost as much as we have see the particularly nasty slice of smile on someone who thinks they're winning when they say "Get over it." This is the thing: If you have the option to not think about or even consider history, whether you learned it right or not, or whether it even deserves consideration, that's how you know you're on board the ship that serves hors d'oeuvres and fluffs your pillows, while others are out at sea, swimming or drowning, or clinging to little inflatable rafts that they have to take turns keeping inflated, people short of breath, who've never even heard of the words *hors d'oeuvres* or *fluff*. Then someone from up on the yacht says, "It's too bad those people down there are lazy, and not as smart and able as we are up here, we who have built these strong, large, stylish boats ourselves, we who float the seven seas like kings." And then someone else on board says something like, "But your father gave you this yacht, and these are his servants who brought the hors d'oeuvres." At which point that person gets tossed overboard by a group of hired thugs who'd been hired by the father who owned the yacht, hired for the express purpose of removing any and all agitators on the yacht to keep them from making unnecessary waves, or even referencing the father or the yacht itself. Meanwhile, the man thrown overboard begs for his life, and the people on the small inflatable rafts can't get to him soon enough, or they don't even try, and the yacht's speed and weight cause an undertow. Then in whispers, while the agitator gets sucked under the yacht, private agreements are made, precautions are measured out, and everyone quietly agrees to keep on quietly agreeing to the implied rule of law and to not think about what just happened. Soon, the father, who put these things in place, is only spoken of in the form of lore, stories told to children at night, under the stars, at which point there are suddenly several fathers, noble, wise forefathers. And the boat sails on unfettered.

If you were fortunate enough to be born into a family whose ancestors directly benefited from genocide and/or slavery, maybe you think the more you don't know, the more innocent you can stay, which is a good incentive to not find out, to not look too deep, to walk carefully around the sleeping tiger. Look no further than your last name. Follow it back and you might find your line paved with gold, or beset with traps.

Last Names

We didn't have last names before they came. When they decided they needed to keep track of us, last names were given to us, just like the name *Indian* itself was given to us. These were attempted translations and botched Indian names, random surnames, and names passed down from white American generals, admirals, and colonels, and sometimes troop names, which were sometimes just colors. That's how we are Blacks and Browns, Greens, Whites, and Oranges. We are Smiths, Lees, Scotts, MacArthurs, Shermans, Johnsons, Jacksons. Our names are poems, descriptions of animals, images that make perfect sense and no sense at all. We are Little Cloud, Littleman, Loneman, Bull Coming, Madbull, Bad Heart Bull, Jumping Bull, Bird, Birdshead, Kingbird, Magpie, Eagle, Turtle, Crow, Beaver, Youngblood, Tallman, Eastman, Hoffman, Flying Out, Has No Horse, Broken Leg, Fingernail, Left Hand, Elk Shoulder, White Eagle, Black Horse, Two Rivers, Goldtooth, Goodblanket, Goodbear, Bear Shield, Yellow Man, Blindman, Roanhorse, Bellymule, Ballard, Begay, Yazzie. We are Dixon, Livingston, Tsosie, Nelson, Oxendene, Harjo, Armstrong, Mills, Tallchief, Banks, Rogers, Bitsilly, Bellecourt, Means, Good Feather, Bad Feather, Little Feather, Red Feather.

Apparent Death

We won't have come expecting gunfire. A shooter. As many times as it happens, as we see it happen on our screens, we still walk around in our lives thinking: No, not us, that happens to them, the people on the other side of the screen, the victims, their families, we don't know those people, we don't even know people who know those people, we're once and twice removed from most of what we see on the other side of the screen, especially that awful man, always a man, we watch and feel the horror, the unbelievable act, for a day, for two whole days, for a week, we post and click links and like and don't like and repost and then, and then it's like it didn't happen, we move on, the next thing comes. We get used to everything to the point that we even get used to getting used to everything. Or we only think we're used to it until the shooter, until we meet him in real life, when he's there with us, the shots will come from everywhere, inside, outside, past, future, now, and we won't know right away where the shooter is, the bodies will drop, the depths of the booms will make our hearts skip beats, the rush of panic and spark and sweat on our skin, nothing will be more real than the moment we know in our bones the end is near.

There will be less screaming than we expect. It'll be that prey-silence of hiding, the silence of trying to disappear, to not be out there, we'll close our eyes and go deep inside, hope that it's a dream or a nightmare, hope that in closing our eyes we might wake up to that other life, back on the other side of the screen, where we can watch from the safety of our couches and bedrooms, from bus and train seats, from our offices, anyplace that is not there, on the ground, playing like we're dead so not playing at all, we'll run like ghosts from our own dead bodies in hopes of getting away from the shots and the loud quiet of wait-ing for the next shot to fire, waiting for another sharp hot line to cut across a life, cut off breath, bring too quickly the heat and then cooling of too-soon death.

We've expected the shooter to appear in our lives in the same way we know death is and always has been coming for us, with its decisive scythe, its permanent cut. We half expect to feel the boom of shots firing nearby. To fall to the ground and cover our heads. To feel like an animal, prey in a pile on the ground. We've known the shooter could show up anywhere, anywhere people gathered, we've expected to see him in our periphery, a masked shadow moving through the crowd, picking people off at random, semiautomatic booms putting bodies down, sending them flailing through the broken air.

A bullet is a thing so fast it's hot and so hot it's mean and so straight it moves clean through a body, makes a hole, tears, burns, exits, goes on, hungry, or it remains, cools, lodges, poi-sons. When a bullet opens you up, blood pours like out of a mouth too full. A stray bullet, like a stray dog, might up and bite anyone anywhere, just because its teeth were made to bite, made to soften, tear through meat, a bullet is made to eat through as much as it can.

Something about it will make sense. The bullets have been coming from miles. Years. Their sound will break the water in our bodies, tear sound itself, rip our lives in half. The tragedy of it all will be unspeakable, the fact we've been fighting for decades to be recognized as a present-tense people, modern and relevant, alive, only to die in the grass wearing feathers.

Tony Loneman

THE BULLETS WILL COME from the Black Hills Ammunition plant in Black Hills, South Dakota. They will be packed in boxes of sixteen, driven across the country, and stored in a warehouse in Hayward, California, for seven years, then stocked and shelved and bought in Oakland at a Walmart off of Hegenberger Road by a young man by the name of Tony Loneman. The two boxes of bullets will go into his backpack. He'll take them out again for security to check against the receipt at the exit. Tony will ride his bike down Hegenberger, across the overpass and on the sidewalk past the gas stations and fast-food chains. He'll feel the weight and hear the jangle of the bullets at every bump and crack.

At the coliseum entrance he'll take each of the boxes of bullets out and empty them into a pair of socks. He'll swing and throw the socks one at a time against the wall behind the bushes past the metal detectors. When he's done he'll look back up at the moon, watch the fog of his breath rise between him and everything. His heart will be in his ears thinking about the bullets in the bushes, the powwow. And wondering how he had wound up here under the moon, under the looming coliseum walls, hiding bullets in bushes.

Calvin Johnson

WHEN CALVIN GETS THERE, people are doing what they always do the first hour of every powwow committee meeting he's ever been to: making small talk and dishing up paper plates of catered Mexican food. There's a new guy there. He's big, and the only one without a plate. Calvin can tell he doesn't have a plate because he's one of those big guys who doesn't know how to carry his weight. How to own it. Calvin's on the bigger end of the spectrum himself, but he's tall and wears baggy clothes, so he comes off as big but not necessarily fat.

Calvin sits down next to the big guy and gives him a slight, general whatsup-type head nod. The guy lifts his hand and waves, then seems to immediately regret the wave because he puts his hand back down as fast as it went up and gets out his phone like everyone does now when they want to leave without leaving.

Blue is writing or doodling at the top of a yellow legal pad.

Calvin likes Blue. Her and Maggie used to work together in youth services. She's who got Calvin the job even though he had no experience working with youth. She probably thought Calvin was a youth. Or looks like one. With his Raiders shit and sad goatee. Blue's the head of the powwow committee. She'd asked Calvin to join the committee shortly after he got the job. Blue said they wanted fresh new perspectives. They'd gotten this pretty big event-based grant and wanted to make this powwow big, compete with other big powwows out there. Calvin had stupidly said "Call it the Big Oakland Powwow" in one of the meetings and everyone loved it. He tried to tell them he was just joking, but they kept it anyway.

Thomas, the custodian, comes in talking to himself. Calvin smells it right away. Alcohol fumes. Then, as if Thomas knows Calvin smells him, he walks right past him to the big guy.

"Thomas Frank," he says, and sticks his hand out.

"Edwin Black," he says.

"I'll let you folks get to work," Thomas says as he takes the trash out. "Let me know if you need help cleaning up the leftovers," he says with a tone like: *Save a plate for me.* Dude is weird. Awkward as fuck like he had to make you feel as uncomfortable as he always appeared to be, like he couldn't contain it.

Blue knocks on the table twice and clears her throat. "Okay, you guys," she says, knocking on the table two more times. "Let's start. We have a lot to talk about. It's already January. We have less than five months. We'll start with the two new people, one of whom isn't here yet, so that means you'll start, Edwin. Go ahead and tell everyone a little bit about yourself and what your role's gonna be here at the center."

"Hi, everyone," Edwin says, and puts his hand up and waves

that same wave he'd waved at Calvin. "I'm Edwin Black, and well obviously I work here now, I mean, I guess not obviously, sorry." Edwin shifts in his chair.

"Just tell them where you're from, what's your tribe, and your role here," Blue says.

"Okay, so I grew up here in Oakland, and I'm, um, I'm Cheyenne, well I'm not enrolled yet, but, like, I will be, with the Cheyenne and Arapaho Tribes of Oklahoma, my dad told me we're Cheyenne and not Arapaho, and, sorry, I'm gonna be interning for the next few months leading up to the powwow, I'm here to help with the powwow," Edwin says.

"We're just waiting on one more," Blue is saying when another guy walks into the meeting. "Speak of the devil," Blue says.

He's a young guy in a baseball cap with an indistinct tribal pattern on it. If he didn't have that hat, Calvin doesn't know if he'd have guessed he's Native.

"Everyone, this is Dene Oxendene. Dene Oxendene, this is the powwow committee. Dene's gonna set up a storytelling booth kinda like StoryCorps. Have y'all heard of StoryCorps?"

They all murmur various noncommittal answers.

"Dene," Blue says, "why don't you go ahead and say a few things about yourself before we start."

Dene starts to say something about storytelling, some real heady shit, so Calvin tunes out. He doesn't know what he's gonna say when it comes around to him. He'd been put in charge of finding younger vendors, to support young Native artists and entrepreneurs. But he hadn't done shit.

"Calvin?" he hears Blue say.

Dene Oxendene

❦

DENE CONVINCED BLUE to let Calvin do his interview for the storytelling project during work hours. Calvin keeps crossing and uncrossing his legs and pulling at his hat by the bill. Dene thinks Calvin is nervous, but then Dene is nervous, he is always nervous, so maybe it's projection. But projection as a concept is a slippery slope because everything could be projection. He is regularly subject to solipsism's recursive, drowning affect.

He set up the camera and mic in Blue's office beforehand. Blue's on her lunch hour. Calvin is sitting still now, staring at Dene mess with the recording equipment. Dene figures out what was wrong and hits Record on the camera and on the recording device, then adjusts the mic one last time. Dene learned early on to record everything before and after, as those moments can sometimes be even better than when the interviewee knows they're being recorded.

"Sorry, I thought we were good to go before you came in," Dene says, and sits down to the right of the camera.

"It's cool," Calvin says. "What is this again?"

"You're gonna say your name and tribe. Talk about the place or places you've lived in Oakland, and then if you can think of a story to tell, like something that's happened to you in Oakland that might, like, give a picture of what it's been like for you specifically, growing up in Oakland, as a Native person, what it's been like."

"My dad never talked about being Native and shit to the point that we don't even know what tribe we are on his side. Our mom has Native blood on her Mexican side too, but she doesn't know too much about that either. Yeah and my dad wasn't home hardly ever, then one day he was really gone. He left us. So I don't know, I feel bad sometimes even saying I'm Native. Mostly I just feel like I'm from Oakland."

"Oh," Dene says.

"I got robbed in the parking lot about to go to a powwow at Laney College. It's not really a good story, I just got fucking robbed in a parking lot and then I left. I never made it to the powwow. So this one coming up will be my first one."

Dene isn't sure how to help him get to a story, and he doesn't want to force it. He's glad he's already been recording. Sometimes not having a story *is* the story.

"It's like having him as a dad and not knowing, and how he fucked us up as a dad, I don't wanna come off like I think that's what being Native means. I know there's a lot of Natives living in Oakland and in the Bay Area with similar stories. But it's like we can't talk about it because it's not really a Native story, but then it is at the same time. It's fucked up."

"Yeah."

"When are you gonna start recording for me to say, like, whatever I'm gonna try to say?"

"Oh, I've already been recording."

"What?"

"Sorry, I should've told you."

"Does that mean you're gonna use anything I already said?"

"Can I?"

"I mean, I guess. Is this shit, like, your job?"

"Kind of. I don't have another job. But I'm trying to pay all the participants out of the grant money I got from the city of Oakland. I think I'll make enough to get by," Dene says. And then there's a lull, a silence neither one of them knows how to recover from. Dene clears his throat.

"How'd you end up working here?" Dene says.

"My sister. She's friends with Blue."

"So you don't feel, like, any kind of Native pride or whatever?"

"Honestly?"

"Yeah."

"I just don't feel right trying to say something that doesn't feel true."

"That's what I'm trying to get out of this whole thing. All put together, all our stories. Because all we got right now are reservation stories, and shitty versions from outdated history textbooks. A lot of us live in cities now. This is just supposed to be like a way to start telling this other story."

"I just don't think it's right for me to claim being Native if I don't know anything about it."

"So you think being Native is about knowing something?"

"No, but it's about a culture, and a history."

"My dad wasn't around either. I don't even know who he is. My mom's Native too, though, and she taught me what she could when she wasn't too busy working or just not in the mood. The way she said it, our ancestors all fought to stay alive, so some parts of their blood went together with another Nation's blood and they made children, so forget them, forget them even as they live on in us?"

"Man, I feel you. But then again I don't know. I just don't know about this blood shit."

Jacquie Red Feather

JACQUIE AND HARVEY RIDE in Harvey's Ford pickup through a moon-purple desert on that stretch between Phoenix and Blythe on I-10. The drive so far has been full of long silences Jacquie maintains by ignoring Harvey's questions. Harvey is not the kind of man comfortable with silence. He's a powwow emcee. It's his job to keep his mouth running. But Jacquie is used to silence. She has no problem with it. She'd actually made Harvey promise she wouldn't have to talk. That didn't mean Harvey wouldn't.

"You know, one time I got stuck out here in the desert," Harvey says, keeping his eyes fixed on the road in front of them. "I'd been out drinking with some friends, and we wanted to go for a drive. A night like this would have been perfect. It's not even dark. That full moon on the sand like that?" Harvey says, and looks over at Jacquie, then rolls down his window and sticks a hand out to feel the air.

"Smoke?" Jacquie says.

Harvey pulls out a smoke for himself and makes a vague grunting sound Jacquie has heard other Indian men use before and knows means yes. "I used to drink with these twins, Navajo guys. One of the twins didn't want the truck to smell like smoke, it was his girlfriend's truck, so we pulled over on the side of the highway. We'd brought a handle of tequila along. We drank too much of that, talked nonsense for a couple hours, then decided we needed to distance ourselves from the vehicle. We stumbled out into the desert, ended up getting so far out we couldn't see the truck," Harvey says.

Jacquie isn't listening anymore. She always finds it funny, or not funny but annoying actually, how much people in recovery like to tell old drinking stories. Jacquie didn't have a single drinking story she'd want to share with anyone. Drinking had never been fun. It was a kind of solemn duty. It took the edge off, and it allowed her to say and do whatever she wanted without feeling bad about it. Something she always notices is how much confidence and lack of self-doubt people have. Take Harvey here. Telling this terrible story like it's captivating. There are so many people she comes across who seem born with confidence and self-esteem. Jacquie can't remember a day going by when at some point she hadn't wished she could burn her life down. Today actually, she hadn't had that thought today. That was something. That was not nothing.

"And then even though I can't remember having passed out on the desert floor," Harvey says, "I woke up and the twins were gone. The moon hadn't moved too far, so not too much time had passed, but they were gone, so I walked toward where I thought we'd parked. It was all of a sudden real cold, like I'd never felt before. Like it's cold when you're near the ocean, like it's cold in San Francisco, that moist cold that gets to the bone."

"It wasn't cold before you passed out?" Jacquie says.

"This is where it gets weird. I must have been walking for twenty minutes or so, the wrong way of course, farther into the desert, that's when I saw them."

"The twins?" Jacquie says, and rolls up her window. Harvey does the same.

"No, not the twins," he says. "I know this is gonna sound crazy, but it was two very tall, very white guys with white hair, but they weren't old, and they weren't so tall that it was freakish, just maybe like a foot and a half taller than me."

"This is the part where you tell me you woke up to the twins lying on top of you or something," Jacquie says.

"I thought maybe the twins had slipped me something. I knew they were Native American Church guys, but I'd done peyote before and this was not that. I got maybe ten or so feet away from them and stopped. Their eyes were big. Not in that alien way, just noticeably big," Harvey says.

"Bullshit," Jacquie says. "This story goes: Harvey got drunk in the desert and had a weird dream, the end."

"I'm not joking. These two tall white guys with white hair and big eyes, hunch-shouldered, just staring off, not even at me. I got the hell out of there. And if that was a dream, then so is this, because I never woke up from it."

"You act like when you're drinking your memory is, what, reliable?"

"True enough, but get this, when the internet came out, or when I started using it I guess is a better way to put it, I looked up tall white guys in the desert in Arizona, and it's a thing.

They're called the Tall Whites. Aliens. No joke. You can look it up," Harvey says.

Jacquie's phone vibrates in her pocket. She gets it out knowing Harvey will think it's to look up these Tall Whites. It's an unusually long text message from Opal.

I already assumed you would have told me if you found spider legs in your leg, either when we were younger or when I told you about Orvil's, but that assumption doesn't make sense because I found spider legs in my leg right before everything happened with Ronald. And I never told you I found those legs, I mean until right now. I need to know if it happened to you. I feel like it has something to do with Mom.

"I read one website that said the Tall Whites are controlling America now, d'you see that?" Harvey says. And Jacquie feels sad for Harvey. And for Opal. And about these spider legs. If she'd ever found spider legs in her leg, she probably would have ended it right there and then. She suddenly feels so overwhelmed by all of it that she gets tired. This sometimes happens to Jacquie, and she feels grateful when it does, because most of the time her thoughts keep her up.

"I'm gonna get some sleep," Jacquie says.

"Oh. Okay," Harvey says.

Jacquie leans her head against the window. She watches the white highway line stream and waver. She watches the lines of telephone wires rise and fall in waves. Her thoughts wander, loosen, reach out aimlessly. She thinks about her back teeth, her molars, how they hurt every time she bites into something too cold or hot. She thinks about how long it's been since she's been to the dentist. She wonders about her mom's teeth. She thinks about genetics and blood and veins and why a heart keeps beating. She looks at her head leaned against her head's dark reflection in the window. She blinks an erratic pattern of blinks, which ends with her eyes closed. She falls asleep to the low drone of the road and the engine's steady hum.

PART III

Return

People are trapped in history and history is trapped in them.

—JAMES BALDWIN

Opal Viola Victoria Bear Shield

EVERY TIME she gets into her mail truck Opal does the same thing. She looks into the rearview and finds her gaze looking back at her through the years. She doesn't like to think of the number of years she's been working as a mail carrier for the USPS. Not that she doesn't like the work. It's that it's hard to see the years on her face, the lines and wrinkles that surround her eyes, branch out like cracks in the concrete. But even though she hates to see her face, she's never been able to stop the habit of looking at it when she finds a mirror there in front of her, where she catches one of the only versions of her face she'll ever see—on top of glass.

Opal thinks as she drives of the first time she took the Red Feather boys in for a weekend at the beginning of the adoption process. They were at a Mervyn's in Alameda for new clothes.

Opal looked at Orvil in the mirror, at an outfit she'd picked out for him.

"You like it?" she said.

"What about them?" Orvil said, pointing at himself and Opal's reflection in the mirror. "How do we know it's not one of them doing it and not us copying?"

"Because look, I'm deciding to wave my hand in front of it right now," Opal said, and waved. It was a three-panel mirror outside the dressing room. Loother and Lony were hiding inside a clothes rack nearby.

"*She* could have waved first, then you couldn't help but copy. But look at this," he said, and then he broke out into a wild dance. Arms flailing, he jumped and spun. It looked to Opal like he was powwow dancing. But he couldn't have been. He was just trying to act crazy in front of the mirror to prove no one else was in control but him, the Orvil on this side of the mirror.

Opal is on her route. Same old same old one. But she's paying attention to where she steps. Opal doesn't step on cracks when she walks. She walks carefully because she's always had the sense that there are holes everywhere, cracks you can slip between—the world, after all, is porous. She lives by a superstition she would never admit to. It's a secret she holds so tight to her chest she never notices it. She lives by it, like breathing. Opal drops mail in slots and in boxes trying to remember which spoon she'd eaten with earlier. She has lucky and unlucky spoons. In order for the lucky ones to work, you have to keep the unlucky ones with them, and you can't look to see what you're getting when you pull one out of the drawer. Her luckiest spoon is one with a floral pattern that runs up the handle to the neck.

She knocks on wood to cancel out something she's said she wants or doesn't want to happen, or even if she just thinks it, she'll find wood and knock on it twice. Opal likes numbers. Numbers are consistent. You can count on them. But for Opal, certain numbers are good and others are bad. Even numbers are generally better than odd ones, and numbers that have some kind of mathematical relationship are good too. She reduces addresses to a single number by adding them together, then judges the neighbors based on their reduced number. Numbers don't lie. Four and eight are her favorites. Three and six are no good. She delivers mail on the odd side first, always having believed it's best to get the bad out of the way before getting to the good.

Bad luck or just bad shit happening to you in life can make you secretly superstitious, can make you want to take some control or take back some sense of control. Opal buys scratchers and lottery tickets when the jackpot gets high enough. Her superstition is one she would never call superstition for fear it would lose its power.

Opal is done with the odd side of the street. When she crosses, a car stops for her—the woman inside impatiently waves Opal across like she's doing all of humanity a favor. Opal wants to lift her arm, lift a single finger as she crosses, but instead she slow jogs across in answer to the woman's impatience and feigned generosity. Opal hates herself for the jog. For the smile that came to her face before she could stop it, turn it upside down, straighten it out before it was too late.

Opal is full of regrets, but not about things she's done. That damn island, her mom, Ronald, and then the shuffling, stifling rooms and faces in foster care, in group homes after that. She regrets that they happened. It doesn't matter that she didn't cause them to happen. She figures she must deserve it in some way. But she couldn't figure it out. So she bore those years, their weight, and the years bored a hole through the middle of her, where she tried to keep believing there was some reason to keep her love intact. Opal is stone solid, but there is troubled water that lives in her, that sometimes threatens to flood, to drown her—rise up to her eyes. Sometimes she can't move. Sometimes it feels impossible to do anything. But that's okay because she's become quite good at getting lost in the doing of things. More than one thing at a time preferably. Like delivering mail and listening to an audiobook or music. The trick is to stay busy, distract then distract the distraction. Get twice removed. It's about layers. It's about disappearing in the whir of noise and doing.

Opal takes out her earphones when she hears a sound up above somewhere. A nasty buzz slicing through the air. She looks up and sees a drone, then looks around to see who might be flying it. When she doesn't see anyone, she puts her earphones back in. She's listening to Otis Redding's "(Sittin' on) The Dock of the Bay." It's her least-favorite Otis Redding song because it gets played too much. She shuffles her music and it lands on Smokey Robinson's "The Tracks of My Tears." This song gives her that strange mix of sad and happy. Plus it's upbeat. That's what she loves about Motown, the way it asks you to carry sadness and heartbreak but dance while doing so.

Opal was on her route yesterday when her adopted grandson Orvil left her a message telling her he'd pulled three spider legs out of a bump on his leg. He'd scratched it open and out came those spider legs like splinters. Opal covered her mouth as she listened to the message, but she wasn't surprised, not as much as she would have been had this not happened to her when she was around the same age Orvil is now.

Opal and Jacquie's mom never let them kill a spider if they found one in the house, or anywhere for that matter. Her mom said spiders carry miles of web in their bodies, miles of story, miles of potential home and trap. She said that's what we are. Home and trap.

When the spider legs didn't come up at dinner last night, Opal figured Orvil was afraid to bring it up because of the powwow—even though the two things had nothing to do with each other.

A few weeks back she found a video of Orvil powwow dancing in his room. Opal regularly checks their phones while they sleep. She looks at what pictures and videos they take, their text messages, and their browser histories. None of them have shown signs of especially worrisome depravity yet. But it's only a matter of time. Opal believes there is a dark curiosity alive in each of us. She believes we all do precisely what we think we can get away with. The way Opal sees it, privacy is for adults. You keep a close eye on your kids, you keep them in line.

In the video, Orvil was powwow dancing like he knew exactly what he was doing, which she couldn't understand. He was dancing in the regalia she kept in her closet. The regalia was given to her by an old friend.

There were all kinds of programs and events for Native youth growing up in Oakland. Opal first met Lucas at a group home, and then again later at a foster-youth event. For a time, Opal and Lucas were model foster youth, always the first chosen for interviews and photos for flyers. They'd both learned from an elder what goes into making regalia, then helped her make it. Opal helped Lucas prepare for his first powwow as a dancer. Lucas and Opal had been in love. Their love was young and desperate. But it was love. Then one day Lucas got on a bus and moved down to Los Angeles. He'd never even talked about it. He just left. Came back almost two decades later out of nowhere wanting an interview for an Urban Indian documentary he was making and gave her the regalia. Then he died a few weeks later. Called Opal from his sister's house to tell her his days were numbered. That's how he put it. He didn't even tell her why, he just said sorry, and that he wished her the very best.

But last night dinner was quiet. Dinner was never quiet. The boys left the table in the same suspicious silence. Opal called Lony back. She would ask him how their day went—Lony couldn't lie. She'd ask him how he liked his new bike. Plus it was his turn to do the dishes. But Orvil and Loother did something they'd never done before. They helped their little brother dry and put away the dishes. Opal didn't want to force the issue. She really didn't know what to say about it. It was like something was stuck in her throat. It wouldn't come back up and it wouldn't go down. Actually it was like the bump in her leg the spider legs had come out of. The bump had never gone away. Were there more legs in there? Was that the spider's body? Opal had stopped asking questions a long time ago. The bump remained.

When she went to tell the boys to go to bed, she heard one of them shush the other two.

"What's that?" she said.

"Nothing, Grandma," Loother said.

"Don't 'nothing, Grandma' me," she said.

"It's nothing," Orvil said.

"Go to sleep," she said. The boys are afraid of Opal, like she was always afraid of her mom. Something about how brief and direct she is. Maybe hypercritical too, like her mom was hypercritical. It's to prepare them for a world made for Native people not to live but to die in, shrink, disappear. She needs to push them harder because it will take more for them to succeed than someone who is not Native. It's because she failed to do anything more than disappear herself. She's no-nonsense with them because she believes life will do its best to get at you. Sneak up from behind and shatter you into tiny unrecognizable pieces. You have to be ready to pick everything up pragmatically, keep your head down and make it work. Death alone eludes hard work and hardheadedness. That and memory. But there's no time and no good reason most of the time to look back. Leave them alone and memories blur into summary. Opal preferred to keep them there as just that. That's why these damn spider legs have her stuck on the problem. They're making her look back.

Opal pulled three spider legs out of her leg the Sunday afternoon before she and Jacquie left the home, the house, the man they'd been left with after their mom left this world. There'd recently been blood from her first moon. Both the menstrual blood and the spider legs had made her feel the same kind of shame. Something was in her that came out, that seemed so creaturely, so grotesque yet magical, that the only readily available emotion she had for both occasions was shame, which led to secrecy in both cases. Secrets lie through omission just like shame lies through secrecy. She could have told Jacquie about either the legs or the bleeding. But Jacquie was pregnant, was not bleeding anymore, was growing limbs inside her they'd agreed she would keep, a child she would give up for adoption when the time came. But the legs and the blood all ended up meaning so much more.

The man their mom left them with, this Ronald, he'd been taking them to ceremony, telling them it was the only way they would heal from the loss of their mother. All while Jacquie was secretly becoming a mother. And Opal was secretly becoming a woman.

But Ronald started to walk by their room at night. Then he took to standing in their doorway—a shadow framed by the door and the light behind him. On a ride home from ceremony she remembered Ronald mentioning something to them about doing a dream ceremony. Opal didn't like the sound of it. She took to keeping a bat she'd found in their bedroom closet when they first moved in by her side, next to her in bed, had taken to holding the thing like she'd once held Two Shoes for comfort. But where Two Shoes was all talk and no action, the bat, which had written on its butt-end the name Storey, was all action.

Jacquie had always slept hard as night stays until morning comes. One night Ronald went over to the end of her bed— a mattress on the floor. Opal had the mattress across from her. When she saw Ronald pull at Jacquie's ankles, she didn't even have to think. She'd never swung the bat before, but she knew its weight and how to swing it. Ronald was on his knees about to pull Jacquie up to him. Opal got up as quiet as she could, breathed in slow, then raised the bat up high behind her. She came down as hard as she could on top of Ronald's head.

There was a deep, muffled crack, and Ronald landed on top of Jacquie—who woke up and saw her sister standing over them with the bat. They packed their duffel bags as fast as they could, then went downstairs. On the way through the living room, there on the TV was that test-pattern Indian they'd seen a thousand times before. But it was like Opal was seeing him for the first time. Opal imagined the Indian turning to her. He was saying: *Go.* Then the sound of him saying *Go* went on too long and turned into the test tone coming from the TV. Jacquie grabbed Opal's hand and led her out of the house. Opal still had the bat in her hand.

After they left Ronald's they went to a shelter their mom had always taken them to when they needed help or were between houses. They met with a social worker who asked where they'd been but didn't push when they didn't tell her.

Opal carried the weight of Ronald's possible death around with her for a year. She was scared to go back and check. She was afraid that it didn't bother her that he was dead. That she killed him. She didn't want to go and find out if he was still alive. But she didn't really want to have killed him either. It was easier to let him stay maybe dead. Possibly dead.

A year later Jacquie was gone from Opal's life. Opal didn't know where. The last time she'd seen her, Jacquie was getting arrested for what reason Opal couldn't tell. Losing Jacquie into the system was just another shitty loss among Opal's many. But she'd met an Indian boy her age, and he made sense to Opal, he wasn't weird or dark, or he was, but in the same ways Opal was. Plus he never talked about where he came from or what happened to him. They shared that omission like soldiers back from war, all the way up until an afternoon Opal and Lucas were hanging out at the Indian Center, waiting for people to show up for a community meal. Lucas was talking about how much he hated McDonald's.

"But it tastes *so* good," Opal said.

"It's not real food," Lucas said as he balanced and walked back and forth on the curb outside.

"It's real if I can chew it up and see it come out the other side," Opal said.

"Gross," Lucas said.

"Wouldn't have been gross if you'd have said it. Girls aren't allowed to talk about farts or poop or curse or—"

"I could swallow pennies and poop them out, that doesn't make them food," Lucas said.

"Who told you it's not real?" Opal said.

"I had half a cheeseburger I forgot was in my backpack for like a month. When I found it, it looked and smelled exactly the same as when I left it. Real food spoils," Lucas said.

"Beef jerky doesn't spoil," Opal said.

"Okay, Ronald," Lucas said.

"What'd you say?" Opal said, and she felt a hot sadness rise up to her eyes from her neck.

"I called you Ronald," Lucas said, and stopped walking back and forth on the curb's edge. "As in, Ronald McDonald." He put his hand on Opal's shoulder and lowered his head a little to try to catch her eyes. Opal pulled her shoulder away. Her face went white.

"What? I'm sorry, geez. I'm joking. If you wanna know what's funny, I ate that cheeseburger, okay?" Lucas said. Opal walked back inside and sat down on a folding chair. Lucas followed her in and pulled up a chair next to her. After some coaxing, Opal told Lucas everything. He was the first person she'd ever told, not just about Ronald but about her mom, the island, what their lives were like before that. Lucas convinced her it would eat her up eventually if she didn't find out for sure about Ronald.

"He's like that cheeseburger in my backpack before I ate it," Lucas said. Opal laughed like she hadn't laughed in a long time. A week later they were on a bus to Ronald's house.

They waited for two hours across the street from Ronald's house, hiding behind a mailbox. That mailbox became the only thing between finding out and not, between seeing him and not, between her and the rest of her life. She didn't want to live, she wanted time to stop there, to keep Lucas there with her too.

Opal went cold when she saw Ronald come home in his truck. Seeing Ronald walk up the stairs to that house, Opal didn't know if she wanted to cry from relief, immediately run away, or go after him, wrestle him to the ground, and finish him off with her bare hands once and for all. Of all that could have occurred to her, what came up in her mind was a word she'd heard her mom use. A Cheyenne word: *Veho*. It means spider and trickster and white man. Opal always wondered if Ronald was white. He did all kinds of Indian things, but he looked as white as any white man she'd ever seen.

When she saw his front door close behind him, it closed the door on all that had come before, and Opal was ready to leave.

"Let's go," she said.

"You don't want to—"

"There's nothing else," she said. "Let's go." They walked the few miles back without saying a word to each other. Opal kept a couple of paces ahead the whole way.

Opal is large. If you want to say bone-structure-wise that's fine, but she's big in a bigger sense than big-bodied or bone-structure-wise. She would have to be called overweight in front of medical professionals. But she got big to avoid shrinking. She'd chosen expansion over contraction. Opal is a stone. She's big and strong but old now and full of aches.

Here she is stepping down from her truck with a package. She leaves the box on the porch and walks back out through the gate of the front yard. There across the street from her is a brown-and-black tiger-striped pit bull baring its teeth and growling a growl so low she can feel it in her chest. The dog is collarless and time seems the same way here, time off its leash, ready to skip so fast she'll be dead and gone before she knows it. A dog like this one has always been a possibility, just like death can show up anywhere, just like Oakland can bare its teeth suddenly and scare the shit out of you. But it's not just poor old Opal anymore, it's what would become of the boys if she were gone.

Opal hears a man's voice boom from down the street some name she can't understand. The dog flinches at the sound of its name coming out of this man's mouth. It cowers and turns around then scurries off toward the voice. The poor dog was probably just trying to spread the weight of its own abuse. There was no mistaking that flinch.

Opal gets into her mail truck, starts it, and heads back to the main office.

Octavio Gomez

BY THE TIME I got back to my grandma Josefina's house I could barely stand. She had to drag me up the stairs. My grandma's old and small, and I was pretty big even then, but Fina's strong. She's got that crazy strength you can't see. It felt like she carried me all the way up the stairs to the extra room and put me in bed. I was hot and cold as fuck, with this deep-ass ache like my fucking bones were being squeezed or drained or fucking stepped on.

"It could just be the flu," my grandma said, like I'd asked her what she thought was wrong with me.

"Or what?" I said.

"I don't know if your dad ever told you anything about curses." She came over to my bed and felt my head with the back of her hand.

"He gave me my mouth."

"Curse words don't count. They can do what they can do, but a real curse is more like a bullet fired from far off." She stood over me, folded a wet towel, and put it on my forehead. "There's someone aiming a bullet meant for you, but with that distance, most of the time it doesn't hit and even if it hits it usually won't kill you. It all depends on the aim of the shooter. You said your uncle never gave you anything, you never took anything from him, right?"

"No," I said.

"We won't know for now," she said.

She came back up with a bowl and a carton of milk. She poured milk into the bowl, then slid the bowl under my bed, stood up, and walked over to a votive candle on the other side of the room. As she lit the candle she turned around and looked at me like I shouldn't have been looking, like I should have my eyes closed. Fina's eyes could bite. They were green like mine, but darker—alligator green. I looked up at the ceiling. She came back over to me with a glass of water.

"Drink this," she said. "My own father cursed me when I was eighteen. Some old Indian curse my mom told me wasn't real. That was how she said it. Like she knew enough to know it was Indian, and enough to know it wasn't real, but not enough to do anything other than tell me it was an old Indian curse that wasn't real." Fina laughed a little.

I handed the glass to her, but she pushed it back toward me like: *Finish it.*

"I thought I was in love," Fina said. "I was pregnant. We were engaged. But he left. I didn't tell my parents at first. But one night my dad came to me to ask if I would name his grandson—he was sure it would be a grandson—if I would name the boy after him. I told him then that I wasn't getting married, that the guy had left, and that I wasn't going to have the baby either. My dad came after me with this big spoon he sometimes hit me with—he'd sharpened the handle to threaten me with it when he beat me—but this time he came at me with the sharp end. My mom stopped him. He'd cross anyone, any line, but not through her. The next morning I found a braid of his hair under my bed. That's where my shoes went, so when I went for them the next morning I found the braid. When I got downstairs my mom told me I had to go." Fina walked over to the window and opened it. "It's better if we get some air in here. This room needs to breathe. I can get you more blankets if you get cold."

"I'm fine," I said. Which wasn't true. A breeze came in and it felt like my arms and back were being scraped by it. I pulled the blankets up to my chin. "This was in New Mexico?"

"Las Cruces," she said. "My mom put me on a bus out here to Oakland, where my uncle owned a restaurant. When I got here I got the abortion. And then I got real sick. Off and on for about a year. Worse than you are now, but the same kind of thing. The kind of sick that knocks you down and doesn't let you up. I wrote my mom to ask for help. She sent me a clump of fur, told me to bury it at the western base of a cactus."

"Clump of fur?"

"About this big." She made a fist and held it up for me to see.

"Did that work?"

"Not right away. Eventually I stopped getting sick."

"So was the curse just that you got sick?"

"That's what I thought, but now, with everything that's happened . . ." She turned and looked to the door. The phone was ringing downstairs. "I should get that," she said, and stood up to leave. "Get some sleep."

I stretched and a hard shiver ran through me. I pulled the blankets over my head. This was that part of the fever where you get so cold you gotta sweat to break it. Hot and cold, with sweat shiver running through and over me, I thought about the night that broke through the windows and walls of our house and brought me to the bed I was doing my best to get better in.

Me and my dad had both moved from the couch to the kitchen table for dinner when the bullets came flying through the house. It was like a wall of hot sound and wind. The whole house shook. It was sudden, but it wasn't unexpected. My older brother, Junior, and my uncle Sixto had stolen some plants from someone's basement. They'd come home with two black garbage bags full. Hella stupid. That much weight, like some shit wasn't tied to it. Sometimes I'd crawl through the living room to get to the kitchen, or watch TV on my stomach on the floor.

That night, whoever got their shit stolen by my stupid-ass brother and uncle, they rolled up on our house and emptied their guns into it, into the life we'd known, the life our mom and dad spent years making from scratch. My dad was the only one to get hit. My mom was in the bathroom, and Junior was in his room at the back of the house. My dad put himself in front of me, blocked the bullets with his body.

Lying in bed wishing for sleep, I didn't want to but couldn't help but think of Six. That's what I used to call him. My uncle Sixto. He called me Eight. I hadn't really known him growing up, but after my dad died he started to come around a few days every week. Not that we said much to each other. He'd come over and turn on the TV, smoke a blunt, drink. He let me drink with him. Passed me the blunt. I never liked getting high. Shit just made me feel hella nervous, made me think too much about the speed of the beat of my heart—was it too slow, would it stop, or was it too fast, would it fucking attack? I liked to drink though.

After the shooting Junior stayed out even more than usual, claimed he was gonna fuck those guys up, that it meant war, but Junior was all talk.

Sometimes me and Six would be watching TV in the afternoon, and the sun would come in through one of the bullet holes, one of the ones in the wall, and I could see the fucking dust in the room float in a bullet-hole-shaped ray of light. My mom had replaced the windows and the doors, but she hadn't bothered to fill the holes in the walls. Hadn't bothered or didn't want to.

After a few months, Sixto stopped coming over and Fina told me to spend more time with my cousins Manny and Daniel. Their mom had called Fina to ask for help. That made me wonder if my mom had called Fina to ask for help after my dad died, and was that why Six came over? Fina had a hand in everything. She was the only one trying to keep us all together, keep us all from falling through the holes life opened up out of nowhere like those bullets that ripped through the house that night.

Manny and Daniel's dad had lost his job, and had been going harder at the drink. At first I went over out of duty. You did what Fina told you to do. But then I got close with Manny and Daniel. Not that we talked. Mostly we played video games together in the basement. But we spent almost all our free time together— when we weren't in school—and it turns out that *who* you spend time with ends up mattering more than *what you do* with that time.

One day we were down in the basement when we heard

a noise upstairs. Manny and Daniel looked at each other like they knew what it was and like they didn't want it to be that. Manny bolted up from the couch. I ran behind him. When we got upstairs the first thing we saw was their dad throwing their mom against the wall, then slapping her once with each hand. She pushed him and he laughed. I'll never forget that laugh. And then how Manny took that laugh right the fuck out of him. Manny came up from behind his dad and pulled back on his neck like he was trying to rip all the breath he'd ever taken out of him. Manny was bigger than his dad. And he pulled back hard. They stumbled backward into the living room.

I heard Daniel coming up the stairs. I opened the door and put my hand up like: *Stay down here.* Then I heard the sound of glass crashing. Manny and his dad had gone through the glass table in the living room. In their struggle Manny had managed to turn them around, so he landed on top of his dad on the glass table. Manny was cut a little on his arms, but his dad was all sliced up. He got knocked out too. I thought he was fucking dead. "Help me get him in the car," Manny said to me. And I did. I picked his dad up from under his arms. On our way out the front door, when I was almost out the door, with Manny at the other end, holding his dad's legs, I saw Daniel and Aunt Sylvia watch us carry him out of the house. Something about them seeing us. Crying because they wanted him gone. Crying because they wanted him back the way he used to be. That shit killed me. We dropped their dad off in the front of Highland, where the ambulances come in. Left him on the ground. Honked the horn once real long, then drove off.

.   .   .

I was around more after that. We didn't even know if we killed him or not until a week later. The doorbell rang and it was like Manny knew, like he felt it. He tapped my knee twice and sprang up. At the front door, we stood there and didn't have to say a thing. We stood there like: *What? What the fuck do you want? Go.* His face was all bandaged. He looked like a fucking mummy. I felt bad for him. Sylvia came up behind us with a trash bag full of his clothes yelling, *"Move!"* So we moved out of the way, and she threw the bag at him. Manny closed the door and that was that.

It was around that time that me and Manny stole our first ride. We took BART to downtown Oakland. There were certain pockets of uptown where people had nice cars and people like me and Manny could be seen without someone calling the cops right away. Manny wanted a Lexus. Just nice enough but not too nice. Not noticeable either. We found a black one with gold lettering and tinted windows. I don't know how long Manny had been stealing cars, but he got in quick with a coat hanger, then with a screwdriver in the ignition. The inside smelled like cigarettes and leather.

We rode down East Fourteenth, which had been International, but shit got so bad all up and down International that they changed the name to something without the history. I rummaged through the glove box and found some Newports. We both thought it was weird for someone we assumed was white to be smoking Newports. Neither one of us smoked cigarettes, but we smoked those, blasted the radio, and didn't say a single word to each other the whole ride. There was something about that ride though. It was like we could put on someone else's clothes, live in someone else's house, drive their car, smoke their smokes—even if just for an hour or two. Once we made it deep enough east we knew we'd be fine. We parked it at the Coliseum BART Station parking lot and walked back to Manny's house high on having gotten away with it so easily. The system scared you so you thought you had to follow the rules, but we were learning that that shit was fucking flimsy. You could do what you could get away with. That's where it was at.

I was at Manny's house when Sylvia called down into the basement to tell me Fina was on the phone. She never called me there. Daniel took the controller from me before I went up.

"He killed them," Fina said.

I couldn't even understand what she meant.

"Your uncle Sixto," she said. "He crashed his car with both of them in it. They're dead."

I ran out the front door, got on my bike, and hurried the fuck home. My heart was some crazy mix of fuck-no-fuck-this and like it had slipped out of me. Before I got to Fina's I thought, *Well then Six better be fucking dead too.*

Fina was standing in her doorway. I jumped off my bike in one motion and ran inside the house like I was gonna find someone else there. My mom and brother. Sixto. I had to believe it was a joke or any fucking thing other than what Fina's face was telling me in that doorway that it was.

"Where is he?"

"They took him to jail. Downtown."

"What the fuck." My knees gave out on me. I was on the ground, not crying, but like I couldn't move, and I got real fucking sad for a minute, but then that shit did a one-eighty and I yelled some shit I don't remember. Fina didn't do or say anything when I got back on my bike and left. I can't remember what I did or where I went that night. Sometimes you just go. And you're gone.

After the funerals I moved in with Fina. She told me Sixto was out. They gave him a DUI. He lost his license. But they let him go.

Fina told me not to go see him. Never to go see him, to let it be. I didn't know what I would do if I went over there, but there wasn't shit she could do to stop me.

On the way over to his house I stopped in the parking lot of a liquor store I knew wouldn't check my ID. I went in and bought a fifth of E&J. That was what Six drank. I didn't know what I meant to do going over there. In my mind I had it like I would get him drunk and fucking beat the shit out of him. Maybe kill him. But I knew it wouldn't be like that. Six had his ways about him. Not that I wasn't mad enough to do it. I just didn't know what it would be like. On my way out of the store I heard a mourning dove somewhere nearby. The sound gave me goose bumps—not the cold kind, and not the good kind either.

We had mourning doves in our backyard for as long as I can remember—under the back porch. My dad once said to me, when we were in the backyard trying to fix my bike, he said, "Their sound is so sad you almost want to kill them for it." Once my dad was gone, I felt like I heard them more, or it was just that they reminded me of him and his attitude toward most kinds of sadness. I didn't wanna feel sad then either. And it was like those fucking birds were making me feel it. So I went into the backyard with the BB gun I got for Christmas when I was ten. One of them was facing the wall, like he'd really been singing toward me inside. I shot it in the back of the head and then in the back twice. The bird flew up right away, its feathers rising then falling slow while it flapped in a flash of crooked downward spirals. It landed in the next-door neighbor's yard. I waited to hear if it would move. I thought about how it would have felt. The sting in the head and the back, after it flew up over me. I didn't feel even a little bit sorry for the bird because of how sad it made me feel ever since my dad got shot, when I had to look down and see my dad's eyes blink in disbelief, my dad looking back up at me like *he* was the one who was sorry, sorry that I had to see him go like that, with no control over the wild possibilities reality threw into our lives.

At Sixto's house I knocked on his door. "Eh, Six, eh!" I said. I backed away from the house, looked at the upstairs window. I heard footsteps. Loud and slow. When Six opened the door, he didn't even look at me or wait for me to say or do anything, he just walked back into the house.

I followed him to his bedroom, found a place to sit on an old office chair he kept in the corner. I was surprised to find it empty considering the state of the rest of the room—clothes, bottles, trash, and a light sprinkling of tobacco, weed, and ash all over everything. He was hella fucking sad-seeming. And I hated that I wanted to say something to make him feel better. That was the first time I saw it different. Like felt for him and how he must've felt about what he did.

"I got us a bottle," I said. "Let's go in the back." I heard him get up and follow me as I walked out of the room.

Six had a few chairs back there in that overgrown, crooked-fenced yard, between two fruitless orange and lemon trees that I remembered used to be full. We drank for a while in silence. I watched him smoke a blunt. I kept expecting him to start the conversation. Say something about what happened to my mom and brother, but he didn't. Six lit up a cigarette.

"When we were kids," Sixto said, "me and your dad, we used to sneak into your grandma's closet. She had an altar set up in there. All sorts of crazy shit on that altar. Like, she had a skull. It was the skull of what they call *little people*. She told us the little people stole babies and kids. She had jars full of powders and different kinds of herbs and stones. One time she caught me and your dad in there. She told your dad to go home. He ran like hell. She can get pretty crazy in her eyes. They go all dark like she keeps a darker pair behind the green ones you usually see. I had that little skull in my hand. She told me to put it down. She told me I had something in me I wasn't gonna be able to get out this time around. She told me I could handle it like a man. Die with it. But that I could also share it with family. I could give it away over time. Even to strangers. It was some old dark leftover thing that stayed with our family. Some people get diseases passed down in their genes. Some people get red hair, green eyes. We got this old thing that hurts real fucking bad, makes you mean. That's what you got. That's what your grandpa had in him. Be a man, she told me. Keep it to yourself." Sixto picked up the bottle, took a deep pull from it. I looked at Six, looked at his eyes to see if he expected me to say anything. Then he dropped the bottle on the grass and stood up. I couldn't believe he hadn't brought up my mom and brother. Or was that what he was trying to get at? Was this some long explanation for why all the shit that happened to our family happened the way it did?

"Let's go," he said to me like we'd just been talking about going somewhere. He brought me to his basement. He pulled out a wooden box that looked like a toolbox. Said it was his medicine box.

"You're gonna have to help me out here," he said, his words dragging a little behind. He pulled out a dried plant with red rope tied around it. He lit it. The smell and smoke were thick. It smelled like musk and earth and Fina. I didn't know anything about ceremony—whatever he was doing—but I knew we shouldn't have been drunk for it.

"This comes from a long way back," Six said, and poured some powder into his hand. Then he gestured for me to move my head closer, as if to see it better. Then he took a big breath in and blew it all in my face. It was thick as sand and some got in my mouth, up my nose. I choked and kept blowing out my nose like a dog.

"We got bad blood in us," Sixto said. "Some of these wounds get passed down. Same with what we owe. We should be brown. All that white you see that you got on your skin? We gotta pay for what we done to our own people." Sixto's eyes were closed, his head bent down a little.

"Fuck this shit, Six," I said through a cough, then stood up.

"Sit down," Six said, with a tone he'd never used with me before. "It's not all bad. It's power too."

I sat down but then stood right back up. "I'm fucking going."

"I said sit down!" Six blew on that plant again. The smoke

rose thick. I felt sick right away. Weak. I made it out to the front of the house, got on my bike, and rode to Fina's.

When I woke up the next day, Fina came in and shook her car keys at me. "Get up, let's go," she said. I was still pretty tired, but the fever had broken. I thought we were maybe going to get groceries. When we got past Castro Valley I knew it wasn't groceries or any kind of errand. We just kept driving, through the hills with all those windmills. I fell asleep looking at one of them that looked like a coin from *Mario Brothers*.

When I woke up we were in a field with orchards on either side of it. Fina was on top of the hood of the car, she was looking down at something. I opened my door, and when I did I saw Fina's hand wave me back, so I sat down without closing the door. Through the windshield, I saw my grandma get onto her knees and yank something with a thread or fishing line, something I couldn't see, until the creature came scrambling up on the windshield.

"Get his fur, get some of his fur!" Fina yelled at me. But I couldn't move. I just stared at it. The fuck was it? A raccoon? No. And then Fina was on top of the thing. It was black with a white stripe that went from its nose to the back of its neck. The thing was trying to bite and claw her, but she had her hand on its back, and it couldn't grip the metal hood. When it seemed to calm down, she lifted it up by its neck with the fishing line. "Come get some of its fur," she said.

"How—" I said.

"Rip its fucking fur off with your hands!" Fina said.

That was enough to get me going. I got out of the car and tried to get behind the thing, but it was onto me. I swiped twice but didn't want to get bit. Then on the third try I pulled a big clump from its side.

"Now get back in the car," Fina said, and got to her feet. She let the thing down to the ground. She walked with it farther into the field and then into the orchard at the edge of the field.

When she got back into the car I was just sitting there with my hand up in a fist, holding the clump of fur. Fina pulled out a leather bag with beadwork and fringes on it, opened it, and gestured for me to put the fur inside.

"What was that?" I said once we were on the road.

"Badger."

"Why?"

"We're gonna set up a box for you."

"What?"

"We're gonna make you a medicine box."

"Oh," I said, like that was all the explanation I needed.

We drove for a while in silence, then Fina looked over at me. "Long time ago they didn't have a name for the sun." She pointed up to the sun, which was in front of us. "They couldn't decide if it was a man or a woman or what. All the animals met about it, and a badger came out of a hole in the ground and called out the name, but as soon as he did, he ran. The other animals came after him. That badger went underground and stayed there. He was afraid they would punish him for naming it." Fina flipped on her blinker and switched lanes to pass a slow truck in the right lane. "Some of us got this feeling stuck inside, all the time, like we've done something wrong. Like we ourselves are something wrong. Like who we are deep inside, that thing we want

to name but can't, it's like we're afraid we'll be punished for it.
So we hide. We drink alcohol because it helps us feel like we can
be ourselves and not be afraid. But we punish ourselves with it.
The thing we most don't want has a way of landing right on top
of us. That badger medicine's the only thing that stands a chance
at helping. You gotta learn how to stay down there. Way deep
down inside yourself, unafraid."

I turned my head. Looked down at the gray streak of road. It
hit me somewhere in the middle of my chest. All that she'd said
was true. It hit me in the middle, where it all comes together
like a knot.

"Six have a box?" I said even though I knew.

"You know he does."

"D'you help him make it?"

"That boy never let me help him make anything," she said,
her voice breaking. She wiped her eyes. "He thinks he can make
it all up himself, but look where that got him."

"I been meaning to tell you. I went over there to see him."

"How did he seem?" Fina asked real quick like she'd been
waiting for me to bring it up.

"He was all right. But we drank. And then he brought me to
the basement, started talking about giving me some shit, lighting this plant in a shell, and then he blew some powder stuff in
my face."

"How do you feel?"

"Like I wanna fucking kill him. For real."

"Why?"

"What you mean why?"

"He didn't do any of it on purpose," Fina said. "He's lost."

"He fucked up."

"So did your brother."

"Six was part of that too."

"So? We all fuck up. It's how we come back from it that matters."

"I don't know what the fuck I'm supposed to do then. I can't get him back, I can't get them back. I don't know what the fuck any of this is about."

"You're not supposed to," she said, and rolled down her window.

It was getting hot. I rolled mine down too.

"That's the way this whole thing is set up," she said. "You're not ever supposed to know. Not all the way. That's what makes the whole thing work the way it does. We can't know. That's what makes us keep going."

I wanted to say something but couldn't. I didn't know what to say. It seemed both right and like the wrongest shit possible. I stayed quiet—the rest of the car ride and then for weeks after that. And she let me.

Daniel Gonzales

THE GUYS LOST their shit when I showed them the gun. Pushed each other and laughed like they hadn't done since forever ago. Everything got so fucking serious after Manny died. Which it should have. I'm not saying it shouldn't have. But he would have loved to see them like that. He would have loved the gun too. It was a real gun. As real as any gun. But it was white, and plastic, and I printed it from a 3-D printer in my room, which is the basement, which used to be Manny's room. I still can't think of him as gone. For now Manny's not here or there. He's in the middle of the middle, where you can only be when you can't be anywhere.

The gun only took three hours to print. My mom made tacos for the guys while they watched the Raiders game. I stayed downstairs and watched the gun spool out in layers. When they came down we watched the last of it get printed in silence. I knew they wouldn't know what to think. That's why I had a YouTube video pulled up to show them. A thirty-second time-lapse of a guy 3-D printing then firing a gun. Once they saw that, that's when they all lost their shit. They yelled and pushed at each other like they were kids again. Like it used to be over simpler shit like video games, like when we used to have all-night *Madden* tournaments and someone would win at four in the morning and we'd be all loud and my dad would come down with that little metal bat he kept by his bed—it was the bat he taught us to hit with when we were younger, an aluminum bat—and he'd hit us with that shit too, that same bat we got for free at that A's game where they were giving them away and we showed up early to be sure to get one.

Manny wouldn't like that Octavio came over so much after he died. I mean, in a big way it was Octavio's fault. But he's our cousin. And him and Manny had become like brothers. All three of us had. It's true, Octavio shouldn't have run his mouth at that party. For a while I hated him for it. Blamed him too. But he kept coming back around. Making sure we were okay. Me and my mom. Then the more I got to thinking about it, it wasn't all on him. Manny's the one who fucked that kid up. It was on all of us really. We turned our heads. Looked the other way when Manny fucked that kid up so bad on the front lawn. The blood stained brown on the yellow grass there until I got the mower out and cut it. And then when it was good, when money came in, before Manny died, we didn't ask where it was coming from. We took the TV and the random cash he left on the kitchen table in envelopes. We allowed the shit in and only wanted it out when it took him from us.

.   .   .

I knew they believed in the white gun for real when I picked it up and pointed it at them. They flinched, put their hands up. Not Octavio though. He told me to put it down. There were no bullets in the gun, but I hadn't felt in control for so long. I know guns are stupid. But that doesn't mean they don't make you feel in control when you're holding one. Octavio pulled the gun out of my hands. He looked down the barrel, pointed it at us. That's when it was my turn to get scared. Octavio holding it made it even more real. Made the white of it creepy—like some plastic message from the future about shit getting into the wrong hands.

After the guys left that night, I decided to write my brother an email. I'd helped him set it up. A Gmail account. Manny barely used it, but sometimes he wrote me. And when he did he said shit he never would have said in real life. That's what was cool about it.

I opened up my Gmail and replied to the last email my brother sent. *No matter what happens you know I'll always be here for you.* He was talking about fights he was getting in with our mom. She kept threatening to kick him out after he beat that kid up. The cops had come. Way too late, but they'd come, asked questions. She could sense shit was getting more serious. A tension was building in him. I could feel it too but didn't know what to say. It was like he'd been moving toward that bullet, toward the front yard, way before he got there.

I scrolled down to reply.

Hey brother. Damn. I know you're not there. But writing
you at your email, with that last message up there, it feels

like you're still here. Being around the guys feels like that too. You must be wondering what I've been up to. Maybe you see. Maybe you know. If you do, you must be like, what the fuck? 3-D printed gun? Shit. I felt the same way when I first saw it, just laughing like a crazy person when it came out. And I know you wouldn't approve. I'm sorry but we need the money. Mom lost her job. After you died she just stayed in bed. I couldn't get her out. I don't know where rent's coming from next month. We'll get an extra month if we get evicted, but shit, we been in this house our whole lives. Your pictures are still up. I still have to see you everywhere in here. So we're not just gonna go. We been here our whole lives. We don't have anywhere to go.

You know what's funny? I'm all, like, street and shit in real life. But online I don't talk like that, like I am now, so it feels weird to. Online I try to sound smarter than I am. I mean I choose what I type carefully, cuz that's all people know about me. What I type, what I post. It's pretty weird on there. Here. The way you don't know who people are. You just get their avatar names. Some profile picture. But if you post cool shit, say cool shit, people like you. Did I tell you about the community I got into? The name of the place, the online community is: Vunderkode. It's fucking Norwegian. You probably don't know what code is. I got way into it after you died. I didn't feel like going out or going to school or nothing.

When you spend enough time online, if you're looking, you can find some cool shit. I don't see it as that much different from what you did. Figuring out a way around a big fucking bully system that only gives those that came from money or power the means to make it. I learned from YouTube how to code. Shit like JavaScript, Python, SQL, Ruby, C++, HTML, Java, PHP. Sounds like a different language, right? It is. And you get better by putting in the time and taking to heart what all the motherfuckers have to say about your abilities on the forums. You have to know how to tell the difference. Whose criticism to take and whose to ignore. Long story short, though, is that I got hooked into this community, and I realized I could get whatever I wanted. Not drugs and shit. I mean I could but that's not what I want. The 3-D printer I got was itself printed by a 3-D printer. No shit, a 3-D printer printed by a 3-D printer. Octavio fronted me the money.

Part of what kills me about you being gone is that I never really said anything to you. Even when you emailed me. I didn't even really know how much I wanted to say to you until the day you left. Until I felt that feeling of losing you on the lawn out there, right on that same spot where that boy's blood stained the grass. But you showed me. I knew how much you loved me. You did shit like, like how you got me that expensive-ass Schwinn. Probably used to be some hipster's bike, you probably stole it, but still, you stole it for me, and in some ways that's even better than if you bought it. Especially if it was from one of those white boys trying to take Oakland over from the West. You should know they haven't made it to the Deep East yet. Probably never will. Shit's mean out here. But everything from High Street to West Oakland, that shit seems doomed to me. Anyway, I mostly see Oakland from online now. That's where we're all gonna be mostly eventually. Online. That's what I think.

We're already kinda moving in that direction if you think about it. We're already like fucking androids, thinking and seeing with our phones all the time.

You might wanna know more about some other shit, like, what's going on with Mom. She gets out of bed more now. But she just moves to the TV. She looks out the window a lot too, peeks out the curtains like she's still waiting for you to come home. I know I should be around her more, but she makes me feel hella sad. The other day she dropped a votive candle on the kitchen floor. Shit shattered, and she just left it there in pieces. Like shit's broken but we can't just leave it broken, all out there in the living room like your picture on the mantel, shit feels like it cuts me whenever I see it, how you graduated from high school and we all thought shit would be okay from then on because you did.

After you died I had this dream. It started off I was on an island. I could just barely see that there was another island across the way. There was hella fog in the way, but I knew I had to get over there, so I swam over. The water was warm and really blue, not gray or green like the bay. When I got over to the other side I found you in a cave. You had all these fucking pit bull puppies in a shopping cart. You were duplicating them in the cart. The pit bulls. You were handing me the puppies as they duplicated in your shopping cart. You were making all those pit bulls for me.

So when I first heard about this 3-D printer that could print a version of itself I thought of you and the pit bulls. The idea about the gun came later. I learned to be okay with Octavio. He started talking to me like I wasn't just your little brother. He asked me if I needed work. I told him about Mom being in bed all the time and he cried. He

wasn't even drunk. I needed to figure out a way to support
me and Mom. I know you wanted me to get an education.
Go to college. Get a good job. But I wanna be able to help
right now. Not in four years. Not owing hella money just
to work in an office somewhere. So then I got to thinking
about how I might help. I'd read about these guns you could
print. I didn't know then what they might be used for. I got
the .cad file, the G-code. After I got the printer I printed
a gun—first thing I printed. Then I made sure it would
work. I rode my bike over near the Oakland airport. That
spot you took me to one time where you can see the planes
come down close. I figured I could fire one off there and no
one would hear it. A big-ass Southwest 747 came down and
I shot a bullet into the water. It hurt my hand, and the gun
got a little hot, but it worked.

Now I've got six of these pieces. Octavio said he'd give
me five thousand for all of them. He's got something going.
All my shit's untraceable. So I'm not worried about the
government coming after me. I am worried about what
the guns will do. Where they'll end up. Who they might
hurt or kill. But we're family. I know Octavio can be a
mean motherfucker. So could you. But here it is. Manny,
he said they're gonna rob a fucking powwow. Crazy, right?
Shit sounded fucking stupid to me at first. Then it had me
fucked up cuz of Dad. You remember he used to always
tell us we're Indian. But we didn't believe him. It was like
we were waiting for him to prove it. Doesn't matter. Cuz
of what he did to Mom. To us. That piece of shit. Deserved
what he got. He had it coming. Long time coming. He
woulda killed Mom. Probably you too if you hadn't beat
his ass. I only wish I had a white gun to give you then. So

let them rob a powwow. Whatever. Dad never taught us anything about being Indian. What's that got to do with us? Octavio said they could make fifty thousand. Said he'd give me another five if they pulled it off.

As for me, I mostly spend my time online. I'm gonna graduate from high school. My grades are all right. I don't really like anyone at school. My only friends are your old friends, but they don't really care about me except that I can make them guns now. Except Octavio. I know how much it all messed him up. You gotta know that. You can't think it didn't fuck him up, right?

Anyway, I'll keep writing you here. I'll keep you updated. It's anyone's guess what's gonna happen. For the first time in a long time I got a little hope in my chest. Not that it's gonna get better. Just that it's gonna change. Sometimes that's all there is. Cuz that means there's something going on, somewhere inside all of it, all that turning the world is always doing, that means it was never supposed to stay the same heat. Miss you.

Daniel

Octavio brought me the first five thousand the day after I showed them all the guns. I left three thousand of it on the kitchen table in a blank envelope like Manny used to do. With the other two thousand I bought a drone and a pair of virtual-reality goggles.

I'd been wanting a drone ever since I found out about the powwow. I knew Octavio wouldn't let me go, but I wanted to see it. To make sure it went all right. Otherwise it was on me. And if shit went wrong, that was it. Octavio's plan was all I had, with my mom like she was. Decent drones are affordable now. And

I'd read that flying one with a camera and live feed, with VR goggles, felt like flying.

The drone I got had a three-mile range and could stay in the air for twenty-five minutes. The camera on it shot 4K resolution. The coliseum was only a mile away from our house on Seventy-Second. I flew it from my backyard. I didn't want to waste any time so I went straight up, about fifty feet in the air, then straight over the BART station. The thing could really move. I was in it. My eyes. The VR goggles.

Out in the back of center field, I went straight up and saw a guy pointing at me from the bleachers. I flew closer to him. He was a maintenance worker—holding a trash-grabber and a trash bag. The old guy got his binoculars out. I went even closer. What could he do? Nothing. I flew almost all the way up to the guy's face, and he tried to reach out to the drone. He got mad. I realized I was messing with him. I shouldn't have. I pulled away and dropped back down to the field. I headed toward the right-field wall, then down the foul line back to the infield. At first base I noticed the drone had ten minutes of battery life left. I wasn't about to lose a thousand dollars out there, but I wanted to finish at home plate. When I got there, just as I was about to turn the drone around, I saw the old guy from the bleachers coming for me. He was on the field and pissed, like he was gonna grab the drone and slam it to the ground—step on it. I backed up but forgot to rise. Luckily I'd been playing video games for long enough that my panicked brain was hardwired to perform well under pressure. But for a second I was close enough to count the wrinkles in the old guy's face. He managed to hit it, which almost caused the drone to come down, but I rose, went straight up, quick, like twenty or forty feet in seconds. I cleared the walls and came straight home to my backyard.

At home I watched the video over and over. Especially the part at the end where the guy almost got me. Shit was exciting. Real. Like I'd been there. I was about to call Octavio to tell him about it when I heard a scream upstairs. My mom.

Ever since Manny got shot I'd felt in a constant state of worry, half expecting some bad shit to happen all the time. I ran up the stairs, and when I got to the top I opened the door and saw my mom holding the envelope, flipping through the cash with her finger. Did she think Manny left it? Like he made it back somehow, or like he was still here? Did she think this was a sign?

I was about to tell her it was me, and Octavio, when she came over and hugged me. She pulled my head into her chest. Just kept saying, "Sorry, I'm so sorry." I thought she meant about how she'd been in bed. How she'd given up. But then as she kept saying it I took it to mean how everything had happened to us. How much we lost, how we'd once been together as a family, how good it'd once been. I tried to tell her it was okay. I kept repeating, "It's okay, Mom"—one for each of her sorrys. But then pretty soon I found myself saying sorry back. And we both said sorry back and forth until we started to cry and shake.

Blue

PAUL AND I GOT MARRIED tipi way. Some people call it the Native American Church. Or peyote way. We call peyote medicine because it is. I still mostly believe that in the same way I believe most anything can be medicine. Paul's dad married us in a tipi ceremony two years ago. In front of that fireplace. That's when he gave me my name. I was adopted by white people. I needed an Indian name. In Cheyenne it's Otá'tavo'ome, but I don't know how to say it right. It means: the Blue Vapor of Life. Paul's dad started calling me Blue for short, and it stuck. Up until then I'd been Crystal.

Almost all I know about my birth mom is that her name is Jacquie Red Feather. My adoptive mom told me on my eighteenth birthday what my birth mom's name is and that she's Cheyenne. I knew I wasn't white. But not all the way. Because while my hair is dark and my skin is brown, when I look in the mirror

I see myself from the inside out. And inside I feel as white as the long white pill-shaped throw pillow my mom always made me keep on my bed even though I never used it. I grew up in Moraga, which is a suburb just on the other side of the Oakland hills—which makes me even more Oakland hills than the Oakland hills kids. So I grew up with money, a pool in the backyard, an overbearing mother, an absent father. I brought home outdated racist insults from school like it was the 1950s. All Mexican slurs, of course, since people where I grew up don't know Natives still exist. That's how much those Oakland hills separate us from Oakland. Those hills bend time.

I didn't do anything about what my mom told me on my eighteenth birthday right away. I sat on it for years. I kept on feeling white while being treated like any other brown person wherever I went.

I got a job in Oakland at the Indian Center and that helped me to feel more like I belonged somewhere. Then one day I was looking on Craigslist and saw that my tribe in Oklahoma was hiring a youth-services coordinator. That's what I was doing in Oakland, so I applied not really thinking I would get it. But I got it and moved out to Oklahoma a few months later. Paul was my boss then. We moved in together just a month after I got there. Super unhealthy from the get-go. But part of why it went so fast is because of ceremony. Because of that medicine.

We sat up every weekend, sometimes it was just me, Paul, and his dad if no one else showed up. Paul took care of the fire and I brought in water for Paul's dad. You don't know the medicine unless you know the medicine. We prayed for the whole world to get better and felt it could every morning when we came out of the tipi. The world just spins, of course. But it all made perfect sense for a while. In there. I could evaporate and drift up and out through the crisscrossed tipi poles with the smoke and prayers. I could be gone and all the way there at once. But after Paul's dad died, everything I'd been praying about all that time got turned upside down and emptied on top of me in the form of Paul's fists.

After the first time, and the second, after I stopped counting, I stayed and kept staying. I slept in the same bed with him, got up for work every morning like it was nothing. I'd been gone since that first time he laid hands on me.

I applied for a job back where I used to work in Oakland. It was the position of events coordinator for the powwow. I had no experience in coordinating events outside of the annual youth summer camps. But they knew me there, so I got the job.

I watch my shadow grow long then flatten on the highway as a car flies by without slowing or seeming to notice me. Not that I want slowing or notice. I kick a rock and hear it ding against a can or some hollow thing in the grass. I pick up my pace and as I do a hot gust of air and the smell of gas blow by with the passing of a big truck.

This morning when Paul said he needed the car all day I decided to take it as a sign. I told him I'd get a ride home with Geraldine. She's a substance abuse counselor where I work. When I walked out the door, I knew everything I left in that house I'd be leaving for good. Most of it was easy to leave. But my medicine box, the one his dad had made for me, my fan, my gourd, my cedar bag, my shawl—these I'll have to learn to leave over time.

I didn't see Geraldine all day and not after work either. But I'd made my decision. I headed to the highway with nothing on me but my phone and a box cutter I took from the front desk before I left.

The plan is to get to OKC. To the Greyhound station. The job doesn't start for a month. I just need to make it back to Oakland.

A car slows then stops ahead of me. I see red brake lights bleed through my vision of the night. I turn around in a panic, then hear Geraldine, so turn to see her old-ass beige Cadillac her grandma gave her for graduating from high school.

When I get in the car Geraldine gives me a look like: *What the fuck?* Her brother Hector is laid out in the backseat, passed out.

"He okay?" I say.

"Blue," she says, scolding me with my name. Geraldine's last name is Brown. Names that are colors is what we have in common.

"What? Where we going?" I say to her.

"He drank too much," she says. "And he's on pain meds. I don't want him to throw up and die in his sleep on our living-room floor, so he's riding with us."

"Us?"

"Why didn't you just ask me for a ride? You told Paul—"

"He called you?" I say.

"Yeah. I was already home. I had to leave early for this fucker," Geraldine says, pointing with her thumb to the backseat. "I told Paul you had to stay late with a youth waiting for an auntie to show up, but that we were leaving soon."

"Thank you," I say.

"So you're going?" she says.

"Yeah," I say.

"Back to Oakland?"

"Yeah."

"OKC Greyhound?"

"Yeah."

"Well shit," Geraldine says.

"I know," I say. And then our saying this makes a silence we drive in for a while.

I see what I think is a human skeleton leaned against a barbed-wire wood-pole fence.

"Did you see that?" I say.

"What?"

"I don't know."

"People think they see stuff out here all the time," Geraldine says. "You know that part of the highway you were walking? Up north a ways, just past Weatherford, there's a town there called Dead Women Crossing."

"Why's it called that?"

"Some crazy white lady killed and beheaded this other white lady and sometimes teenagers go over to where it happened. The woman who got killed had her fourteen-month-old baby with her when she got killed. The baby made it out okay. They say you can hear that woman calling out for her baby at night."

"Yeah, right," I say.

"Ghosts aren't what you have to worry about out here," Geraldine says.

"I brought a box cutter from work," I say to Geraldine, and pull it out of my jacket pocket and slide the plastic clip up to show her the blade—like she doesn't know what a box cutter is.

"This is where they get us," Geraldine says.

"Safer out here than at home," I say.

"You could do worse than Paul."

"I should go back then?"

"Do you know how many Indian women go missing every year?" Geraldine says.

"Do you?" I say.

"No, but I heard a high number once and the real number's probably even higher."

"I saw something too, someone posted about women up in Canada."

"It's not just Canada, it's all over. There's a secret war on women going on in the world. Secret even to us. Secret even though we know it," Geraldine says. She rolls down her window and lights a smoke. I light one too.

"Every single place we get stuck out on the road," she says. "They take us, then leave us out here, leave us to dim to bone, then get all the way forgotten." She flicks her cigarette out the window. She only likes a cigarette for the first few drags.

"I always think of the men who do that kinda thing like, I know they're out there somewhere—"

"And Paul," she says.

"You know what he's going through. He's not who we're talking about."

"You're not wrong. But the difference between the men doing it and your average violent drunk is not as big as you think. Then you've got the sick pigs in high places who pay for our bodies on the black market with Bitcoin, someone way up at the top who gets off on listening to the recorded screams of women like us being ripped apart, knocked against the cement floors in hidden rooms—"

"Jesus," I say.

"What? You don't think it's real? The people who run this shit are real-life monsters. The people you never see. What they want is more and more, and when that isn't enough, they want what can't be gotten easily, the recorded screams of dying Indian women, maybe even a taxidermied torso, a collection of Indian women's heads, there's probably some floating in tanks with blue lights behind them in a secret office on the top floor of an office building in midtown Manhattan."

"You've given this some thought," I say.

"I meet with a lotta women," she says. "Trapped by violence. They have kids to think about. They can't just leave, with the kids, no money, no relatives. I have to talk to these women about options. I have to talk them into going to shelters. I have to hear about when the men accidentally go too far. So no, I'm not telling you that you should go back. I'm taking you to the bus station. But I'm saying you shouldn't be out here on the side of the highway at night. I'm saying you should have texted me, asked me for a ride."

"I'm sorry," I say. "I thought I'd see you after work."

I feel tired and a little annoyed. I always get this way after a cigarette. I don't know why I smoke them. I yawn a big yawn, then lean my head against the window.

I wake up to the blink-blur of a struggle. Hector has his arms around Geraldine—he's reaching for the wheel. We're swerving, no longer on the highway. We're on Reno Avenue just across the bridge over the Oklahoma River, not far from the Greyhound station. Geraldine's trying to get Hector off of her. I slap Hector on his head over and over with both hands to try to stop him. He grunts like he doesn't know where he is or what he's doing. Or like he's woken up from a bad dream. Or like he's still having it. We swerve hard left then harder right and go over the curb, over some grass, and then into the Motel 6 parking lot, right into the front of a truck parked there. The glove compartment comes in and crushes my knees. My hands fly toward the windshield. The seat belt pulls, then cuts into me. We stop and my vision blurs. The world spins a little. I look over and see that Geraldine's face is a bloody mess. Her airbag is out and it looks like it might have broken her nose. I hear the back door open and see Hector fall out of the car, then get up and stumble away. I turn my phone on to call an ambulance, and as soon as I do I see that Paul's calling again. I see his name. His picture. He's in front of his computer at work wearing that I'm-a-hella-hard-Indian-dude look, with his chin lifted. I pick up because I'm this close to the Greyhound. He can't do anything to me now.

"What, what the fuck do you want? We just got in a wreck," I say.

"Where you at?" he says.

"I can't talk. I'm calling an ambulance," I say.

"What are you doing in OKC?" he says, and my stomach drops. Geraldine looks at me and mouths: *Hang up.*

"I don't know how you know that, but I'm hanging up now," I say.

"I'm almost there," Paul says.

I hang up. "Did you fucking tell him where we are?"

"No, I did not fucking tell him where we are," Geraldine says, and wipes her nose with her shirt.

"Then how the fuck does he know we're here?" I say more to myself than to her.

"Shit."

"What?"

"Hector must have texted him. Hector's all fucked up right now. I gotta go after him."

"What about your car? Are you okay?"

"I'll be fine. Get to the bus station. Hide in the bathroom until the bus is ready to leave."

"What are you gonna do?"

"Find my brother. Convince him to not keep doing whatever the fuck it is he thinks he's doing."

"How long has he been back?"

"Only a month," she says. "And he gets deployed again next month."

"I didn't even think we were still over there." I side-hug her.

"Go," she says. I don't let go.

"Go," she says, and pushes me away. My knees are stiff and sore, but I run.

The Greyhound sign stretches up like a beacon. But the lights are out. Is it too late? What time is it? I look at my phone. It's only nine. I'm okay. I look back and see Geraldine's car where we left it. No cops yet. I could call and wait for the police, tell them what happened, tell them about Paul.

The station is empty. I go straight into the bathroom. On my feet, in a crouch, on top of the toilet in one of the stalls, I try to order my ticket on my phone. But he calls. I can't order because his calls keep interrupting me. I see a text at the top of my screen and try to ignore it but can't.

You here? the text says. I know he means the bus station. He must have seen Geraldine's car, seen how close the Greyhound station was.

We're at a bar around the corner from where we crashed, I text.

BULLSHIT, he texts back. Then he calls. I press the top button of my phone in. He's probably here. Walking through the bus station. He's looking for the light of my phone. Listening for its vibration. He won't come into the bathroom. I turn the

vibrate on my phone off. I hear the door to the bathroom open.
My heart is too big and fast to hold in my chest. I take a deep
breath as quiet and slow as I can. Still standing on the toilet seat
I duck my head down to see who came in. I see women's shoes.
It's an old woman. Big, beige, wide, Velcroed shoes step into the
stall next to mine. Paul calls again. I press the top button again.
I see a text come in.

C'mon baby. Come out. Where are you going? the text says. My
legs are tired. My knees throb from the crash. I get down from
the toilet. I pee and try to think of a text that might lead him
away from here.

*I told you we're down the street. Come down. We'll have a drink.
We'll talk through this, okay?* I text him. The door to the bath-
room opens again. I drop my head down again. Fuck. His shoes.
I get back up on the toilet.

"Blue?" His voice booms in the stall.

"This is the women's room, sir," the woman in the stall next
to me says. "There's no one in here but me." And I know she
must have heard me in the next stall when I peed.

"Sorry," Paul says.

There's still too much time before the bus gets here. He'll wait
for the lady to leave and come back in. I hear the door open then
close again.

"Please," I whisper to the woman, "he's after me." And I don't
know what I'm asking her to do.

"What time's your bus leaving, darling?" the woman says.

"Thirty minutes," I say.

"Don't worry. When you get to my age, you can get away with
that much time in here. I'll stay with you," she says, and I start to
cry. Not loud, not a sob, but I know she can hear me. The snot
comes and I sniff in hard so it won't keep coming.

"Thank you," I say.

"This kind of man. They're getting worse."

"I'm gonna have to run out, I think. Run to the bus."

"I carry mace. I been attacked, robbed more than once."

"I'm going to Oakland," I say. And I realize just then that we're no longer whispering. I wonder if he's at the door. My phone isn't ringing anymore.

"I'll walk over with you," she says.

I order the ticket on my phone.

We walk out of the bathroom together. The station is empty. The woman is brown, ethnically ambiguous, and older than I thought even from the shoes. She has those deep wrinkles on her face that seem carved, wooden. She gestures for us to lock arms as we walk.

I climb the steps into the bus, the old woman behind me. I show my ticket to the driver on my phone, then turn it off. I walk to the back and slink way down in my seat, take in a deep breath then let it out, and wait for the bus to start moving.

Thomas Frank

BEFORE YOU WERE BORN, you were a head and a tail in a milky pool—a swimmer. You were a race, a dying off, a breaking through, an arrival. Before you were born, you were an egg in your mom who was an egg in her mom. Before you were born, you were the nested Russian grandmother doll of possibility in your mom's ovaries. You were two halves of a thousand different kinds of possibilities, a million heads or tails, flip-shine on a spun coin. Before you were born, you were the idea to make it to California for gold or bust. You were white, you were brown, you were red, you were dust. You were hiding, you were seeking. Before you were born, you were chased, beaten, broken, trapped on a reservation in Oklahoma. Before you were born, you were an idea your mom got into her head in the seventies, to hitchhike across the country and become a dancer in New York. You were on your way when she did not make it across the country but sputtered and spiraled and wound up in Taos, New Mexico, at a peyote commune named Morning Star. Before you were born, you were your dad's decision to move away from the reservation, up to northern New Mexico to learn about a Pueblo guy's fireplace. You were the light in the wet of your parents' eyes as they met across that fireplace in ceremony. Before you were born, your halves inside them moved to Oakland. Before you were born, before your body was much more than heart, spine, bone, brain, skin, blood, and vein, when you'd just started to build muscle with movement, before you showed, bulged in her belly, as her belly, before your dad's pride could belly-swell from the sight of you, your parents were in a room listening to the sound your heart made. You had an arrhythmic heartbeat. The doctor said it was normal. Your arrhythmic heart was not abnormal.

"Maybe he's a drummer," your dad said.

"He doesn't even know what a drum is," your mom said.

"Heart," your dad said.

"The man said arrhythmic. That means no rhythm."

"Maybe it just means he knows the rhythm so good he doesn't always hit it when you expect him to."

"Rhythm of what?" she said.

But once you got big enough to make your mom feel you, she couldn't deny it. You swam to the beat. When your dad brought out the kettle drum, you'd kick her in time with it, or to her heartbeat, or to one of the oldies mixtapes she had made from records she loved and played to no end in your Aerostar minivan.

Once you were out in the world, running and jumping and climbing, you tapped your toes and fingers everywhere, all the time. On tabletops, desktops. You tapped every surface you found in front of you, listened for the sound things made back at you when you hit them. The timbre of taps, the din of dings, silverware clangs in kitchens, door knocks, knuckle cracks, head scratches. You were finding out that everything makes a sound. Everything can be drumming whether rhythm is kept or strays. Even gunshots and backfire, the howl of trains at night, the wind against your windows. The world is made of sound. But inside every kind of sound lurked a sadness. In the quiet between your parents, after a fight they both managed to lose. You and your sisters listening through the walls for tones, listening for early signs of a fight. For late signs of a fight reignited. The sound of the worship service, that building drone and wail of evangelical Christian worship, your mom speaking in tongues on the crest of that weekly Sunday wave, sadness because you couldn't feel any of it in there and wanted to, felt you needed it, that it could protect you from the dreams you had almost every night about the end of the world and the possibility of hell forever—you living there, still a boy, unable to die or leave or do anything but burn in a lake of fire. Sadness came when you had to wake up your snoring dad in church, even as members of the congregation, members of your family, were being slain by the Holy Ghost in the aisles right next to him. Sadness came when the days got shorter at the end of summer. When the street got quiet without kids out anymore. In the color of that fleeting sky, sadness lurked. Sadness pounced, slid in between everything, anything it could find its way into, through sound, through you.

You didn't think of any of the tapping or knocking as drumming until you actually started drumming many years later. It would have been good to know that you'd always done something naturally. But there was too much going on with everyone else in your family for anyone to notice you should probably have done something else with your fingers and toes than tap, with your mind and time than knock at all the surfaces in your life like you were looking for a way in.

．　　．　　．

You're headed to a powwow. You were invited to drum at the Big Oakland Powwow even though you'd quit drum classes. You weren't gonna go. You didn't wanna see anyone from work since you got fired. Especially anyone from the powwow committee. But there's never been anything like it for you—the way that big drum fills your body to where there's only the drum, the sound, the song.

The name of your drum group is Southern Moon. You joined a year after you first started working at the Indian Center as a janitor. You're supposed to say *custodian* now, or *maintenance person,* but you've always thought of yourself as a janitor. When you were sixteen you went on a trip to Washington, D.C., to visit your uncle—your mom's brother. He took you to the American Art Museum, where you discovered James Hampton. He was an artist, a Christian, a mystic, a janitor. James Hampton would end up meaning everything to you. Anyway, being a janitor was just a job. It paid the rent, and you could have your earphones in all day. No one wants to talk to the guy cleaning up. The earphones are an additional service. People don't have to pretend to be interested in you because they feel bad that you're taking their trash out from under their desk and giving them a fresh bag.

Drum group was Tuesday nights. All were welcome. Not women though. They had their own drum group Thursday nights. They were Northern Moon. You first heard the big drum by accident one night after work. You'd come back because you'd forgotten your earphones. You were just about to get on the bus when you realized they weren't in your ears when you most wanted them, for that long ride home after work. The

drum group played on the first floor—in the community center.
You walked into the room and, just as you did, they started singing. High-voiced wailing and howled harmonies that screamed
through the boom of that big drum. Old songs that sang to the
old sadness you always kept as close as skin without meaning to.
The word *triumph* blipped in your head then. What was it doing
there? You never used that word. This was what it sounded like
to make it through these hundreds of American years, to sing
through them. This was the sound of pain forgetting itself in
song.

You went back every Tuesday for the next year. Keeping time
wasn't hard for you. The hard part was singing. You'd never
been a talker. You'd certainly never sung before. Not even alone.
But Bobby made you do it. Bobby was big, maybe six four, three
fifty. He said he was big because he came from eight different
tribes. He had to fit all of them in there, he said, pointing at
his stomach. He had the best voice in the group, hands down.
He could go high or low. And he was the one who first invited
you in. If it was up to Bobby, the drum would be bigger, would
include everyone. He'd have the whole world on a drum if he
could. Bobby Big Medicine—sometimes a name just fit right.

Your voice is low like your dad's.

"You can't even hear it when I sing," you'd told Bobby after
class one day.

"So what? Adds body. Bass harmony is underappreciated,"
Bobby told you, then handed you a cup of coffee.

"The big drum's all you need for bass," you said.

"Voice bass is different than drum bass," Bobby said. "Drum
bass is closed. Voice bass opens."

"I don't know," you said.

"Voice can take a long time to come all the way out, brother," Bobby said. "Be patient."

You walk outside your studio apartment to a hot Oakland summer day, an Oakland you remember as gray, always gray. Oakland summer days from your childhood. Mornings so gray they filled the whole day with gloom and cool even when the blue broke through. This heat's too much. You sweat easy. Sweat from walking. Sweat at the thought of sweating. Sweat through clothes to where it shows. You take off your hat and squint up at the sun. At this point you should probably accept the reality of global warming, of climate change. The ozone thinning again like they said in the nineties when your sisters used to bomb their hair with Aqua Net and you'd gag and spit in the sink extra loud to let them know you hated it and to remind them about the ozone, how hair spray was the reason the world might burn like it said in Revelation, the next end, the second end after the flood, a flood of fire from the sky this time, maybe from the lack of ozone protection, maybe because of their abuse of Aqua Net—and why did they need their hair three inches in the air, curled over like a breaking wave, because what? You never knew. Except that all the other girls did it too. And hadn't you also heard or read that the world tilts on its axis ever so slightly every year so that the angle made the earth like a piece of metal when the sun hits it just right and it becomes just as bright as the sun itself? Hadn't you heard that it was getting hotter because of this tilt, this ever increasing tilt of the earth, which was inevitable and not humanity's fault, not our cars or emissions or Aqua Net but plain and simple entropy, or was it atrophy, or was it apathy?

. . . .

You're near downtown, headed for the Nineteenth Street BART Station. You walk with a slightly dropped, sunken right shoulder. Just like your dad's. The limp too, right side. You knew this limp could be mistaken for some kind of affect, some lame attempt at gangsta lean, but on some level that you maybe didn't even acknowledge, you knew that walking the way you walk is a way of subverting the straight-postured upright citizenly way of moving one's arms and feet just so, to express obedience, to pledge allegiance to a way of life and to a nation and its laws. Left, right, left, and so on. But had you really cultivated this lean, this drop-shouldered walk, this way of swaying slightly to the right in opposition? Is it really some Native-specific countercultural thing you're going for? Some vaguely anti-American movement? Or do you only walk the way your dad walked because genes and pain and styles of walking and talking get passed down without anyone even trying? The limp *is* something you've cultivated to look more like a statement of your individual style and less like an old basketball injury. To get injured and not recover is a sign of weakness. Your limp is practiced. An articulate limp, which says something about the way you've learned to roll with the punches, all the ways you've been fucked over, knocked down, what you've recovered from or haven't, that you've walked or limped away from with or without style—that's on you.

You pass a coffee shop you hate because it's always hot and flies constantly swarm the front of the shop, where a big patch of sun seethes with some invisible shit the flies love and where there's always just that one seat left in the heat with the flies, which is why you hate it, on top of the fact that it doesn't open until ten in the morning and closes at six in the evening to cater to all the hipsters and artists who hover and buzz around Oakland like flies, America's white suburban vanilla youth, searching for some invisible thing Oakland might give them, street cred or inner-city inspiration.

Before getting to the Nineteenth Street Station you pass a group of white teenagers who size you up. You're almost afraid of them. Not because you think they'll do anything. It's how out of place they are, all the while looking like they own the place. You want to run them down. Scream something at them. Scare them back to wherever they came from. Scare them out of Oakland. Scare the Oakland they made their own out of them. You could do it too. You're one of these big, lumbering Indians. Six feet, two thirty, chip on your shoulder so heavy it makes you lean, makes everyone look at it, your weight, what you carry.

Your dad is one thousand percent Indian. An overachiever. A recovering alcoholic medicine man from the rez for whom English is his second language. He loves to gamble and smoke American Spirit cigarettes, has false teeth and prays for twenty minutes before every meal, asks for help from the Creator for everyone, beginning with the orphan children and ending with the servicemen and servicewomen out there, your one thousand percent Indian dad who only cries in ceremony and has bad knees that took a turn for the worse when he laid concrete in your backyard for a basketball court when you were ten.

You know your dad could once play ball, knew the rhythm of the bounce, the head-fake and eye-swivel, pivot shit you learned how to do by putting in time. Sure he leaned heavily on shots off the glass, but that was the way it used to be done. Your dad told you he hadn't been allowed to play ball in college because he was Indian in Oklahoma. Back in 1963, that was all it took. No Indians or dogs allowed on courts or in bars or off the reservation. Your dad hardly ever talked about any of it, being Indian or growing up on the rez, or even what he felt like now that he's a certifiable Urban Indian. Except sometimes. When he felt like it. Out of nowhere.

You'd be riding in his red Ford truck to Blockbuster to rent a movie. You'd be listening to your dad's peyote tapes. The tape-staticky gourd-rattle and kettle-drum boom. He liked to play it loud. You couldn't stand how noticeable the sound was. How noticeably Indian your dad was. You'd ask if you could turn it off. You'd make him turn off his tapes. You'd put on 106 KMEL—rap or R & B. But then he'd try to dance to that. He'd stick his big Indian lips out to embarrass you, stick one flat hand out and stab at the air in rhythm to the beat just to mess with you. That's when you'd turn the music off altogether. And that was when you might hear a story from your dad about his childhood. About how he used to pick cotton with his grandparents for a dime a day or the time an owl threw rocks at him and his friends from a tree or the time his great-grandma split a tornado in two with a prayer.

The chip you carry has to do with being born and raised in Oakland. A concrete chip, a slab really, heavy on one side, the half side, the side not white. As for your mom's side, as for your whiteness, there's too much and not enough there to know what to do with. You're from a people who took and took and took and took. And from a people taken. You were both and neither. When you took baths, you'd stare at your brown arms against your white legs in the water and wonder what they were doing together on the same body, in the same bathtub.

. . .

How you ended up getting fired was related to your drinking, which was related to your skin problems, which was related to your father, which was related to history. The one story you were sure to hear from your dad, the one thing you knew for sure about what it means to be Indian, was that your people, Cheyenne people, on November 29, 1864, were massacred at Sand Creek. He told you and your sisters that story more than any other story he could muster.

Your dad was the kind of drunk who disappears weekends, lands himself in jail. He was the kind of drunk who had to stop completely. Who couldn't have a drop. So you had it coming in a way. That need that won't quit. That years-deep pit you were bound to dig, crawl into, struggle to get out of. Your parents maybe burned a too-deep, too-wide God hole through you. The hole was unfillable.

Coming out of your twenties you started to drink every night. There were many reasons for this. But you did it without a thought. Most addictions aren't premeditated. You slept better. Drinking felt good. But mostly, if there was any real reason you could pinpoint, it was because of your skin. You'd always had skin problems. Since you can remember. Your dad used to rub peyote gravy on your rashes. That worked for a while. Until he wasn't around anymore. The doctors wanted to call it eczema. They wanted you hooked on steroid creams. The scratching was bad because it only led to more scratching, which led to more bleeding. You'd wake up with blood underneath your fingernails—a sharp sting wherever the wound moved, because it moved everywhere, all over your body—and blood ended up on your sheets, and you'd wake up feeling like you'd dreamed something as important and devastating as it was forgotten. But there was no dream. There was only the open, living wound, and it itched somewhere on your body at all times. Patches and circles and fields of red and pink, sometimes yellow, bumpy, pus-y, weeping, disgusting—the surface of you.

If you drank enough you didn't scratch at night. You could deaden your body that way. You found your way in and out of a bottle. Found your limits. Lost track of them. Along the way you figured out there was a certain amount of alcohol you could drink that could—the next day—produce a certain state of mind, which you over time began to refer to privately as *the State*. The State was a place you could get to where everything felt exactly, precisely in place, where and when it belonged, you belonged, completely okay in it—almost like your dad used to say, "In'it, like, isn't that right? Isn't that true?"

But each and every bottle you bought was a medicine or a poison depending on whether you managed to keep them full enough. The method was unstable. Unsustainable. To drink enough but not too much for a drunk was like asking the evangelical not to say the name Jesus. And so playing drums and singing in those classes had given you something else. A way to get there without having to drink and wait and see if the next day the State might emerge from the ashes.

The State was based on something you read about James Hampton years after your trip to D.C. James had given himself a title: Director of Special Projects for the State of Eternity. James was a Christian. You are not. But he was just crazy enough to make sense to you. This is what made sense: He spent fourteen years building a massive piece of artwork out of junk he collected in and around the garage he rented, which was about a mile from the White House. The piece was called *The Throne of the Third Heaven of the Nations' Millennium General Assembly.* James made the throne for Jesus's second coming. What you get about James Hampton is his almost desperate devotion to God. To the waiting for his God to come. He made a golden throne from junk. The throne *you* were building was made of moments, made of experiences in the State after excess drinking, made of leftover, unused drunkenness, kept overnight, dreamed, moon-soaked fumes you breathed into throne form, into a place you could sit. In the State you were just unhinged enough to not get in the way. The problem came from having to drink at all.

The night before you got fired, drum class had been canceled. It was the end of December. The approach of the new year. This kind of drinking was not about reaching the State. This kind of drinking was careless, pointless—one of the risks, the consequences of being the kind of drunk you are. That you'll always be, no matter how well you learn to manage it. By night's end, you'd finished a fifth of Jim Beam. A fifth is a lot if you don't work your way up to it. It can take years to drink this way, alone, on random Tuesday nights. It takes a lot from you. Drinking this way. Your liver. The one doing the most living for you, detoxifying all the shit you put into your body.

When you got to work the next day you were fine. A little dizzy, still drunk, but the day felt normal enough. You went into the conference room. The powwow committee meeting was happening. You ate what they were calling breakfast enchiladas when they offered them. You met a new member of the committee. Then your supervisor, Jim, called you into his office, called on the two-way you kept on your belt.

When you got to his office he was on the phone. He covered it with one hand.

"There's a bat," he said, and pointed out to the hallway. "Get it out. We can't have bats. This is a medical facility." He said it like you'd brought the bat in yourself.

Out in the hallway, you looked up and around you. You saw the thing on the ceiling in the corner near the conference room at the end of the hall. You went and got a plastic bag and a broom. You approached the bat carefully, slowly, but when you got close it flew into the conference room. Everyone, the whole powwow committee, their heads spinning, watched as you went in there and chased it out.

When you were back out in the hallway, the bat circled around you. It was behind you, and then it was on the back of your neck. It had its teeth or claws dug in. You freaked out and reached back and got the bat by a wing and instead of doing what you should have done—put it in the trash bag you'd been carrying with you—you brought your hands together and with all your strength, everything you had in you, you squeezed. You crushed the bat in your hands. Blood and thin bones and teeth in a pile in your hands. You threw it down. You would mop it up quick. Wipe clean the whole day. Start over again. But no. The whole powwow committee was there. They'd come out to watch you catch the bat after you'd chased the thing into their meeting. Every one of them looked at you with disgust. You felt it too. It was on your hands. On the floor. That creature.

Back in your supervisor's office after you'd cleaned up the mess, Jim gestured for you to sit down.

"I don't know what that was," Jim said. Both hands were on top of his head. "But it's not something we can tolerate in a medical facility."

"The thing fucking . . . Sorry, but the thing fucking bit me. I was reacting—"

"And that would have been okay, Thomas. Only co-workers saw. But you smell like alcohol. And coming to work drunk, I'm sorry, but that's a fireable offense. You know we have a zero-tolerance policy here." He didn't look mad anymore. He looked disappointed. You almost told him that it was just from the night before, but that maybe wouldn't have made a difference, because you could have still blown an over-the-limit blood alcohol level. The alcohol was still in you, in your blood.

"I did not drink this morning," you said. You almost crossed your heart. You'd never even done that when you were a kid. It was something about Jim. He was like a big kid. He didn't want to have to punish you. Crossing your heart seemed like a reasonable way to convince Jim you were telling the truth.

"I'm sorry," Jim said.

"So that's it? I'm being fired?"

"There's nothing I can do for you," Jim said. He stood up and walked out of his own office. "Go home, Thomas," he said.

You get down to the train platform and enjoy the cool wind or breeze or whatever you call the rush of air the train brings before it arrives, before you even see it or its lights, when you hear it and feel that cool rush of air you especially appreciate because of how much it cools your sweaty head.

You find a seat at the front of the train. The robot voice announces the next stop, by saying, or not saying exactly, but whatever it's called when robots speak, *Next stop Twelfth Street Station*. You remember your first powwow. Your dad took you and your sisters—after the divorce—to a Berkeley high-school gym where your old family friend Paul danced over the basketball lines with that crazy-light step, that grace, even though Paul was pretty big, and you'd never thought of him as graceful before. But that day you saw what a powwow was and you saw that Paul was perfectly capable of grace and even some kind of Indian-specific cool, with footwork not unlike break dancing, and that effortlessness that cool requires.

The train moves and you think of your dad and how he took you to that powwow after the divorce, how he had never taken you before when you were younger, and you wonder if it was your mom and Christianity, the reason why you didn't go to powwows and do more Indian things.

The train emerges, rises out of the underground tube in the Fruitvale district, over by that Burger King and the terrible pho place, where East Twelfth and International almost merge, where the graffitied apartment walls and abandoned houses, warehouses, and auto body shops appear, loom in the train window, stubbornly resist like deadweight all of Oakland's new development. Just before the Fruitvale Station, you see that old brick church you always notice because of how run-down and abandoned it looks.

You feel a rush of sadness for your mom and her failed Christianity, for your failed family. How everyone lives in different states now. How you never see them. How you spend so much time alone. You want to cry and feel you might but know you can't, that you shouldn't. Crying ruins you. You gave it up long ago. But the thoughts keep coming about your mom and your family at a certain time when the magical over- and underworld of your Oakland-spun Christian evangelical end-of-the-world spirituality seemed to be coming to life to take you, all of you.

You remember it so clearly, that time. It never moved far from you no matter how much time had carried you away from it. Before anyone was awake, your mom was crying into her prayer book. You knew this because teardrops stain, and you remember tearstains in her prayer book. You looked into that book more than once because you wanted to know what questions, what private conversations, she might have had with God, she who spoke that mad-angel language of tongues in church, she who fell to her knees, she who fell in love with your dad in Indian ceremonies she ended up calling demonic.

Your train leaves the Fruitvale Station, which makes you think of the Dimond district, which makes you think of Vista Street. That's where it all happened, where your family lived and died. Your older sister, DeLonna, was heavily into PCP, angel dust. That was when you found out you don't need religion to be slain, for the demons to come out with their tongues. One day after school DeLonna smoked too much PCP. She came home and it was clear to you that she was out of her mind. You could see it in her eyes—DeLonna without DeLonna behind them. And then there was her voice, that low, deep, guttural sound. She yelled at your dad and he yelled back and she told him to shut up and he did shut up because of that voice. She told him that he didn't even know which God he was worshipping, and soon after that DeLonna was on the floor of your sister Christine's room, foaming at the mouth. Your mom called an emergency prayer circle and they prayed over her and she foamed and writhed and eventually stopped when that part of the high wore off, the drug dimmed, her eyes closed, the thing was done with her. When she woke up they gave her a glass of milk, and when she was back with her normal voice and eyes, she didn't remember any of it.

Later you remember your mom saying to take drugs was like sneaking into the kingdom of heaven under the gates. It seemed to you more like the kingdom of hell, but maybe the kingdom is bigger and more terrifying than we could ever know. Maybe we've all been speaking the broken tongue of angels and demons too long to know that that's what we are, who we are, what we're speaking. Maybe we don't ever die but change, always in the State without hardly ever even knowing that we're in it.

When you get off at the Coliseum Station, you walk over the pedestrian bridge with butterflies in your stomach. You do and don't want to be there. You want to drum but also to be heard drumming. Not as yourself but just as the drum. The big drum sound made to make the dancers dance. You don't want to be seen by anyone from work. The shame of your drinking and showing up to work with the smell still on you was too much. Getting attacked by the bat and crushing it in front of them was part of it too.

You go through the metal detector at the front and your belt gets you another go-through. You get the beep the second time because of change in your pocket. The security guard is an older black guy who doesn't seem to care much about anything but avoiding the beeping of the detector.

"Take it out, anything, anything in your pockets, take it out," he says.

"That's all I got," you say. But when you walk through it beeps again.

"You ever have surgery?" the guy asks you.

"What?"

"I don't know, maybe you have a metal plate in your head or—"

"Nah, man, I got nothing metal on me."

"Well, I gotta pat you down now," the guy says, like it's your fault.

"All right," you say, and put your arms up.

After he pats you down, he gestures for you to walk through again. This time when it beeps he just waves you through.

About ten feet away you're looking down as you walk and you realize what it was. Your boots. Steel toe. You started wearing them when you got the job. Jim recommended it. You almost go back to tell the guy, but it doesn't matter anymore.

You find Bobby Big Medicine under a canopy. He nods up, then tilts his head toward an open seat around the drum. There's no small talk.

"Grand Entry song," Bobby says to you because he knows everyone else knows. You pick up your drumstick and wait for the others. You hear the sound but not the words the powwow emcee is saying, and you watch for Bobby's stick to go up. When it does, your heart feels like it stops. You wait for the first hit. You pray a prayer in your head to no one in particular about nothing in particular. You clear a way for a prayer by thinking nothing. Your prayer will be the hit and the song and the keeping of time. Your prayer will begin and end with the song. Your heart starts to hurt from lack of breath when you see his drumstick go up and you know they're coming, the dancers, and it's time.

PART IV

Powwow

A man must dream a long time in order to act with grandeur, and dreaming is nursed in darkness.

—JEAN GENET

Orvil Red Feather

INSIDE THE COLISEUM, the field is already packed with people, with dancers, tables, and canopies. Packed to the stands. Camping chairs and lawn chairs are scattered across the field, with and without people sitting in them—saved spots. On top of the tables and hung on the backs and sides of canopy walls are powwow hats and T-shirts with slogans like *Native Pride* written in capital block letters gripped by eagle talons; there are dream catchers, flutes, tomahawks, and bows and arrows. Indian jewelry of every kind is splayed and hung everywhere, crazy amounts of turquoise and silver. Orvil and his brothers stop for a minute at the table with beaded A's and Raiders beanies, but they really want to check out the line of food tables in the outfield.

They spend their fountain money and go up to the second deck to eat. The fry bread is wide and the meat and grease are deep.

"Man. That's goot," Orvil says.

"Pffft," Loother says. "Quit trying to talk Indian."

"Shut up. What am I supposed to sound like, a white boy?" Orvil says.

"Sometimes you sound like you wanna be Mexican," Lony says. "Like when we're at school."

"Shut up," Orvil says.

Loother elbows Lony and they both crack up at Orvil. Orvil takes off his hat and hits them both on the back of the head with it. Then Orvil takes the taco and steps over the row to sit behind them. After sitting in silence for a while, he hands the taco to Lony.

"How much you say you could win if you win?" Loother asks Orvil.

"I don't wanna talk about it. It's bad luck," Orvil says.

"Yeah but you said it was like, five thou—" Loother says.

"I said I don't wanna talk about it," Orvil says.

"'Cuz you think it'll jinx it, huh?"

"Loother, shut the fuck up."

"All right," Loother says.

"All right then," Orvil says.

"But imagine how much cool shit we could get with that kinda money," Loother says.

"Yeah," Lony says, "we could get a PS4, a big TV, some J's—"

"We would give it all to Grandma," Orvil says.

"Aw man, that's weak," Loother says.

"C'mon, you know she likes to work," Lony says, still chewing the last of the taco.

"There's probably other stuff she'd rather do if she could," Orvil says.

"Yeah, but we could just keep some of it," Loother says.

"Shit," Orvil says, looking down at the time on his phone. "I gotta get down to the locker room!"

"What you want us to do?" Loother asks.

"Stay up here," Orvil says. "I'll come get you after."

"What? C'mon," Lony says.

"I'll come get you after, it won't take that long," Orvil says.

"But we can't barely see shit from up here," Loother says.

"Yeah," Lony says.

Orvil walks away. He knows the more he argues, the more rebellious they'll get.

The men's locker room is loud with laughter. At first Orvil thinks they're laughing at him, but then realizes someone had told a joke just before he got in, because more jokes come as he sits down. Mostly it's older guys, but there are a few young men in there too. He puts his regalia on slow, carefully, and puts his earphones in, but before he can put a song on he sees a guy across from him gesturing for him to take them out. It's this huge Indian guy. He stands up, he's in full regalia, and he picks his feet up one at a time, which makes his feathers shake, which sort of scares Orvil. The guy clears his throat.

"Now you young men in here, listen up. Don't get too excited out there. That dance is your prayer. So don't rush it, and don't dance how you practice. There's only one way for an Indian man to express himself. It's that dance that comes from all the way back there. All the way over there. You learn that dance to keep it, to use it. Whatever you got going on in your life, you don't leave it all in here, like them players do when they go out on that field, you bring it with you, you dance it. Any other way you try to say what you really mean, it's just gonna make you cry. Don't act like you don't cry. That's what we do. Indian men. We're crybabies. You know it. But not out there," he says, and points to the door of the locker room.

A couple of the older guys make this low *huh* sound, then another couple of guys say *aho* in unison. Orvil looks around the room, and he sees all these men dressed up like him. They all needed to dress up to look Indian too. There's something like the shaking of feathers he felt somewhere between his heart and his stomach. He knows what the guy said is true. To cry is to waste the feeling. He needs to dance with it. Crying is for when there's nothing else left to do. This is a good day, this is a good feeling, something he needs, to dance the way he needs to dance to win the prize. But no. Not the money. To dance for the first time like he learned, from the screen but also from practice. From the dancing came the dancing.

There are hundreds of dancers in front of him. Behind him. To his left and right. He's surrounded by the variegation of color and pattern specific to Indianness, gradients from one color to the next, geometrically sequenced sequined shapes on shiny and leathered fabrics, the quill, bead, ribbon, plume, feathers from magpies, hawks, crows, eagles. There are crowns and gourds and bells and drumsticks, metal cones, sticked and arrowed flickers, shag anklets, and hairpipe bandoliers, barrettes and bracelets, and bustles that fan out in perfect circles. He watches people point out each other's regalia. He is an old station wagon at a car show. He is a fraud. He tries to shake off the feeling of feeling like a fraud. He can't allow himself to feel like a fraud because then he'll probably act like one. To get to that feeling, to get to that prayer, you have to trick yourself out of thinking altogether. Out of acting. Out of everything. To dance as if time only mattered insofar as you could keep a beat to it, in order to dance in such a way that time itself discontinued, disappeared, ran out, or into the feeling of nothingness under your feet when you jumped, when you dipped your shoulders like you were trying to dodge the very air you were suspended in, your feathers a flutter of echoes centuries old, your whole being a kind of flight. To perform and win you have to dance true. But this is just Grand Entry. No judges. Orvil hops a little and dips his arms. He puts his arms out and tries to keep light on his feet. When he starts to feel embarrassed, he closes his eyes. He tells himself not to think. He thinks the thought *Don't think* over and over. He opens his eyes and sees everyone around him. They're all feathers and movement. They're all one dance.

When Grand Entry is over, the dancers disperse, moving out in every direction in a ripple of chatter and bells, headed for the vendors, or to find family, or to walk around, giving and accepting compliments, acting normal, like they don't look like what they look like. Indians dressed up as Indians.

Orvil's stomach rumbles and shudders. He looks up to see if he can find his brothers.

Tony Loneman

TO GET TO THE POWWOW Tony Loneman catches a train. He gets dressed at home and wears his regalia all the way there. He's used to being stared at, but this is different. He wants to laugh at them staring at him. It's his joke to himself about them. Everyone has been staring at him his whole life. Never for any other reason than the Drome. Never for any other reason than that his face told you something bad happened to him—a car wreck you should but can't look away from.

No one on the train knows about the powwow. Tony's just an Indian dressed like an Indian on the train for no apparent reason. But people love to see the pretty history.

Tony's regalia is blue, red, orange, yellow, and black. The colors of a fire at night. Another image people love to think about. Indians around a fire. But this isn't that. Tony is the fire and the dance and the night.

He's standing in front of a BART map. An older white woman sitting across from him points to the map and asks him where to get off if she's going to the airport. She knows the answer to this question. She would have already looked it up on her phone numerous times to be sure. She wants to see if the Indian speaks. It's the next question she means to get to. The face behind the face she makes says it all. Tony doesn't answer about the airport right away. He stares at her and waits for what she'll say next.

"So you're . . . a Native American?"

"We get off at the same exit," Tony says. "Coliseum. There's a powwow. You should come." Tony walks to the door to look out the window.

"I would, but . . ."

Tony hears that she's responding, but he doesn't listen. People don't want any more than a little story they can bring back home with them, to tell their friends and family around the dinner table, to talk about how they saw a real Native American boy on a train, that they still exist.

Tony looks down and watches the tracks fly by. He feels the train pull him back as it slows. He grips the metal handle, shifts his weight to the left, then rocks back to his right when the train comes to a complete stop. The woman behind him is saying something, but it can't matter what. He steps off the train and when he gets to the stairs he takes off, skipping two steps the whole way down.

Blue

BLUE IS DRIVING to pick up Edwin. It's that weird night-morning color, that deep blue-orange-white. The day she's been anticipating for almost a year is just starting.

It feels good to be back in Oakland. All the way back. She's been back a year. On a regular paycheck now, in her own studio apartment, with her own car again for the first time in five years. Blue tilts the rearview down and looks at herself. She sees a version of herself she thought was long gone, someone she'd left behind, ditched for her real Indian life on the rez. Crystal. From Oakland. She's not gone. She's somewhere behind Blue's eyes in the rearview.

Blue's favorite place to smoke a cigarette is in the car. She likes how the smoke escapes when all the windows are down. She lights one. She tries to at least say a little prayer every time she smokes. It makes her feel less guilty for smoking. She takes in a deep drag and holds it. She says *thank you* as she blows out the smoke.

She'd gone all that way to Oklahoma to find out where she came from and all she'd gotten for it was a color for a name. No one had heard of any Red Feather family. She'd asked around plenty. She wonders if maybe her birth mom made it up— maybe she didn't know her own tribe either. Maybe she had been adopted too. Maybe Blue would end up having to make up her own name and tribe too, pass that on to her possible children.

Blue throws her cigarette out the window as she passes the Grand Lake Theatre. The theater meant many things to her over the years. Right now she's thinking of the awkward, clearly stated non-date date she recently went on with Edwin. Edwin's her intern, her assistant for the powwow event coordination for this past year. The movie was sold out so they walked around the lake instead. The awkward silence that was the entire walk was intense. They both kept starting sentences and stopping them short, then saying "Never mind." She liked Edwin. She likes him. There's something about him that feels like family. Maybe because he has a similar background. In Edwin's case, he hadn't known his dad, who is Native, who happens to be the emcee at the powwow. So they had that in common, sort of, but not much else. She definitely does not like Edwin as anything more than a co-worker and possible future friend. She'd told him a thousand times with her eyes that there's no way—in what her eyes didn't do, in how they looked away when his tried to stay.

When Blue pulls up to his house, she calls him from her car. He doesn't answer. She walks up and knocks on his door. She should have texted that she was outside the minute she left her house. The drive to West Oakland took about fifteen minutes without traffic. Why didn't she make him take BART? Right, it's too early. But the bus? No, he had a bad experience on the bus he won't even tell her about. Does she baby him? Poor Edwin.

He really does try. He really doesn't know how he comes off to other people. He's so painfully aware of his physical size. And he makes too many comments about himself, his weight. It makes people as uncomfortable as he appears to be most of the time.

Blue knocks again, hard to the point that it would have been rude except that Edwin was making her wait outside his door on this day they'd both been planning and working hard toward for so many months.

Blue looks at her phone for the time, then checks her email and texts. When nothing of interest comes up, she checks her Facebook. It's a tired feed she'd read last night before going to bed. No new activity. Old comments and posts she'd already seen. She presses the Home button and for a second, just for a small moment, thinks she should open her *other* Facebook feed. On that other Facebook, she'd find the information and media she'd always been looking for. On that other Facebook feed, she'd find true connection. That is where she'd always wanted to be. Is what she'd always hoped Facebook would turn out to be. But there is nothing else to check, there *is* no other Facebook, so she clicks the screen off and puts the phone back in her pocket. Just as she's about to knock again, Edwin's big face appears before her. He's holding two mugs.

"Coffee?" he says.

Dene Oxendene

DENE IS IN a makeshift storytelling booth he built to record stories. He aims the camera at his face and presses Record. He doesn't smile or speak. He's recording his face as if the image, the pattern of light and dark arranged there, might mean something on the other side of that lens. He's using the camera his uncle gave to him before he died. The Bolex. One of Dene's favorite directors, Darren Aronofsky, used a Bolex in his movies *Pi* and *Requiem for a Dream*—which Dene would say is one of his favorite movies, though it's hard to call such a fucked-up movie a favorite. But that for Dene is what is so good about the movie, aesthetically it's rich, so you enjoy the experience, but you don't exactly come away from the film glad that you watched it, and yet you wouldn't have it any other way. Dene believes this kind of realness is something his uncle would have appreciated. This unflinching stare into the void of addiction and depravity, this is the kind of thing only a camera can keep its eye wide open for.

Dene turns the camera off and sets it up on a tripod to point at the stool he has placed in the corner for the storytellers. He flips one switch on his cheap lighting gear for soft light behind the stool, then the other switch for the harder lighting he has behind him. He'll ask everyone who comes into his booth why they've come to the powwow, what powwows mean to them. Where do they live? What does being Indian mean to them? He doesn't need more stories for his project. He doesn't even need to show a product at the end of the year for the grant money he's received. This is about the powwow, the committee. It's about documentation. For posterity. It might end up in his final production, whatever that might be—he still doesn't know. He's still letting the content direct the vision. Which is *not* just another way of saying he's making it up as he goes along. Dene walks through the black curtains out into the powwow.

Opal Viola Victoria Bear Shield

⟫⟪

OPAL IS SITTING alone in plaza infield, second deck. She's watching from up there so as to not be seen by her grandsons. By Orvil especially. It would mess with him if he saw her there.

She hasn't been to an A's game in years. Why did they stop going to games? Time only seems to have skipped, or to have sped by without you when you looked the other way. That's what Opal had been doing. Closing her eyes and ears to the closing of her eyes and ears.

Lony was just starting to walk on his own the last time they were here. Opal is listening to the drum. She hasn't heard a big drum like that since she was young. She scans the field for the boys. It's a blur. She should probably get glasses. Probably should have gotten glasses a long time ago. She would never tell anyone this, but she enjoys the distance being a blur. She can't tell how crowded it is. Certainly not the same crowd as at a baseball game.

She looks up at the sky, then at the empty third deck. That's where they'd watched the game from with the boys. She sees something fly over the edge of the rim of the coliseum. Not a bird. Its movement is unnatural. She squints to try to see it better.

Edwin Black

EDWIN HANDS BLUE a coffee he made for her just minutes
before she came and knocked at his door. French-pressed organic
dark roast. He'd guessed a moderate dose of sugar and milk. He
doesn't smile or make small talk as they walk to her car together.
Today means everything for them. The countless hours they put
in. All the different drum groups and vendors and dancers they
had to call and convince to come, that there was prize money
to be had, money to be made. Edwin's made more phone calls
this year than he has in his whole life. People didn't really want
to sign on for a new powwow. Especially one in Oakland. If it
doesn't go well, the powwow won't happen again next year. And
they'll be out of a job. But this means more than a job for Edwin
at this point. This is a new life. Plus his dad will be there today.
It's almost too much to think about. Or maybe Edwin just drank
too much coffee this morning.

The drive to the coliseum feels slow and tense. Every time he
thinks to say something he takes a sip of coffee instead. This is

only the second time they're spending time together outside of work. She has NPR on so low it's unintelligible.

"I started writing a story the other day," Edwin says.

"Oh yeah?" Blue says.

"It's about a Native guy, I'll call him Victor—"

"Victor? Really?" Blue says, with comically half-closed eyelids.

"Fine, his name is Phil. You wanna hear it?"

"Sure."

"Okay, so Phil lives in a nice apartment in downtown Oakland he got grandfathered into, it's a big place with fixed rent. Phil works at Whole Foods. One day a white guy he works with, I'll call him John, he asks Phil if he wants to hang out after work. They hang out, go to a bar, have a good time, then John ends up spending the night at Phil's. The next day when Phil comes home from work, John's still there, only he has a couple of friends over. They brought a bunch of their stuff too. Phil asks John what's going on and John tells Phil he figured since there's so much extra room that Phil wasn't using, that it would be okay. Phil doesn't like it, but he's not one for confrontation so he lets it go. Over the next few weeks, and then months, the house fills up with squatters, hipsters, corporate tech nerds, and every kind of young white person imaginable. They're either living in Phil's apartment or just sort of hanging out indefinitely. Phil doesn't understand how he let it get so out of control. Then just when he gets up the nerve to say something, to kick everyone out, he gets really sick. Someone had stolen his blanket, and when he asked John about it, John gave him a new blanket. Phil believes that blanket made him sick. He's in bed for a week. By the time he comes out, things have changed. Progressed, you might say. Some of the rooms have been turned into offices.

John's running some kind of start-up out of Phil's apartment. Phil tells John he has to go, everyone has to leave, and that Phil had never agreed to any of this. That's when John provides some paperwork. Phil had signed something, apparently. Maybe in a fever dream. But John won't show him the papers. Trust me, bro, John says. You don't wanna go there. Oh and by the way, you know that spot under the stairs, John says. Spot? Phil says. That room? He means the closet under the stairs. Phil knows what's coming next. Let me guess, you're moving me to that spot under the stairs, that's my new room, Phil says. You guessed it, John says. This is my apartment, my grandfather lived here, he passed it on to me to take care of, Phil says. It's for my family, if anyone needs a place to stay, that's what it's supposed to be here for. And here John produces a gun. He points it at Phil's face, then proceeds to walk Phil to the closet under the stairs. Told you, bro, John says. Told me what? Phil says. You should have just joined the company. We could have used someone like you, John says. You never asked me anything, you just came to my apartment and stayed here, then took over, Phil says. Whatever, bro, my record keepers have it going down differently, John says, and nods with his head at a couple of guys on a couch in the downstairs living room furiously typing on their Apple computers what Phil assumes is a different version of the events happening just then. Suddenly feeling very tired, and hungry, Phil retreats to his under-the-stairs closet-room. That's it, that's what I have so far."

"That's funny," Blue says. Like she doesn't think it's funny, but feels like that's what he wants her to say.

"It's stupid. Sounded a lot better in my head," Edwin says.

"So much is like that, right?" Blue says. "I feel like something like that actually happened to a friend of mine. I mean, not exactly like that, but like a warehouse in West Oakland she inherited from her uncle got taken over by squatters."

"Really?"

"That's their culture," Blue says.

"What is?"

"Taking over."

"I don't know. My mom's white—"

"You don't have to defend all white people you think aren't a part of the problem just because I said something negative about white culture," Blue says. And Edwin's heart rate goes up. He'd heard her get mad on the phone, at other people, but never at him.

"Sorry," Edwin says.

"Don't apologize," Blue says.

"Sorry."

Edwin and Blue set up the tables and canopies together in the early-morning light. They unpack folding tables and chairs. When everything is set, Blue looks at Edwin.

"Should we just leave the safe in the car until later?" she says.

It's a small safe they got from Walmart. It wasn't easy to convince the grantees to cut them a check they could cash. Cash was a problem when it came to grants and how nonprofits managed their money. But after the phone calls and emails, all the explanations and testimony about the people who come to powwows to compete, people who want to win cash because they prefer cash, sometimes don't have bank accounts, and don't want to lose the three percent cash-checking services take, they finally agreed on Visa gift cards. A whole mess of them.

"There's no reason not to get it now," Edwin says. "I'm sure it'll get crazy later and we won't wanna go all the way out to the parking lot when it's time to hand out the prizes."

"True," Blue says.

They pull the safe out of her trunk, then walk with it together, not because it's so heavy but because it's so wide.

"I've never held this much money," Blue says.

"I know it's not that heavy, but it feels super heavy, right?" Edwin says.

"Maybe we should've gotten money orders," Blue says.

"But we advertised cash. That's one of the ways to draw people. You said that."

"I guess."

"No, but I mean, you said that. It was your idea."

"Just seems a little flashy," Blue says as they approach the table.

"Powwows are all about flash, aren't they?"

Calvin Johnson

~❧~

THEY'RE ALMOST DONE with their breakfast before anyone says anything. They're at the Denny's next to the coliseum. Calvin got eggs over easy with sausage and toast. Charles and Carlos both got the Grand Slam. And Octavio ordered oatmeal, but he's mostly just been drinking coffee. Shit had gotten more serious as the day drew closer, and as it got more serious, they all got quiet about it. But Calvin is more worried about making sure they steal the money sooner than later. He's more worried about *getting away with it* than getting the money. He's still pissed at Charles for involving him in this shit plan. That Charles had smoked up all his shit. That *that's* why they're here. He couldn't get over it. But he couldn't get out of it either.

Calvin cleans up his yolk with toast, washes it down with the last of his orange juice. It's sour, sweet, salty, and that thick specifically yolk flavor all at once.

"But we all agree it needs to happen sooner than later, right?" Calvin says out of the blue.

"How's she not gonna come around to ask about refills after this long?" Charles says, holding his empty coffee mug in the air.

"We just won't tip, that'll be like getting our coffee for free," Carlos says.

"Fuck that," Octavio says.

"The tip is supposed to mean something. People have to be held fucking accountable," Charles says.

"That's right," Carlos says.

"She already refilled you twice, motherfucker," Octavio says. "Now shut the fuck up about the tip. You said they're keeping it in a safe?"

"Yeah," Calvin says.

"Big dude we'll recognize 'cuz he's big," Octavio says. "And like a forty-something-year-old woman with long black hair, kinda pretty but not, with bad skin?"

"Right," Calvin says.

"I say we just take the safe and figure out how to open that shit later," Charles says.

"We're not gonna rush it," Octavio says.

"It's probably better to do it sooner than later, right?" Calvin says.

"There's gonna be a lotta people with phones who could call the cops while we wait for some fat ass to cough up the combination. Charles is right," Carlos says.

"We're not gonna rush it if we don't have to," Octavio says. "If we can get the combination, we're gonna get it and not fucking walk out of the place with a fucking safe."

"Did I tell you guys it's all in gift cards? Like a whole bunch of Visa gift cards," Calvin says.

"Same as cash," Octavio says.

"Why the fuck is it all in gift cards?" Charles says.

"Yeah, why the fuck is it—" Carlos says.

"Would you shut the fuck up already, Charlos? Just keep your mouth shut and think before you speak. It's the exact same fucking thing as cash," Octavio says.

"They needed receipts, for the grant," Calvin says, then takes a last bite and looks to see how Charles is taking what Octavio just said. Charles is staring off, out the window. He's pissed.

Daniel Gonzales

❧

DANIEL BEGS to go. To see it happen. He never begs. Octavio says no. Says no again every time after. Up until the night before. It's just the two of them in the basement.

"You know you have to let me go," Daniel says from his computer. Octavio is on the couch staring at the table.

"What I have to do is make sure this shit goes right. So we get that money," he says, and walks over to Daniel.

"I'm not even talking about going, I'll be here. I can fly the drone over to the coliseum from here. Or let me go then—"

"Hell no, you're not going," Octavio says.

"So just let me fly the drone over."

"Man, I don't know," Octavio says.

"C'mon. You owe me," Daniel says.

"Don't make this shit about—"

"I'm not making shit about shit," Daniel says, and turns around. "It's *been* about it. You fucked this family up."

Octavio walks back to the couch. "Fuck!" he says, and kicks

the table. Daniel goes back to mindlessly playing chess on his computer. He suicides a bishop for his opponent's knight to mess up his formation.

"You gotta stay here. You gotta get that fucking thing outta there and not get caught up, they can trace that shit back if it falls."

"I got it. I'll stay here. So we good?" Daniel says.

"Are we good?" Octavio says. Daniel gets up and walks over to him. Sticks his hand out.

"You wanna fucking shake on it?" Octavio says, laughing a little. Daniel keeps his hand out.

"All right," Octavio says, and shakes Daniel's hand.

Jacquie Red Feather

JACQUIE AND HARVEY GET into Oakland the night before the powwow. Harvey offers his room to Jacquie, mentioning it having two queens.

"It doesn't have to be any kinda way. The other bed is open, free of charge," he says.

"I'm not poor," Jacquie says.

"Have it your way," Harvey says. That was the problem with men like Harvey. As much as he might have appeared to change for the better, you can't ever get the pig all the way out. Jacquie could care less if he thought it was gonna be one way and now it's another. That's his shit. She'd carried their child, given birth, and gave her away. Their baby. He can be uncomfortable. He should be.

When Jacquie wakes up it feels way too early, but she can't get back to sleep. When she opens the curtains she sees the sun is just about to come up. It's that dark and light blue gradient that meets somewhere in the middle. She's always loved that blue. She should watch the sunrise. How long had it been since she'd done that? Instead she closes the curtains and turns on the TV.

At some point a couple of hours later a text comes in from Harvey about getting breakfast.

"You nervous?" Jacquie says as she stabs a piece of link sausage and dips it into a puddle of syrup.

"I haven't gotten nervous in a long time," Harvey says, and takes a sip of coffee. "It's where I do my best thinking. Out loud. I just talk out what I see and it comes easy because of how many powwows I done. It's like all the sports announcers you hear filling the game with their nonsense, it's the same thing, except there are times when I'm talking about what's happening out there, as the dancers come in, sometimes it can feel like a prayer. But you can't be too serious. A powwow emcee is supposed to be irreverent. It's a big event for a lotta people trying to win money. It's a competition. So I have to try to keep it light like a sports announcer." He mixes his whole plate up—eggs, biscuits, gravy, sausage. He stabs a forkful of the mix. When he's done, he sops up what's left with a piece of toast. Jacquie sips her coffee and watches Harvey eat his soaked toast.

At the powwow, Jacquie sits next to Harvey under a canvas canopy with the sound system and mixing board, the mic cord snaking out of it.

"Will you have all the names and dancers' numbers somewhere, like on a piece of paper in front of you, or do you memorize?" Jacquie says.

"Memorize? Pssh. Here," Harvey says, and hands her a clipboard with a long list of names and numbers on it. She absently looks down the list.

"We're okay, Harvey," Jacquie says.

"I know," Harvey says.

"Well you shouldn't," Jacquie says.

"It was more than forty years ago," Harvey says.

"Forty-two," she says. "She's forty-two years old. Our daughter."

Jacquie's about to hand the clipboard back to Harvey when she sees Orvil's name on the list. She pulls the clipboard closer to her eyes to be sure. She reads his name over and over. *Orvil Red Feather*. It's there. Jacquie gets out her phone to text her sister.

Octavio Gomez

EVEN THOUGH the guns are plastic, going through the metal detectors still makes Octavio sweat. Nothing happens though. On the other side, Octavio looks around to see if anyone is paying attention to them. The security guard is reading a newspaper next to the detector. Octavio walks over to the bushes and sees the black socks. He reaches down for the pair.

In the bathroom, Octavio fishes around in one of the socks and grabs a handful of bullets, then passes the socks under the stall to Charles, who does the same then passes them under to Carlos, who passes them under the last stall to Calvin. As Octavio puts the bullets in his gun, he feels a dread move all the way from his toes to the top of his head. The dread keeps going, moves out of him, like he had his chance with what it was telling him but he missed it, because just as he feels it a bullet drops and rolls out in front of him, out of the stall. Hears the squeak of shoes. Must be Tony here to get his bullets. Everyone goes quiet at the sound of that bullet rolling.

Edwin Black

BLUE AND EDWIN SIT at the table and canopy they'd set up earlier. They watch the dancers come out for Grand Entry. Blue tilts her head up at them.

"You know anyone out there?" Blue says.

"Nah. But listen," Edwin says, and points up, at the sound of the powwow emcee's voice.

"Your dad," Blue says, and they listen for a second.

"Weird, right?" Edwin says.

"Totally weird. But wait, did you find out before or after you got the internsh . . . I mean the job or—"

"No, I knew. I mean, part of taking the job had to do with finding out who he is."

They watch the dancers enter. The veterans first, with their flags and staffs. Then a long line of bouncing dancers. Edwin had avoided watching powwow footage to preserve this moment. Let it be new, even after Blue insisted he watch some powwow footage on YouTube so he'd know what he was getting into.

"You know anyone out there?" Edwin says.

"A lotta the kids I knew when I used to work here are all grown up, but I haven't seen any of them around," Blue says. She looks at Edwin, who's just stood up.

"Where you going?"

"Get a taco," Edwin says. "You want one?"

"You're gonna go walk past your dad again, aren't you?"

"Yeah, but I'm really getting a taco this time."

"And you got one last time."

"Did I?" Edwin said.

"Just go talk to him."

"It's not that easy," Edwin says, and smiles.

"I'll go with you," Blue says. "But you have to actually talk to him."

"Okay."

"Okay," Blue says, and stands up. "Didn't you guys plan to meet up here anyway?"

"Yeah, but then we didn't talk after that," Edwin says.

"So," Blue says.

"It's not on me. Imagine it. Your son gets ahold of you, your son who you didn't know existed, then you just . . . stop communicating? You don't just say, yeah, hey, let's meet up, then not make plans."

"Maybe he figured he'd wait until you could meet in person," Blue says.

"We're already walking over there, aren't we?" Edwin says. "So let's stop talking about it. Let's act like we're talking about something else."

"We should probably not *act* like we're talking about something else and just talk about something else," Blue says. But this makes it impossible to think of anything else to talk about.

They walk in silence, past tables and canopies. As they get closer to Edwin's dad's canopy, Edwin turns to Blue. "So the dancers who win just take the cash, no taxes, no hidden fees?" he says, like they were in the middle of a conversation.

"Okay, so you're acting like we've been talking," Blue says. "Well then it doesn't matter what I say. This right here, what I'm saying now, is probably enough, right?" She's not even looking at Edwin.

"Yes, perfect. But no more. Okay, you wait back here," Edwin says.

"Okay," Blue says in a robotically obedient voice.

Edwin approaches Harvey, who's just put his mic down. Harvey turns to him and sees him right away for who he is. He shows this by taking off his hat. Edwin sticks out his hand for a shake, but Harvey grabs Edwin behind his head and brings him in for a hug. They hold the hug for longer than Edwin is comfortable with, but he doesn't break it either. His dad smells like leather and bacon.

"When did you get here?" Harvey says.

"I was the first one, well, one of two of the first people here," Edwin says.

"You pretty serious about powwows then?" Harvey says.

"I helped put this all together. Remember?"

"That's right. Sorry. Oh, this here's Jacquie Red Feather," Harvey says, pointing to the woman sitting down next to where Harvey was sitting before he stood up to give Edwin a hug.

"Edwin," Edwin says, and reaches his hand out to her.

"Jacquie," she says.

"Blue," Edwin says with a hand half cupped around his mouth like she's far away, and like he's yelling it.

Blue walks over. She looks stressed.

"Blue, meet my dad, Harvey, and this is his, his friend Jacquie, what was it?"

"Red Feather," Jacquie says.

"Right, and this is Blue," Edwin says.

Blue's face goes white. She reaches out her hand and goes for a smile, but it looks more like she's trying not to throw up.

"It's so nice to meet you both, but, Edwin, we should get back—"

"C'mon, we just got here," Edwin says, and looks at his dad like: *Right?*

"I know, and we can come back, we have the whole day, we'll just be right over there," Blue says, pointing to where they'd come from.

"All right," Edwin says, and reaches out one more time for a shake with his dad. Then they both wave and walk away.

"Okay, two things," Blue says as they walk back to their table.

"That was crazy," Edwin says. He's smiling a smile he can't contain.

"I think that woman was my mom," Blue says.

"What?"

"Jacquie."

"Who?"

"The woman with your dad just now?"

"Oh. Wait, what?"

"I know. I don't know. I don't know what the fuck is happening right now, Ed."

They walk back to the table. Edwin looks over to Blue and tries for a smile, but Blue, she's ghost-white.

Thomas Frank

———

"YOU GOOD?" Bobby Big Medicine says after the song is over. Thomas had been looking off, or not off but down and like he could see through the ground and like he could see something specific there.

"I think. Getting somewhere," Thomas says.

"Still drinking?" Bobby says.

"Doing better," Thomas says.

"Get all that junk out for this one," Bobby says, and rotates his drumstick in a circle.

"I feel good," Thomas says.

"It's not enough to feel good. You gotta drum good for them," he says, and points with his drumstick out at the field.

"Do I know all the songs we're gonna sing today?"

"Most. You'll catch up," he says.

"Thanks, brother," Thomas says.

"Put your thanks in there," Bobby says, and points to the middle of the drum.

"I just mean for asking me to come out here," Thomas says, but Bobby doesn't hear. He's talking to one of the other drummers. Bobby's like that. With you all the way and then gone. He doesn't think of it like doing a personal favor. He wanted a drummer. He likes the way Thomas drums and sings. Thomas stands up to stretch. He really does feel good. Singing and drumming had done that thing, that all-the-way-there thing he needs to feel that full, that complete feeling, like you're right where you're supposed to be right now—in the song and about what the song's about.

Thomas walks around to various vendors, jewelry and blanket booths. He's keeping an eye out for anyone from the Indian Center. He should just find Blue and apologize. It would make drumming the rest of the day better. It would make his drumming better, more true. He sees her. But there's someone yelling. Thomas can't tell from where.

Loother and Lony

─◆─

THE SUN BEAT DOWN on Loother and Lony up in the stands. They'd run out of things to complain about to each other, and lost patience for the silence slowly growing between them. Without having to say it, they stand up and walk down to look for Orvil. Lony had said he wanted to get closer to the drum, see what it sounds like up close.

"It's just hella loud," Loother had said.

"Yeah, but I wanna see."

"You wanna hear," Loother said.

"You know what I mean."

They make their way toward the drum—Loother's head on a swivel looking for Orvil. He told Lony they could go listen if they could stop to get a lemonade first. Lony hadn't shown interest in any of the powwow stuff Orvil had gotten into until this moment. Something about the drum, he'd said. He hadn't realized it'd be so loud, and that the singers sounded like that in real life.

"It's the singing, you hear that?" he'd said to Loother before they went down.

"Yeah, I hear it, and it sounds just like we heard a hundred times coming from Orvil's earphones," Loother said.

They pass dancers and look up and almost flinch. People don't notice them, which makes them have to dodge the dancers coming their way. Lony keeps drifting toward the drum. And Loother keeps grabbing him by the shirt to pull him toward the lemonade. They're almost to the lemonade stand when they both turn around at what they think is the sound of people screaming.

Daniel Gonzales

DANIEL HAS HIS VR goggles on. They weigh his head down a little. But that's the same angle the drone flies—top heavy. In that way he feels as if he's flying as he flies toward the coliseum.

Daniel is waiting before flying the drone over. He's waiting because of the battery life. He doesn't want to miss anything. He wants it to go right. He wants them to pull it off, but more so he doesn't want the guns to get used. He'd been waking up in the middle of the night the week leading up to the pow-wow. Dreams of people running in the streets and gunfire all around. He'd thought they were the usual zombie-apocalypse-type dreams he'd always had, until he noticed the people were Indian. Not dressed like Indians, but he just knew like you just know stuff in dreams. The dreams all ended the same. Bodies on the ground. The silence of death, the hot stillness of all the bullets lodged in the bodies.

.   .   .

The day is bright, and as he comes over the top of the coliseum, he hears his mom coming down the stairs. This doesn't make any sense as she hadn't come down those stairs since Manny died.

"Not right now, Mom," he says. Then feels bad and adds, "Hold on a second." Daniel lands the drone in the upper deck, which is empty if seagulls don't count. He doesn't want her to see the goggles because he knows she'll think they look expensive.

"You okay?" Daniel says to her from the bottom of the stairs. She's halfway down.

"What are you doing down there?"

"Same thing I'm always doing, Mom, nothing," Daniel says.

"Come up here and eat with me. I'll make you something."

"Can you wait?" Daniel says, and knows he says it impatiently. He wants to get back to the drone, which is sitting by itself on the third deck of the coliseum wasting its battery.

"Okay, Daniel," his mom says. And it's almost sad enough, the sound in her voice, to make him want to leave the drone up there, leave it all alone and just go eat with her.

"I'll be up pretty soon, Mom. Okay?"

She doesn't respond.

Blue

BLUE DIDN'T KNOW WHY she became so aware of the safe. Or she did know why, but she didn't want to know why she began to think of the safe. The money. All morning it hadn't come up. And leading up to the powwow it hadn't been a thing either. There were gift cards, and a heavy safe, and who would rob a powwow? There were other things to think about. She'd just seen her mom. Maybe. There are a few thuggish-looking guys standing nearby. Blue is bothered that she is bothered by their presence.

Edwin is next to her chewing and swallowing sunflower seeds. This almost bothers her more than anything else because you're supposed to do the work of splitting the shells and reaping the seed benefit, and he's just shoving handfuls in his mouth and chewing them up until he can swallow them shell and all.

These guys keep getting closer to the table. Kind of creeping up. She asks herself again: Who would rob a powwow? Who would even know to rob a powwow? Blue lets go of the whole idea but looks under the table to make sure the safe is still covered with the little red, yellow, and turquoise Pendleton blanket. Edwin looks over at her and smiles a rare proud-toothed smile. His teeth are covered in sunflower-seed shells. She hates and loves him for it.

Dene Oxendene

DENE IS IN his booth when he hears the first shots. A bullet whizzes through the booth. He moves to the corner and puts his back to the wooden pole there. He feels something hit his back, then the black curtain walls of the booth collapse around him.

The whole shoddily built booth is on top of him. He doesn't move. Can he? He doesn't try. He knows or thinks he knows he won't die from whatever hit him. He reaches back and feels the piece of wood, one of four thicker poles that held the thing up. As he pushes the piece of wood away, he feels something hot lodged in it. A bullet. It'd gone all the way through and almost all the way out, almost into him. But it stopped. The pole saved him. The booth he built is all that came between him and that bullet. The shots keep coming. He crawls out through the black curtains. For a second the brightness of the day blinds him. He rubs his eyes and sees across from him something that doesn't make any sense for more than one reason. Calvin Johnson, from the powwow committee, is firing a white gun at a guy on the ground, and two other guys are shooting on his left and right. One of them is in regalia. Dene gets on his stomach. He should have stayed under his collapsed booth.

Orvil Red Feather

ORVIL IS WALKING BACK out onto the field when he hears the shots. He thinks of his brothers. His grandma would kill him if he survived and they didn't. Orvil breaks out into a run when he hears a boom that fills his body with a sound so low it pulls him to the ground. He smells the grass inches from his nose and he knows. He doesn't want to know what he knows but he knows. He feels the blood-warm wetness with his fingers when they reach for his stomach. He can't move. He coughs and isn't sure if what comes out of his mouth is blood or spit. He wants to hear the drum one more time. He wants to stand up, to fly away in all his bloodied feathers. He wants to take back everything he's ever done. He wants to believe he knows how to dance a prayer and pray for a new world. He wants to keep breathing. He needs to keep breathing. He needs to remember that he needs to keep breathing.

Calvin Johnson

❦

CALVIN IS STANDING, head bent to his phone, but his eyes keep looking up from it. His hat is pulled low, and he's standing behind where Blue and Edwin are sitting so they won't see him. He looks over to Tony, who's bouncing a little—he's light on his feet like he's ready to dance. Tony's supposed to do the actual robbing. The rest of them are there in case anything goes wrong. Octavio never explained why he wants Tony in regalia, and why he should be the one to take the money. Calvin assumes it's because someone in regalia would be harder to identify, and ultimately harder to investigate.

Octavio, Charles, and Carlos are near the table looking antsy. Calvin gets a group text from Octavio that just says *We all good Tony?* Calvin can't help but start walking toward the table when he sees Tony doing it too. But Tony stops. Octavio, Charles, and Carlos watch him stop, watch him stand there, bouncing a little. Calvin's gut spins. Tony backs off, still facing them, then he turns around and walks the other way.

It doesn't take Octavio long to make the next move. Calvin's never held a gun before this. There's a gravity to it. A weight pulling him closer to Octavio, who's now pointing his gun at Edwin and Blue. He's pointing at the safe with the gun. He's calm about it. Calvin has his hand on his gun through his shirt. Edwin crouches down to open the safe.

Octavio looks to his right then left, bag of gift cards in his hand, when stupid-ass Carlos turns his gun on Octavio. Calvin sees it before Octavio does. Charles points his gun at Octavio too. Charles is yelling for Octavio to put down his gun and give him the bag. Carlos is yelling the same thing behind him. Fucking Charles.

Octavio throws the bag of gift cards at Charles, and as he does he fires a few shots at him. Charles stumbles back and starts firing. Octavio gets hit and fires a few more back at Charles. Calvin sees a kid in regalia go down ten or so feet behind Charles. This is fucked up, but Calvin doesn't have time to think of it that way because Carlos puts three or four into Octavio's back. He might've fired more, but Daniel's drone plane comes crashing down on his head and Carlos goes down. Calvin has his gun pointed at no one, finger on the trigger, ready, when he feels the first bullet hit him in his hip, the bone. Down on one knee, Calvin gets another one in the gut, and he feels a sick weight there like he'd swallowed too much water at once. How could a hole make him feel more full? As he goes down, Calvin sees Carlos get hit with bullets coming from Tony's direction.

From the ground Calvin sees his brother firing bullets at Tony. He feels each tiny blade point of grass pushing into his face. It's all he can feel, those blades of grass. And then he doesn't hear any more firing. He doesn't hear anything.

Thomas Frank

HE DOESN'T THINK of the shots being fired as shots being fired. He waits for it to be anything else. But then he sees people run and stumble and drop and scream and generally lose their shit because soon, very soon, after what he at first thought must have been something else and not gunfire became in his mind and before his eyes definite gunfire. Thomas ducks incomprehensibly. Squats down and watches dumbly. He can't find the shooter, or shooters. So stupid is he that he stands up to see better what's happening. He hears a sharp whiz nearby, and as soon as he realizes that it's the sound of bullets missing him, one hits him in the throat. He should have been keeping as low as possible, he should have dropped to the ground, played dead, but he didn't and now he's on the ground anyway, holding his neck where the bullet went in. He can't figure out where the bullet came from, and it doesn't matter because he's bleeding badly into the hand that holds his burst neck.

All he knows is that the bullets are still flying and people are screaming and someone is behind him, his head is in their lap but he can't open his eyes and it burns like hell where he knows or feels he knows the bullet exited. The person whose lap he is in is maybe wrapping something around his neck and tightening it, maybe it's a shirt or a shawl, they are trying to stop the bleeding. He doesn't know if his eyes are closed or if all of this has suddenly blinded him. He knows he can't see anything and that sleep feels like the best idea he's ever had, like no matter what that sleep could mean, even if it means *only* sleep, dreamless sleep from here on out. But a hand is slapping his face and his eyes open and he's never believed in God until this moment, he feels God is in the feeling of his face being slapped. Someone or something is trying to make him stay. Thomas tries to lift his whole body up, but he can't. Sleep floats beneath him somewhere, seeps into his skin, and he's losing the rhythm in his breath, breathing fewer breaths, his heart, it'd been beating for him all this time, his whole life, without even trying, but now he can't, he just can't do anything but wait for the next breath to come—hope that it will. He's never in his life felt as heavy as he feels now, and it burns, the back of his neck, like no burn he's ever felt. Thomas's childhood fear of eternity in hell comes back to him and it's right there in the burn and the cool of the hole in his neck. But just as that fear comes it goes, and he arrives. In the State. It doesn't matter how he got here. Or why he's here. And it doesn't matter how long he stays. The State is perfect and is all he could ever ask for, for a second or a minute or a moment, to belong like this is to die and live forever. So he's not reaching up, and he's not sinking down, and he's not worried about what's coming. He's here, and he's dying, and it's okay.

Bill Davis

BILL HEARS MUTED SHOTS fire behind the thick concrete walls that separate everyone else from the coliseum employees. He thinks of Edwin before he can even register what the muted booms might mean. What happens to him right away, though, is that he stands up and moves toward the sounds. He runs through the door that leads out to the concession stands. He smells gunpowder and grass and soil. A mix of dread and long-dormant courage in the face of danger moves over the top of his skin like a nervous sweat. Bill sets off at a run. His heartbeat is in his temples. He's skipping stairs to get down to the field. As he approaches the infield wall, his phone vibrates in his pocket. He slows. It could be Karen. Maybe Edwin called her. Maybe Edwin is calling him. Bill drops to his knees, crawls between the second and first rows. He looks at his phone. It's Karen.

"Karen."

"I'm on my way there now, sweetie," Karen says.

"No. Karen. Stop. Turn around," Bill says.

"Why? What's—"

"There's a shooting. Call the police. Pull over. Call them," Bill says.

Bill puts the phone against his stomach and lifts his head up to look. Right away he feels a sting-burn explode on the right side of his head. He puts his hand to his ear. It's flat. Wet. Hot. Not thinking to put it to his other ear, Bill puts the phone to the place where his ear had been.

"Kare—" Bill starts but can't finish. Another bullet. This one hits above his right eye—makes a clean hole through. The world tips over.

Bill's head slams against the concrete. His phone is on the ground in front of him. He watches the numbers count up— the time of their call. Bill's head throbs, not with pain, just a big throbbing that turns into a full-on swelling. His head is an expanding balloon. The word *puncture* occurs to him. Everything is ringing. There's a deep whooshing sound coming from somewhere beneath him, waves or a white noise coming on— a buzz he can feel in his teeth. He watches his blood seep out from under his head in a half circle. He can't move. He wonders what they'll use to clean it. Sodium peroxide powder is best for concrete stains. Bill thinks: *Please not this.* Karen is still there; the seconds are still counting up. He closes his eyes. He sees green, all he can see is a green blur, and he thinks he's looking out onto the field again. But his eyes are closed. He remembers another time he saw a green blur like this. A grenade had landed nearby. Someone yelled for him to take cover, but he froze. He wound up on the ground then too. Same ringing in his head. Same buzz in his teeth. He wonders if he ever made it out of there. It doesn't matter. He's dimming. He's leaving. Bill is going.

Opal Viola Victoria Bear Shield

GUNFIRE BOOMS THROUGHOUT the stadium. Screams fill the air. Opal is already going as fast as she can down the steps to the first level. She's getting pushed from behind. She shuffles along with everyone else. Opal doesn't know how she didn't think to do it, but as soon as she does she gets her phone out. She calls Orvil first but his phone just rings and rings. Next she calls Loother. She gets through but the call breaks up. She can only hear parts of words. A broken sound. She hears him say, *Grandma*. She puts her hand over her mouth and nose, sobs into her hand. She keeps listening to see if it will clear up. She wonders, she has the thought, *Did someone really come to get us here? Now?* She doesn't know what she means.

As soon as she gets outside the front entrance, Opal sees the boys. But it's just Loother and Lony. She runs to them. Loother's still holding his phone. He's pointing to it. She can't hear him but she sees him mouthing, *We been trying to call him.*

Jacquie Red Feather

━━◆━━

HARVEY'S HAND IS on Jacquie's shoulder, pushing down. He's trying to get Jacquie to go down with him. Jacquie looks at him. His eyebrows are furrowed intensely to indicate how serious he is about this push down. Jacquie walks toward the sound and his hand slips off of her.

"Jacquie," she hears him whisper-scream behind her. She can hear the bullets, the boom and the whizzing. It's close. She hunches a little but keeps walking. There's a whole bunch of people on the ground. They look dead. She's thinking about Orvil. She'd just watched him go by for the Grand Entry.

For a second Jacquie thinks it might be some kind of performance-art piece. All these people in regalia on the ground like it's a massacre. She remembers what her mom told her and Opal about Alcatraz, how a small group of Indians first took over Alcatraz, just five or six of them, took it over as a piece of performance art five years before it really happened. It had always fascinated her. That it started that way.

She sees the shooters, then scans the field of bodies to find the colors of Orvil's regalia on the ground. His colors stand out because there's a bright orange in it, a particular almost pink orange you don't normally see in regalia. She doesn't like the color, which makes it easier for her to spot.

Before she acknowledges to herself that it's him, before she can feel or think or decide anything, she's already moving toward her grandson. She knows the risk of walking out there. She's walking toward the gunfire. It doesn't matter. She keeps an even pace. She keeps her eyes locked on Orvil.

His eyes are closed when she gets to him. She puts two fingers to his neck. There's a pulse. She screams out for help. The sound she makes is not a word. The sound she makes comes from below her feet, from the ground, and with the sound Jacquie lifts Orvil's body. She can hear the shots behind her as she carries her grandson's body through the crowd toward the exit. "Excuse me," she says as she moves through the crowd. "Please," she says.

"Someone!" she hears herself cry out as she comes out through the entrance. Then she sees them there. Just outside the entrance. Loother and Lony.

"Where's Opal?" she says to them. Lony is crying. He points out toward the parking lot. Jacquie looks down at Orvil. Her arms are shaking. Loother comes over and puts an arm around Jacquie, looks down at his brother.

"He's white," Loother says.

When Opal pulls up, Jacquie sees Harvey come running out toward them. She doesn't know why he should come, or why she calls out his name, waves him over. They all get into the back of Opal's Ford Bronco and Opal puts her foot on the gas.

Blue

BLUE AND EDWIN MANAGE to get out to Blue's car without having to stop. Edwin is out of breath and starting to look pretty pale. Blue puts Edwin's seat belt on, starts the car, and heads for the hospital. She leaves because she hasn't even heard sirens yet. She leaves because Edwin is officially slumped in his seat, his eyelids half-closed. She leaves because she knows the way and can get there sooner than someone not even here yet.

After the shooting stopped, Blue could barely make out what Edwin was yelling at her from the ground.

"We gotta go," Edwin said. He was talking about the hospital. He wanted her to take him. He was right. They wouldn't get enough ambulances there in time. Who knows how many people had been shot. For Edwin, it was just one shot—in the stomach.

"Okay," Blue said. She tried to help him up, wrapped his arm over her shoulder and pulled. He winced a little but for the most part was pretty unfazed.

"Hold it with pressure so it doesn't bleed too much," Blue said. He was holding three or four Big Oakland Powwow T-shirts against his stomach. He reached behind his back and the color went out of his face.

"It went through," Edwin said. "Out the back."

"Fuck," Blue said. "Or good? Shit. I don't know." Blue put an arm around him and let his arm hold on to her. They hobbled out of the coliseum like that, all the way out to Blue's car.

When Blue pulls into Highland, Edwin is passed out. She'd been telling him, yelling at him, screaming at him to stay awake. There was probably a closer hospital, but she knew Highland. She keeps her hand on the horn, to try to wake Edwin up and to get someone to come out to help. She reaches her hand over and slaps Edwin a few times on the cheek. Edwin shakes his head a little.

"You gotta wake up, Ed," Blue says. "We're here."

He doesn't respond.

Blue runs inside to get someone with a stretcher to come out and help.

When she comes out through the emergency room automatic double doors, she sees a Ford Bronco pull up. All the doors open at once. She sees Harvey. And Jacquie. Jacquie's holding a boy, a teenager in regalia. As Jacquie passes Blue, two nurses come out with a stretcher for Edwin. Blue knows right away there will be confusion. Should she allow Jacquie and the boy to go in Edwin's place? It doesn't matter what Blue has or hasn't decided. She watches the nurses load the boy and take him away on the stretcher. Harvey walks up to Blue and looks at Edwin in the car. He nods his head sideways at Edwin like: *Let's pick him up.*

Harvey slaps Edwin a few times on the cheek and he rustles a little but can't pick his head up. Harvey yells some incomprehensible thing about getting someone out here to help, then gets Edwin halfway out of the car and puts Edwin's arm around him. Blue squeezes between the car and Edwin and takes his other arm and puts it around her shoulder.

Two orderlies settle Edwin on the gurney. Blue and Harvey run alongside as they roll him through the halls, and then he's through the swinging doors.

Blue sits next to Jacquie, who's looking down at that angle, at the ground, elbows to knees in that position you take when you're waiting for death to leave the building, for your loved one to come out in a wheelchair with a broken smile, for a doctor with a sure step to come for you with good news. Blue wants to say something to Jacquie. But what? Blue looks at Harvey. He really does look like Edwin. And if Harvey and Jacquie are together, then does that mean . . . ? No. Blue doesn't allow that thought to finish. She looks across from her. There are two younger boys and a woman who looks a little like Jacquie, but bigger. The woman looks at Blue and Blue averts her eyes. She wants to ask the woman why she's here. She knows it has to do with the pow-wow, the shooting. But there's nothing to say. There's nothing to do but wait.

Opal Viola Victoria Bear Shield

OPAL KNOWS Orvil's gonna make it. She's telling herself that in her head. She would scream the thought if you could scream thoughts. Maybe you can. Maybe that's what she's doing to make herself believe there's reason to hope despite there maybe being no reason to hope. Opal wants Jacquie and the boys to see it on her face too, this belief despite everything, which is maybe what faith is. Jacquie doesn't look okay. She looks like if Orvil doesn't make it, she won't either. Opal thinks she's right. None of them will make it back from this if he doesn't. Nothing will be okay.

Opal looks around the room and sees that everyone in the waiting room, everyone's head is down. Loother and Lony aren't even on their phones. This makes Opal sad. She almost wants them to be on their phones.

But Opal knows this is the time, if there ever was one, to believe, to pray, to ask for help, even though she'd abandoned all hope for outside help on a prison island back when she was eleven. She tries her best to keep quiet and close her eyes. She hears something coming from a place she thought she'd closed off forever a long time ago. The place where her old teddy bear, Two Shoes, used to speak from. The place she used to think and imagine from when she was too young to think she shouldn't. The voice was hers and not hers. But hers, finally. It can't come from anywhere else. There is only Opal. Opal has to ask. Before she can even think to pray, she has to believe she can believe. She's making it come but also letting it come. The voice pushes through and she thinks: *Please. Get up,* she says, this time out loud. She's talking to Orvil. She's trying to get her thoughts, her voice, into that room with him. *Stay,* Opal says. *Please.* She says it all out loud. *Stay.* She recognizes that there is power in saying the prayer out loud. She cries with her eyes shut tight. *Don't go,* she says. *You can't.*

A doctor comes out. Just one doctor. Opal thinks that might be good, they probably report death in pairs, for moral support. But she doesn't want to look up at the doctor's face. She does and doesn't want to know. She wants to stop time, have more time to pray, to prepare. But all time has ever done is to keep going. No matter what. Before she can think to do it, Opal is counting the swings of the double doors. Every swing in counts as one. The doctor is saying something. But she can't look up yet, or listen. She has to wait and see what the number of swings will say. The doors come to a rest on the number eight, and Opal breathes in deep, then lets out a sigh and looks up to see what the doctor has to say.

Tony Loneman

TONY TURNS AROUND at the sound of gunfire, thinking they might be shooting at him. He sees a kid in regalia get shot behind Charles, sees him go down. Tony lifts his gun and moves toward them—unsure of who to aim at. Tony watches Carlos shoot Octavio in the back, then a drone lands on Carlos's head. Tony's gun works long enough for him to hit Carlos two or three times, enough times that he stops moving. Tony knows Charles is firing at him, but he hasn't felt anything yet. The trigger's stuck. The gun is too hot to hold, so Tony drops it. As he does the first bullet hits him. The bullet feels fast and hot in his leg even though he knows the bullet can't be moving anymore. Charles keeps shooting at him and missing. Tony knows this means he might be hitting other people behind him, and his face gets hot. A kind of hardening is happening all over his body. Tony knows this feeling. He sees black in his periphery. Some part of him is trying to leave, into the dark cloud he's only ever emerged from later. But Tony means to stay, and he does. His vision brightens.

He builds up to a run. Charles is about thirty feet away. Tony can feel all his fringes and ties flapping behind him. He knows what he's running into, without a gun, but he feels harder than anything that might come at him, speed, heat, metal, distance, even time.

When the second bullet hits him in his leg, he stumbles but doesn't lose speed. He's twenty feet away, then ten. Another hits his arm. A couple get him in his stomach. He feels them and he doesn't. Tony charges, ducks his head into it. The hot heavy weight and speed of the bullets do their best to push him back, pull him down, but he can't be stopped, not now.

When he's a few feet away from Charles, Tony notices something so quiet and still inside him it feels like it's emanating out into the world, quieting everything down to nothing—molten silence. Tony means to sink through anything that gets in his way. He's making a sound. It starts in his stomach, then comes out through his nose and mouth. A roar and rumble of blood. Tony drops a little lower just before he reaches Charles, then dives into him.

Tony lands hard on top of Charles with the last of his strength. Charles reaches up for Tony's throat. He grips it. Tony sees darkness creeping in around his vision again. He's pushing up against Charles's face. He gets a thumb in his eye and pushes. He sees Charles's gun on the ground next to his head. With all he has left in him, Tony shifts his weight and falls sideways, then grabs the gun. Before Charles can look over, or reach back out toward Tony's neck, Tony fires a shot into the side of Charles's head, then watches it drop and his body go lifeless.

Tony rolls onto his back and right away he's sinking. Quicksand slow. The sky darkens, or his vision darkens, or he's just sinking deeper and deeper in, headed for the center of the earth, where he might join the magma or water or metal or whatever is there to stop him, hold him, keep him down there forever.

But the sinking stops. He can't see. He hears something that sounds like waves, then he hears Maxine's voice somewhere in the distance. Her voice is echoey, like it used to sound when she was in the kitchen and he was nearby, under the table or slapping magnets on the fridge. Tony wonders if he's dead. If Maxine's kitchen is where he'd end up after. But Maxine's not even dead. It's definitely her voice. She's singing an old Cheyenne hymn she used to sing when she did the dishes.

Tony realizes he can open his eyes again, but he keeps them closed. He knows he's full of holes. He can feel each one of those bullets trying to pull him down. He watches himself go up, out of himself, then he watches himself from above, looks at his body and remembers that it was never actually really him. He was never Tony just like he was never the Drome. Both were masks.

Tony hears Maxine singing in the kitchen again and then he's there. He's there and he's four years old, the summer before going into kindergarten. He's in the kitchen with Maxine. He's not twenty-one-year-old Tony thinking about his four-year-old self—remembering. He's just there again, all the way back to being four-year-old Tony. He's on a chair helping her wash dishes. He's dipping his hand into the sink and blowing bubbles at her out of the palm of his hand. She doesn't think it's funny but she doesn't stop him. She keeps wiping the bubbles on the top of his head. He keeps asking her: *What are we? Grandma, what are we?* She doesn't answer.

Tony dips his hand back into the sink of bubbles and dishes and blows them at her again. She has some on the side of her face and she doesn't wipe them off, just keeps a straight face and keeps on washing. Tony thinks this is the funniest thing he's ever seen. And he doesn't know if she knows this is happening, or if they're really not there. He doesn't know that he's not there, because he's right there, in that moment which he can't remember as having happened because it's happening to him now. He's there with her in the kitchen blowing sink bubbles.

Finally, after catching his breath and containing his laughter, Tony says, "Grandma, you know. You know they're there."

"What's that?" Maxine says.

"Grandma, you're playing," Tony says.

"Playing what?" Maxine says.

"They're right there, Grandma, I see them with my own eyes."

"You go play now and let me finish these in peace," Maxine says, and smiles a smile that tells him she knows about the bubbles.

Tony plays with his Transformers on the floor of his bedroom. He makes them fight in slow motion. He gets lost in the story he works out for them. It's always the same. There is a battle, then a betrayal, then a sacrifice. The good guys end up winning, but one of them dies, like Optimus Prime had to in *Transformers,* which Maxine let him watch on that old VHS machine, even though she said she thought he was too young. When they watched it together, at the moment they realized Optimus had died, they looked over to each other and saw they were both crying, which then made them laugh for a few seconds, for just that singular moment, both of them together in the dark of Maxine's bedroom, laughing and crying at the exact same time.

As Tony has them walk away from the battle, they talk about how they wish it didn't have to be that way. They wish they could all have made it. Tony has Optimus Prime say, "We're made of metal, made hard, able to take it. We were made to transform. So if you get a chance to die, to save someone else, you take it. Every time. That's what Autobots were put here for."

Tony is back on the field. Every hole is a burn and a pull. Now he feels as if he might not float up but instead fall inside of something underneath him. There is an anchor, something he's been rooted to all this time, as if in each hole there is a hook attached to a line pulling him down. A wind from the bay sweeps through the stadium, moves through him. Tony hears a bird. Not outside. From where he's anchored, to the bottom of the bottom, the middle of the middle of him. The center's center. There is a bird for every hole in him. Singing. Keeping him up. Keeping him from going. Tony remembers something his grandma said to him when she was teaching him how to dance. "You have to dance like birds sing in the morning," she'd said, and showed him how light she could be on her feet. She bounced and her toes pointed in just the right way. Dancer's feet. Dancer's gravity. Tony needs to be light now. Let the wind sing through the holes in him, listen to the birds singing. Tony isn't going anywhere. And somewhere in there, inside him, where he is, where he'll always be, even now it is morning, and the birds, the birds are singing.

Acknowledgments

To my wife, Kateri, my first (best) reader/listener, who believed in me and the book from the very beginning, and to my son, Felix, for all the ways he helps and inspires me to be a better human and writer; to them both, for whom I'd give my own heart's blood. I couldn't have done it without them.

There were many people and organizations that helped get this book out into the world. I'd like to thank from the innermost reaches of my heart all of the following: The MacDowell Colony, for supporting my work long before it came to be what it is now. Denise Pate at the Oakland Cultural Arts Fund, for funding a storytelling project that never came to fruition except for in fiction— i.e., in a chapter of this novel. Pam Houston, for all she's taught me, and for being the first person to believe in this book enough to send it out herself. Jon Davis, for all the ways he's supported me and the MFA (Institute of American Indian Arts) program I graduated from in 2016, for all the copyediting help, and for believing in me from the get-go. Sherman Alexie, for how he helped this become a better novel, and for all the unbelievable support he's given me once the book was bought. Terese Mailhot, for all she's done to make it so our lives as writers have paralleled each other, and for all the support and encouragement she's always given me, for being the unbelievably amazing writer she is. The Yaddo Corporation, for the time and space to finish this book before it got sent out. Writing By Writers and the fellowship they gave me in 2016. Claire Vaye Watkins, for hearing me read and believing in the book enough to send it to her agent. Derek Palacio, for helping guide the manuscript, and for all the advice and support he gave me post-graduation. All the many writers and teachers at IAIA, who taught me a tremendous amount. My brother, Mario, and his wife, Jenny, for letting me sleep on their couch whenever I came into town, and for their love and support. My mom and dad for always believing in me no matter what I tried to do. Carrie and Ladonna. Christina. For all that we've been through and how we've always helped each other along the way. Mamie and Lou, Teresa, Bella, and Sequoia, for helping to make our family what it is. For helping to give me the time I needed to write. For being sweet, caring, and loving to my son during those times when I was away to write. My uncle Tom and aunt Barb, for all the ways they help and love everyone in our family. Soob and Casey. My uncle Jonathan. Martha, Geri, and Jeffrey, for being there for my family when we needed them most. My editor Jordan, for loving and believing in the book, and helping me to make it as good as it could possibly be. My agent Nicole Aragi, for reading the manuscript too late one night, or too early one morning, when it seemed the world was falling apart, for everything she's done for me and the book since. Everyone at Knopf for all their undying support. The Native community in Oakland. My living Cheyenne relatives, and my ancestors who made it through unimaginable hardship, who prayed hard for us next ones here now, doing our best to pray and work hard for those to come.